Joanna Johnson lives in a pretty Wiltshire village with her husband and as many books as she can sneak into the house. Being part of the Mills & Boon family is a dream come true. She has always loved writing, starting at five years old with a series about a cat imaginatively named Cat, and keeps a notebook in every handbag—just in case. In her spare time she likes finding new places to have a cream tea, stroking scruffy dogs and trying to remember where she left her glasses.

Also by Joanna Johnson

The Marriage Rescue
Scandalously Wed to the Captain
His Runaway Lady
A Mistletoe Vow to Lord Lovell

Discover more at millsandboon.co.uk.

THE RETURN OF HER LONG-LOST HUSBAND

Joanna Johnson

MILLS & BOON

First Published in Great Britain 2022
by Mills & Boon, an imprint of HarperCollins*Publishers* Ltd,
1 London Bridge Street, London, SE1 9GF

www.harpercollins.co.uk

HarperCollins*Publishers*
1st Floor, Watermarque Building,
Ringsend Road, Dublin 4, Ireland

The Return of Her Long-Lost Husband © 2022 Joanna Johnson

ISBN: 978-0-263-30152-6

01/22

To everyone who struggled, felt frightened, lonely
or sad over the difficult past year and a bit:
this one's for you.

Prologue

December 1816

The sky above stretched out in infinite darkness, the pale gleam of a crescent moon lighting the way for a ship cutting steadily through icy waves. Only one passenger still stood on its deck, alone beneath the stars, breathing in salt-tinged air and watching in silence as at long last the white cliffs of Dover hove into view.

Home again once more.

Chapter One

A stiff breeze blew by Hester Honeywell's ear, insistently tugging at a dark blonde ringlet, but her blue eyes never strayed from their target. The string of the bow clasped between her fingers strained for release and Hester took a breath to steady herself.

Careful. Take your time.

She could sense the onlookers ranged on either side, eight or so faces pink from the cold. Her younger sister, Diana, host for the afternoon and young mistress of the Farleigh estate, was the only person not watching intently for the shot, far too busy charming the sole single man in attendance with her wit and gleaming smile—although not, Hester thought wryly, for her *own* benefit.

Poor Diana. She won't be able to rest until she's found me another husband. If only she'd believe me when I tell her she's wasting her time.

What was this one's name? Hester could hardly remember, more interested in the tiny cloud each breath made as it rose from her mouth. Another man to be danced beneath her nose, her well-meaning but meddling sister hell-bent on marrying her off once again, whether Hester wanted it or not.

And she most certainly did not. Widowhood had suited her very well indeed these past five years, and the freedom to live without an unreliable man's hand on her shoulder was something far too precious to give up—even if it had come at the ultimate cost.

'Are you going to shoot any time this decade? The Regent will be crowned before you let that arrow loose!'

The voice of Diana's husband, Lord Lavendon, issued at Hester's back and she tensed her jaw on a retort. Closing one eye, she surveyed the distance between her and the target set a good fifty yards away, trusting the calm rhythm of her pulse for the perfect chance to strike.

On the next beat—now!

She slackened her gloved fingers and watched as the arrow sliced through the chill air, flying straight and true to bury its head in the very centre of the painted circle. The collection of bystanders broke into polite applause and, turning, Hester raised a brow at her brother-in-law.

'Was that worth the wait?'

'Not too bad, I suppose.' Lord Lavendon gave a grudging smile, no stranger to their good-natured rivalry. 'But still room for improvement.'

'Improvement?' Diana piped up indignantly from her perch, immersed beneath several blankets on a chair beside Sir What's-His-Name. 'Hester is the best shot of all of us. Don't you think she has a fine arm, Sir Matthew?'

Hester battled the instinct to roll her eyes.

I think it's time for me to leave. A well-timed headache should do it.

'Thank you, Diana. I can always count on you to think the best of me. With that in mind, I'm sure you'll forgive me for breaking up the party—I'd like to return to Shardlow House now, before the wind grows stronger. My head is beginning to ache.'

She surrendered her bow to her brother-in-law, answering the goodbye bows and nods of those standing about her with a neat curtsey. Out of the corner of her eye she saw Diana rise quickly.

'You'll stay a while longer?' Diana's voice was low and warm with persuasion. 'We haven't even had luncheon. I'd planned to seat you by Sir Matthew. You've so much in common, and I know you'd find each other good company. You can't mean to leave already, surely?'

'I'm afraid I do. You know better than anyone that I can't bear the cold.'

'Then we'll go inside into the warm! I daresay nobody else wants to shoot anyway.'

Hester glanced over her sister's shoulder at her unwitting suitor, who seemed mercifully oblivious to Diana's plans. Broad and florid of face, with dark hair rather than fair, the difference between this man and the one Diana schemed to replace was so stark Hester might have allowed herself a grim laugh. There was no likeness whatsoever between Sir Matthew and the late Nathaniel Honeywell, the latter tall and fair and handsome beyond all sense. Surely Hester could be forgiven for having fallen in love with him at first sight, an eighteen-year-old's innocence giving her no clue as to what would come after he'd slipped a ring onto her shaking finger.

The split-second memory of that fateful moment never failed to make Hester's throat tighten, this time no exception, but there was little point in revisiting that day. Ambitious, cold-hearted Nathaniel lay somewhere at the bottom of the Atlantic along with the *Celeste* and her crew, with no trace left behind to mark the exact spot where the Honeywell Trading Company's merchant ship had sunk, and his untimely death had set Hester free of one who had brought her so much pain with his indifference and pride.

Diana pursed her lips, thankfully unaware of the direction of her sister's thoughts. 'You're quite sure you won't stay? Not even another hour?' One look at Hester's face, however, was enough to make her sigh. 'Very well. At least let me walk with you to the gate.'

Arm in arm they crossed the sparkling lawns, the wind flattening their skirts against chilled legs. Hester's feigned headache threatened to become real as a draught whistled in her ears, dull pain beginning to gnaw her already frayed temper. Thoughts of Nathaniel never improved her mood, a complex mixture of resentment and regret only fanned by her sister's unwanted meddling.

'I wish you'd stop interfering, Diana. When you invite me I never know whether it's for my company or an ambush. I won't keep coming if you carry on.'

Diana's smooth brow creased in unconvincing confusion. 'In what possible way am I interfering? Or ambushing you? I can't think what you mean.'

They had reached the gate that led on to Farleigh's kitchen gardens and Hester laid her hand firmly on the latch, barring the way forward. The metal glittered beneath her fingertips, the crisp scent of frost and damp earth a delicious combination that still couldn't soothe her irritation.

'Husband-hunting. As well you know. I've money and a house of my own now—there's nothing any match could bring that I don't have already, aside from more disappointment and grief. Why would I ever be fool enough to allow another man the chance to promise so much yet deliver so little? I had enough of that with Nathaniel—enough to last a lifetime.'

She caught the determined jut of her sister's chin, the same movement their mother made when Father dared cross her. At barely twenty Diana might be a full five years younger than her, but at times she managed to make those years seem irrelevant, and Hester's heart sank as she recognised the light of battle in Diana's eye.

'Not every marriage is like that—nor every husband. Lavendon certainly isn't.'

'Lavendon married you because he loved you—not to secure a deal between ambitious men! A merchant's daughter could never rise so high as to marry a lord if there wasn't real affection there, no matter how wealthy Father's business made us. You know that's the truth.'

'Even so. You shouldn't let your experience with Nathaniel cloud your judgement. Don't you want to ease Mother and Father's worries? I know how much they regret brokering the match now, considering the outcome.'

Diana attempted to walk on, but Hester stopped short, jerking them both to an abrupt halt. 'Mother and Father think *they* have regrets?' Her eyebrows rose so high they were almost lost among her curls. 'They weren't the ones who had to live with that mistake for *two years*, hanging their hopes on a smile rather than a scowl from a man who quite clearly never wanted a wife in the first place. Nathaniel only married me for what he stood to gain from our match, and he left me at the very moment I needed him most.'

When she thought now about the first golden weeks of her marriage, when the future had seemed so bright and endless possibilities had stretched out before her, Hester felt an ache beneath the bodice of her gown.

Heaven help her. She'd honestly believed that perfection was real, with her new husband so attentive and her feelings for him blossoming like a flower each time he brushed her fingers or shot her the sideways smile that had never failed to make her melt. She could have watched him for hours, drinking in every line of his beloved face, and the nights when he'd visited her bed were still as vivid in her mind now as they had been then…two sets of uncertain but eager hands, venturing further each time, until every question was answered and the last mystery was solved in a rush of wordless heat now too painful to recall.

Young and naïve as she'd been, how could she have known she was on borrowed time until Nathaniel's façade of kindness was swallowed up by neglect, all warmth and promise snuffed out like a candle in the rain to leave her nothing but smoke and ruins?

His father's example. I know that now. If Mr Honeywell were cut open there would be an accounts book in place of a heart, and he made damn sure to bring up his only son in his own bitter image.

The day after Nathaniel returned from a meeting with the cold, intimidating man who had sired him had been the same day Hester watched the door to her husband's office close in her face and saw how easily she had been fooled. From that moment on everything had changed: far from seeking her out during the day as he had for their month-long marriage Nathaniel had hardly deigned to speak to her at all, instead spending almost every waking hour cloistered away about business he refused to share, and Hester had realised the cruel truth.

All that charm and attention had been nothing but a ruse to trick her papa into entrusting her to Nathaniel's keeping, bringing the Townsend trading contacts along with her, and once she was safely wed the mask of decency could finally slip. Every act of consideration, every tender glance, even the gentlemanly hand to guide her through a door that had made her blood burn hot…each wonderful hint that he might feel something for her had disappeared overnight, and Hester's lonely heart had broken at the knowledge he had never intended to return her love. All he'd thought about was the business, withdrawing completely from the girl who would have given him everything if only he'd asked, and his rejection had continued right up until that final day when her life had hung in the balance and *still* he hadn't cared.

Would he have mourned if that fever had carried me away? Hester wondered now, perhaps for the thousandth time. *I doubt it. After the funeral he would have barely given me a second thought. Only of one thing can I be certain.*

'Do you recall that he never came to see me—not even when I was so ill the doctor couldn't say whether I'd live or die?' Hester fought to keep her voice steady, unaware that it strayed instead into harshness. 'We'd been wed for *two years* by then and *still* the business came first, killing once and for all any hope of reviving what I thought, in my stupidity, we could build together. Leaving me a home and my widow's jointure were the only good things he ever did for me—a better husband dead than alive.'

A climbing vine spread across the crumbling brick wall near to Hester's shoulder and she turned to it, more to hide her face from Diana than to inspect its brown fronds. The sweet call of birdsong echoed in her ears but Hester was deaf to anything but the memory of her own sobs, those of barely more than a girl as she'd lain alone in her great bed and fear had gripped her, terror her only companion as she'd waited in vain for her husband to come to her side.

At least that will never happen again.

From suffering came strength, and from that strength a spine of pure steel and self-respect no man's indifference could erode. She was her own mistress—a world away from the trusting girl Nathaniel's deceit and then apathy had slowly but surely moulded into a dignified woman. Perhaps one day she'd even be able to thank him for it; but not today, when the memories of what had been lost seemed so cold and cruel. For those few glorious weeks she'd dared to dream that happiness might be within her grasp, before he had taken her love and cast it out to moulder like rotting fruit.

A light touch on Hester's arm drew her away from the shadows of the past, gentle fingertips anchoring her back to the present. Diana hovered at her side, some measure of Hester's unhappiness reflected back in a matching pair of blue eyes.

'I'm sorry, Hess. I thought finally, after all this time, perhaps you might consider... But I never should have pushed. I won't do it again.'

Hester swallowed, her throat tight and head thumping harder than ever. Even Diana's soft voice, usually so soothing, couldn't calm the rough sea that churned now in Hester's stomach, and she shook her head.

'Is that a promise? I might ask for it in writing. I'm not sure I can trust your word.'

Without waiting for a reply she walked on ahead, fixed now on the gravel path that would lead her to freedom. She might have pleaded a headache, but in truth she simply wanted to be alone, to outrun memories of her previous life and turn her back on days she had no desire to revisit.

'Hester? At least let's part as friends?'

The plaintive entreaty in her sister's voice made Hester turn just before she escaped the garden. Diana stood where she had left her, one hand toying with the leaves of the sleeping vine and looking so earnest Hester felt a sudden rush of love that helped lighten some of the weight pressing on her heart.

Meddlesome, interfering, maddening—but still my sister, and always with my wellbeing at the forefront of her mind.

'We're always friends. You know that. But please, Diana, no more talk of husbands. There's nothing in the world I desire less than a man in my house—and let that be the end of it.'

The carriage juddered violently as it hit yet another pothole, but the man wrapped tightly in a well-worn cloak didn't complain. Anything was better than that blasted boat. The weeks spent pitching and yawing were mercifully behind him now, and never—never!—to be repeated. The only way he'd set foot on another ship was if he were carried, and it was unlikely anybody looking at his hulking frame would dare to try.

Perhaps it was the broad shoulders that made his fellow passengers in the carriage give him a wide berth, or maybe the leather patch covering one ruined eye was more off-putting. Whatever the reason, nobody seemed eager to speak to him, and he was thankful for the silence as he mulled over the events that had brought him to this point.

Like something out of a novel. Shipwrecks, kidnap, and a man wondering if he can change for the better.

He folded his arms, gazing up at the roof of the carriage as it shuddered down yet another chilly country lane. It was far colder than Algiers, and he almost smiled at the notion of actually appreciating an English winter following his perilous escape. Perhaps there were other things he'd be thankful for now he'd returned, more ready than before to count his blessings…and might that even extend to people, to the faces held in his memory blurred now by the passage of so much time?

I wonder if my parents missed me. For certain Mother did, but Father?

A momentary frown crossed his face, his uncovered eye narrowing slightly as he considered the father who had taught him so harshly what it meant to be a man. From the moment he'd been able to hold a pen he'd been moulded into a copy of that severe figure—an unsmiling giant bent over accounts books with never a kind word to spare for his own child.

There was only one aim in a successful life: to make money, lots of it, and to hold oneself so coldly apart nothing could distract from that single goal. A *real* man was proud and unbending, focused solely on his ambition and holding his head so high no lesser person would cross him. Sentiment was a useless waste of time, reserved for weak-willed women, and no male of substance would allow it any space in his mind.

A silent grimace twisted his grim mouth.

No doubt my disappearance was taxing more for the lost cargo than a lost son. I would have written to warn them of my return if only I'd had half an idea of what to say in circumstances that defy description.

Outside the carriage window the skeletal trees began to thin as another quaint village rolled into view—a handful of thatched cottages sprinkled with sparkling white. For a moment the scene distracted him from uncomfortable thoughts, something in the peaceful prettiness reminding him of the one other person to whom his mind had so often turned throughout both his captivity and the long journey to freedom.

What would *she* think of all this?

He leaned forward, resting his elbows on his knees and making the passenger beside him shift uneasily.

Not something I intended to consider again after those first weeks. A clean break was what I wanted, after I remembered where my concerns should lie—and that was exactly what I managed.

A fleeting picture flashed through his mind of rustling skirts and glossy hair, topped off by a smile that could light up a room better than any fire.

Loveliest girl I'd ever seen, and clever into the bargain. Small wonder my head was turned and I had to act fast to save myself from being carried away completely.

His mistake had been in getting distracted, getting too close despite his father's strict instruction and example, and the conversation that had reminded him of his priorities had not been pleasant.

A wife wasn't someone to dally with—as he should have known. His own parents rarely spent more than a few minutes in each other's company, and there was no accord between them whatsoever. Pulling away from the intriguing young woman who had made his pulse race and his attention wander from his work had been absolutely necessary, his reluctance all the proof he'd needed that it was the right course. Placing profit over people was the only way to conduct himself if he was to live up to the expectations placed on him since birth. There was no room for anything else but pure business—including the curious sensation that had shaken him every time she'd entered a room—and he needn't forget it.

And he hadn't forgotten again, just as he'd sworn he wouldn't after that unforgivable lapse in concentration at the start. Not for one single day: until his whole life had been turned upside down and he'd realised nothing would be the same again.

The cottages slid away to be replaced once more by trees clawing at the vast grey sky, their limbs waving in a biting wind, but he looked through them as though they weren't even there.

There were more important things to consider, other questions to pose. *Such as wondering what she'll say and whether I'm different enough now to make amends.*

He'd know soon enough. With every clip of the horses' hooves he drew closer to home—to the place and people he'd dreamed of for five long years—and there was nothing to do but wait.

Shardlow House stood only a few minutes' walk from Farleigh, a smaller but still impressive residence standing tall above the other roofs of Thame Magna barely twenty miles from London. Nestled behind immaculate hedges its white walls were partially hidden by swathes of ivy, the emerald leaves waving to Hester as she crunched up the wide drive towards them.

It was a house pulled directly from a fairy tale, she'd always thought, although Nathaniel had poured scorn over that particular observation when she'd ventured to make it—as Hester recalled now, with a frown that made her headache worse as she pushed open the green front door.

'Fairy stories are for children, Hester. It was the price that attracted me to Shardlow House and nothing more.'

She couldn't help a scowl as an image of Nathaniel's damnably handsome face uttering those very words flickered before her like the light of a match—one she blew out at once.

I've spent long enough thinking of him today.

Hester glowered to herself as the sound of quick footsteps signalled the approach of Arless, her lady's maid.

Nathaniel took up quite enough room in my thoughts while he was alive. There can be no need for him to linger now he's dead. All the same...

Diana's meddling had woken something in Hester that she'd managed to keep undisturbed, locked away in the darkness, but now vague snippets of memories stirred at the back of her mind like fallen leaves.

The first instant she'd seen him, standing so tall and proud in his expensive coat that her heart had almost leaped out of her chest; how her pulse had galloped at Father's declaration the Townsend and Honeywell trading empires were to be connected by a marriage; the warmth of Nathaniel's hand as he'd slid it around her waist in a darkened room and sent a thrill down her spine as his lips touched hers for the very first time...

Each memory lasted mere seconds—the blink of an eye in the grand scheme of Hester's life—and yet they were imprinted into her mind like a blacksmith's brand. At one time they had been like treasured jewels, but now she wanted nothing more than to forget the very things she'd once thought would always bring her joy, their sparkle dulled by the unhappy years that had followed.

'Are you unwell, ma'am? You've returned sooner than I expected.'

Turning, Hester saw the concern in Arless' face, kind as always beneath her lace cap. She'd been a loyal presence ever since Hester's marriage, and her calm competence was something even fine ladies could aspire to.

Hester forced a smile, knowing it must look unnatural as the weight in her gut pressed painfully. 'A slight headache from the cold wind, that's all. Nothing a short lie-down won't cure.'

Arless watched her young mistress narrowly, but said nothing as Hester crossed the impressive hall and made for the stairs. The pale greens and blues of her rooms would be soothing to a troubled soul; or so she hoped, the prospect of an afternoon spent raking over the past something she had no desire to suffer.

'Could you please see I'm not disturbed? I'll be up in time for luncheon.'

'Very good, ma'am. I'll make sure you're left in peace.'

The room was warm, with a fire dancing merrily in the grate, and with a sigh Hester folded down onto the embroidered coverlet of her bed. Gazing upwards, she stared at the canopy, its floral pattern so familiar she could have described it with her eyes shut.

Perhaps I ought to shut them now. I might be permitted to sleep instead of being tormented by memories I don't want, and when I wake Nathaniel's face might not loom so large as to obliterate all other thought.

It was worth a try. The man who had so enticed and then wounded her might retreat into the shadows if she sought escape in sleep—unless the usual nightmare, of his ghostly hand reaching for her from beneath the sea, returned to frighten her once more. It came less often these days, but all the same Hester shuddered at the idea, a cold chill running through her despite the lively flames.

Drowning was a terrible death, Nathaniel's

naval acquaintances had murmured when they'd come to pay their respects. The thought of it clamped Hester's chest in a vice of horror and squeezed until she could barely breathe.

'However badly he hurt me, I would never have wished that end on him,' Hester murmured, only the damask bed curtains and rich pillows catching her low words. 'Lost beneath the waves with no hope of proper burial. Never even recovering his body…'

The moment her father had come to Shardlow House at dawn, face white as parchment and his hat in his hand, tried to push itself forward, but Hester swatted it away immediately as though it were a fly.

No. I won't think of it. I won't relive the morning Father came to tell me I was a widow at barely twenty years old.

She screwed her eyes closed. Diana had a lot to answer for, her interference poking the hornets' nest Hester had to conceal each day. It writhed inside her now, insistent, trying to find her weakest point.

Father's shaking voice. Mother's stunned silence. My realisation that I'd never see Nathaniel again, would have no chance at all of recapturing what I thought we'd once had—and a split second of guilt, when I wondered if I ought to be weeping instead of simply numb…

The sudden knock at Hester's bedroom door

couldn't have been less welcome, the prospect of anyone entering her sanctuary at that precise moment one that made her grimace.

'Ma'am?' Arless' voice came from the landing. 'Ma'am, are you awake?'

'So much for being left in peace,' Hester mumbled into her pillow, eyes still closed. The throbbing behind them had hardly abated, and Hester knew she sounded a fraction too sharp when she called out to her unwanted visitor. 'Unfortunately. Come in.'

Hester heard the door open and turned her head to see the maid enter—then sat up, sudden alarm sweeping through her as she saw Arless' face.

'You're as white as a sheet!'

She slid from the bed and crossed the room, catching hold of the maid's arm and guiding her into a chair beside the hearth. The other woman's face was indeed the colour of sour milk, pale and wan as she gazed up so blankly that Hester's fears grew.

'What is it? What's wrong?'

Hester watched the shake of a lace-capped head. Whatever had happened to make the servant look like a frightened child must have been dire, and Hester's stomach tightened as dread circled inside her.

'You're starting to worry me. What's amiss? You look as though you've seen a ghost!'

The lady's maid passed a hand across her brow and Hester saw how violently it shook, Arless' usual serene presence deserting her completely. The servant took an unsteady breath, seemingly to gather herself, and when she met her eye Hester felt a chill run the length of her spine at the stark fear she saw in their depths.

'I'm very much afraid I may have done just that. There's someone waiting for you down in the parlour, ma'am. It's Mr Honeywell—he's back from the dead!'

Pulling the patch a little lower to fully cover his useless eye, Nathaniel allowed the remaining one to explore the stylish parlour.

Redecorated since I was last here. Hester must have grown into a woman of good taste.

He shifted a little in his seat, bones still aching and jangled from the long carriage ride from Dover. Poor Arless certainly hadn't looked thrilled to see him; something of an understatement, seeming as though she might pass out at the first sight of his now crooked smile. It was his home, and he had every right to be there, but for a long while it had been ruled by Hester alone... and they hadn't quite parted as friends.

Still...

Nathaniel stretched the stiffness of travelling out of his strong arms, feeling the release of tight muscles. Once Hester got over the shock he was positive she'd be delighted to see him. Her adoration had never been a secret, after all.

That's the Hester I remember—always watching me walk across a room and blushing when I caught her staring, even after any interest was entirely one-sided. At the time it was an irritation I didn't want, but perhaps now I might even find it endearing.

He tapped the fingers of his right hand against his knee, the index conspicuous by its absence. The poorly cauterised stump still itched occasionally and he scratched it now—more for something to occupy his restless hands than anything else. The last time he'd seen Hester he'd been complete, proud of the comely face he had known made his shy wife flush with admiration, not possessing the hard, work-honed muscles of a slave nor the new sense of shame that sat like a permanent weight in his belly.

Did he look much older, only twenty-six but so scarred from life's harshness that he might be a decade more? Even his skin was different, darkened by the Algerian sun that had the opposite effect on his already fair hair, now bleached from toiling all day in the fierce heat.

She might not even recognise him, Nathaniel mused—and would he know *her*, the infatuated young wife he had all but abandoned? In those days he'd barely cared for anyone but himself, Hester's obvious fancy for him an irrelevant nuisance once he'd been reminded that other things were more important. But after what he had endured at the hands of his cruel keepers...

It was not a pleasant thought, and Nathaniel rose from the sofa and paced about the room as though he could outrun it.

Leaving in the manner I did was possibly not my finest hour, he admitted as he walked, *but wouldn't most rational men have done the same?*

All that fuss over some trifling cold Hester claimed to have had in a ploy to stop him from going to sea... Nonsense, of course, that Father had swiftly assured him was just a cunning female ruse, and as always Nathaniel had trusted that clear reasoning. Why would he not?

Even now he could remember his relief at hearing Shardlow's door close behind him as he escaped her tears, glad his father had been there to guide him away from any misplaced concern and back towards the trade where his interest belonged—just as had been necessary the month after Nathaniel had wed, when for a moment it seemed he might waver from his proper course.

He huffed out a heavy breath.

Profit over people. Allow no distractions.

The mantra had been drilled into him ever since he could remember, along with stories of his great-grandfather dragging himself up from nothing to build wealth and status, told so often Nathaniel could recite them word for word. By that reckoning he'd been right to crush his developing feelings for the girl who had become his wife. Money was all that mattered, capital and ambition placed above all else: even one's own family, something Nathaniel had learned to accept as soon as he was old enough to understand.

Mr Honeywell gave no affection and wanted none in return—not from his son and certainly not from the wife he scorned for her inane chatter and pointless emotion. Caught between his mother's love and his father's coldness, Nathaniel had followed the path he understood, shaped by duty and greed and the ruthless ambition for *more*. Life was a cut-throat business, only lived right if one remained strong and unbroken and proud. Honeywells never bent the knee to anyone, instead crushing others beneath their far superior boots.

Now Nathaniel caught his reflection in the ornate mirror hanging above the fireplace and saw shame in his tanned, weather-beaten face. Doubtless his father would be horrified, then, to learn how deeply he had despaired in the days of his captivity, when his keepers had sought to break his spirit with humiliation and suffering.

He'd been brought lower than he'd known possible, living like an animal rather than a human being, and it made him grimace to think what his father would say if he ever learned of his son's disgrace. It flew in the face of everything

Nathaniel knew a man should be, such repulsive subservience deserving of nothing but contempt and it had left a stain on his character he could never hope to wash clean.

He passed a rough hand across his face, feeling the scratch of stubble as the same dark memories returned to harry him like a wolf among sheep. Everything in Algiers had been so *hard*— a million miles away from the comfort he'd always taken for granted and stripping away his pride until it lay in tatters. The work, his captors, finding the will to get through each brutal day with no hope of escape…

His fellow slaves—in particular a steadfast Scot named Jacob Morrow—had been the only thing that had kept him alive on days when he would rather have died than bear the shame of what he'd become, and their friendship and kindness was something without which he would not have survived until the sails of *HMS Queen Charlotte* had crested the horizon and Nathaniel had known he was saved.

Something his father had always taught him was a weakness had in fact been his salvation. The compassion and humanity of the other captives had been a strength, not a failing. It was a valuable lesson to learn, and perhaps one he might even share with Hester now fate had brought them together once again.

'I've been granted a second chance,' he muttered, taking another turn of the familiar room. 'The least I can do is try to offer her my friendship—although of course that's as far as I'm willing to go.'

Nathaniel shook his head, dismissing echoes of the past that had no place in the present. Any feelings he might once have entertained as a lad of barely eighteen lay forgotten, cut off and left to wither as useless baggage. The Honeywell Trading Company still came first despite his long absence and he knew his responsibilities, although it crossed his mind that this time it might be possible to treat Hester with some of the kindness he had learned, rather than the outright neglect his father favoured for wives.

She wouldn't be allowed to become a distraction again—a laughable notion, since he had packed that weakness into a box and buried it so deep there was no possibility it had survived— but he could extend an olive branch she'd be delighted to accept, her eagerness to please him vaguely touching now he was more inclined to be generous.

Abruptly Nathaniel ceased his pacing, ears straining hard.

Was that footsteps outside the door?

He hardly had time to wonder before it flew open and Hester stood square on the threshold, and the stiff smile he had forced froze fast on his lips.

'Nathaniel?'

She stared at him, eyes wide; eyes just as blue as the last time he'd seen them, although in that moment he couldn't remember why their attention had ever irritated him. They were piercing, any naivety replaced now by a keen understanding that caught him off guard, and he blinked as an unexpected whip-crack flared in his stomach. Outlined in sunlight she looked older, no longer a shy girl, with her fair hair a halo and the porcelain contours of her face lit like something from a painting.

Can this truly be the same woman I left behind?

Secreted beneath his shirt, Nathaniel felt his heart-rate pick up. However he'd expected to feel on seeing Hester again, it hadn't been *this*—wordless surprise and the sudden feeling he wished he'd thought to comb his hair after the long journey from the ship.

'Hello, Hester.'

He too stood still, aware of how he towered above his stunned wife. She would scarcely reach up to his shoulder if they stood closer together, some part of him registered, although by the look on her face he thought she might faint if he tried.

I forgot how small she is. Or—more likely— perhaps I never bothered to notice...

Ignoring the thought, he offered a bow, feeling her stare boring into the top of his head as he bent forward. 'It's been a long time since we last met. I'm happy to see you're looking considerably better than I am.'

The Hester he remembered would be quick to jump in with some clumsy compliment to deny his self-reproach—but no such thing came.

'I thought… We all thought…'

Hester's face was still milk-white, her hand gripping the parlour door as though she might break it off; but then her eyes hardened. All of a sudden she looked nothing like the timid, unwanted wife he'd left behind, and Nathaniel's brow contracted in a frown.

'You're supposed to be *dead*!'

Her gaze fixed on his with such steely focus that another man might have taken a step backwards. It was a world away from the reaction he had expected, and for a moment Nathaniel was at a loss for a reply.

'Well…' He pushed back his shaggy hair, watching the snap of Hester's gaze move from his patch to the missing finger of his right hand.

Periwinkle-blue? Or perhaps more cornflower? More comely than I remember, at any rate.

He almost felt as though he should apologise for *not* having drowned, and he couldn't keep a touch of confusion from his voice. 'Not the warmest of welcomes a man might hope for, especially from his wife.'

Hester's mouth twisted, the small movement of her lips attracting Nathaniel's attention at once.

'Your eye...your hand...'

She shook her head, slim neck moving at the lace collar of her cream dress and drawing his eye like a magnet. Had she always possessed a freckle at her throat, or that intriguing dip between her collar bones?

If she did I never noticed... Why did I never notice?

At least to that question he could provide an answer.

Probably because I only shared her bed for that first month, and in my boyish eagerness I didn't take the time for a comprehensive study. After I came to my senses I thought the required heir would follow later...when I found the time.

Those pretty lips were moving again, still demanding answers, and he dismissed the wayward thought. Hester and beds didn't belong in the same sentence, surely? And yet...

'Why did you not send word you survived the *Celeste*'s sinking? Not a single letter to anybody in all this time! How could you allow the mistake to go on so long?'

Nathaniel folded his arms, hardly knowing where to begin. Where were the happy tears he had prepared himself to endure with his new-found patience? Of all the possible receptions he had imagined, *this* had not been one of them.

Hesitant, obliging little Hester, demanding answers? It was unthinkable, impossible, and it momentarily robbed him of the ability to reply.

When he didn't speak Hester drew herself up to her full height, looking at him with all the warmth of a marble statue.

'Forgive me. Perhaps you might want to rest a while before you explain. It must be a long story, and by the look of you your journey home has been longer still.'

If he'd possessed less self-control Nathaniel might have let his mouth fall open.

A rebuke? From Hester?

Who *was* this woman—and what had she done with his wife?

She still watched him, apparently waiting, and Nathaniel mustered a curt nod. 'I won't deny it has taken a long while. A rest would be appreciated.'

Hester lifted her chin, the image of an icily polite hostess. 'Very good. I'll have rooms prepared at once.'

She paused, and Nathaniel felt his pulse quicken once more as she looked him pointedly up and down.

'And hot water sent up so you can wash.'

Again his lips felt in danger of parting by themselves as another flood of disbelief washed over him. Was that disapproval in her eyes as she surveyed him from head to toe? Nathaniel could hardly believe it. Admittedly he was not quite as handsome as he'd been before parts of him were scarred for life, but to see anything but admiration in Hester's face was a surprise—and one that bothered him more than he liked.

Did she only have regard for me when I was whole and unmarked?

The idea rang unpleasantly in his ears and he determined at once to set it aside—although not before it stoked the embers of the shame he carried constantly. Its heat warmed him always, never letting him forget how low he'd sunk, his scars a constant reminder of the depths he'd plumbed to get them.

No doubt Hester would be appalled if she knew the extent of his dramatic fall from grace…but she didn't, and never would—of that he would make certain. A man ought to be proud and upright, not scrabbling in the mud, and even if he was as tainted as he felt his wife would never be given cause to look upon him with anything so humiliating as pity.

She had turned away, moving to leave the room, and Nathaniel called to her before he knew what he was doing. 'We haven't seen each other in five years, Hester. Are you in such a hurry to run away from me again so soon?'

The moment the words left his mouth Nathaniel wished he could call them back. Why had he spoken at all? There was no real answer, but even if there had been he would have forgotten at the slow half-turn of Hester's head. She didn't look him in the eye, instead keeping her face carefully angled away.

'It wasn't me that did the running away, Nathaniel,' Hester replied, her voice as cold as the frosted lawns outside. 'That was you.'

She stepped out, slipping from the room and pulling the door closed behind her. All Nathaniel could do was watch her go, an uncomfortable realisation beginning to unfurl in the pit of his stomach.

It seems I was wrong. Perhaps my homecoming isn't quite as welcome as I thought.

Chapter Two

Hester slumped against the door of her bed-chamber and waited for the room to stop spinning, eyes closed and breathing shallow. Keeping her composure had taken every ounce of strength, and now she felt each muscle tremble as she tried to straighten up, legs weak as if she'd run for miles instead of back upstairs to find a place to hide.

It really is him. I thought for sure Arless was mistaken.

Time had slowed as Nathaniel turned to her, a stiff smile on the tanned face now much more rugged than she remembered. There had been a momentary pause while her brain caught up with the sight before her eyes—and then pure shock, its icy fist closing around her chest. At least she had escaped with some dignity, cutting their meeting short before she betrayed herself; it was a miracle she hadn't collapsed at his feet, all good sense fleeing at a ghost made flesh.

He's so altered I might never have known him. The hair, the patch—and what in heaven's name happened to his hand?

She pressed her palm against her breastbone, feeling the leap of her heart beneath the thin fabric of her gown. Each violent beat was all too reminiscent of how she'd used to feel in her husband's presence, jumping and thrashing with wild confusion.

At least she'd shown none of that bewilderment to Nathaniel. He couldn't have known how her throat had dried at the sight of him, or how her attention had been drawn against her will to the new—impressive, *fascinating*—breadth of shoulder beneath his shirt. It suited him, the way his lightened hair now fell in a perfect sweep below his collar, the one emerald eye left uncovered finding hers and making her swallow as it held her gaze. He looked so different he might almost be another person; but still one who tempted her to stare, static shock crackling through her veins just as it had on their wedding day, and the unwanted fact was enough to focus Hester's mind.

Absolutely not!

She flung herself away from the door, pacing across the room like a caged animal. What kind of perverse thought was *that* at such a moment?

Nathaniel had made her life a misery with his trickery and neglect, and her first thought after all these years was that he was still *handsome*?

Hester laced her hands together behind her head, sinking shaking fingers into her hair. Where had he been all that time? How could he have let his family believe he was dead? Yet more proof of his unthinking selfishness—as if there had ever been any question! And then to stroll back into her home without a word to forewarn her, no doubt expecting to pick his life up again at the very place he had left it five years ago—without ever having cared whether his wife was dead or alive?

She drew in a ragged breath, pausing in her mindless striding about the room.

Dead or alive.

Nathaniel was *alive*, and despite everything Hester wasn't so malicious as to wish him otherwise. His parents would be overjoyed—or at least his mother would. His father would surely keep any pleasure at his heir's return strictly to himself, brooding on it like a dragon with its hoard.

The sound of activity on the other side of Hester's door captured her attention. Light feet on creaking floorboards signalled the busyness of housemaids preparing Nathaniel's rooms—and sent Hester flying out to intercept them.

'Wait, please. Where are you putting Mr Honeywell?'

'In his usual rooms, ma'am.'

'Ah.' Hester smiled painfully to cover a sudden unpleasant jolt in her stomach. Nathaniel had always occupied the rooms next to hers, their bedchambers linked by an adjoining door that, testament to their cold marriage, was kept locked and unused. In the old days she'd learnt to cry quietly as she lay trying to sleep, knowing her husband would hear any sobs louder than a whisper. There was no danger of her crying now, of course—this time her desire for distance from Nathaniel was for a different reason altogether.

That hideous, girlish leap of her pulse when she'd seen him standing in front of the hearth had been a warning bell, chiming loud and clear. Ignoring it would be foolish, and Hester was no longer anyone's fool.

Especially not Nathaniel's.

He would expect things to be just as they were before, Hester mused darkly. He the returning ruler, come to reclaim his place and take back control of her home, her money—and her. She would go back to being the meek little wife she'd always been, looking to her captivating husband for some scrap of kindness to light her lonely life, and he would hold all the power in one tight-fisted hand.

I think not.

Nathaniel would never hold such sway over her ever again. Perhaps once she'd been weak enough to accept her unhappiness without complaint, but that had been before her spine had grown harder and she would not be bending it now.

However, with only a door separating them he was far too close—especially given her discomforting thoughts of how his forearms looked so newly sculpted and strong. With so many months and an ocean between them she'd thought her foolish fancy for that accursed man dead and buried, and to find traces still tried to linger was more than she could stand.

It's the shock. I'm so rattled I barely know which way is up, Hester reassured herself. *But until I'm completely satisfied I have a firm hold on any stupid infatuation I won't put myself in his way. Sleeping so closely to him is only asking for trouble if any spark of that old partiality remains. Not that it'll take long to stamp out.*

'Mr Honeywell has clearly had a long journey and will need his rest. A quieter part of the house will be much more suitable than here, near the bustle of my rooms.'

'Very good, ma'am. I'll see to it at once.'

Hester watched the housemaid go, envious of the other woman's sense of purpose as she collected her assistants. They had a job to do, a task to occupy their thoughts; something Hester would have welcomed. Her own head was so distractingly full that a voice from behind made her jump—and then her pulse followed suit as she saw Nathaniel had appeared on the landing, just as blond and as handsome as she'd feared.

'Sorry. I didn't mean to startle you.'

His faint smile did something strange to Hester's stomach. A flicker leapt up inside, warm as a coal from a fire, making her swallow a gasp at the sudden heat. The curve of Nathaniel's lips was something she'd seen so rarely that part of her wanted to keep looking at it, before a much larger—and more sensible—part snatched back control.

'You didn't,' Hester snapped, knowing she sounded flustered and hating it. 'I was preoccupied, that's all.'

Nathaniel merely inclined his head, although Hester could have sworn she saw a gleam of surprise in his eye at the brusqueness of her tone. If she was right, he wasn't the only one confused.

Nathaniel apologising for startling her? Nathaniel apologising for *anything*?

'Can I be of any assistance in your preoccupation?'

Hester glanced up at him narrowly. What game was he playing? Suddenly so solicitous when once if he'd spoken two words together she would have been pleased. Intense curiosity assailed her, tempting her to ask again… Where had he been? What had happened to keep him from home for five years, and changed him so markedly upon his return?

But in the next breath Hester resolved to do no such thing.

I won't flatter him by begging for answers. If Nathaniel wants to explain himself I shall listen quite calmly, but I won't allow him to think he has my unwavering fascination ever again. He can't behave so selfishly as to let us think he died and then expect me to fall over myself with interest in hearing his story.

The fact that she was interested—burningly, maddeningly so—was neither here nor there, she decided sternly. Nathaniel needn't know how badly she wanted to know why the patch was needed, or the circumstances in which his hand had been maimed. She would display no outward curiosity at all, mirroring the lack of interest with which Nathaniel had so damaged her... before he'd returned so bafflingly different Hester couldn't help another thrill of mistrust. He'd already drawn her in with convincing charm once, when as an innocent girl she hadn't been able to tell false regard from real, and there was no way she'd be falling for the same trick twice.

'No, thank you. I'm more than capable of taking care of arrangements at Shardlow House myself.'

She watched his lips part as if on a reply, but evidently he changed his mind, only a brief furrow of his brows betraying whatever he was thinking. Perhaps he didn't like her newfound assertiveness, Hester wondered with faint triumph, but his next words took the wind from her sails at once.

'The house is so different since I was last here. Perhaps you'd give me a guided tour after I've settled in?'

'Oh.' Hester froze. The uncharacteristic, even suspicious request caught her entirely off guard. 'I'm not sure...'

She groped for an excuse, horribly aware of the blood rushing to her cheeks. That unacceptable reaction to Nathaniel's smile had been enough of a caution to steer clear of him, and yet as she looked up into his face her mind stretched out blank as a side of paper.

The novel tan of his skin contrasted pleasingly with his white shirt, almost the colour of caramelised sugar and, terrifyingly, just as tempting. He'd been so much paler before, but now he looked almost edible—a dangerous thought that made Hester's blood run cold.

Damn. Why couldn't she think up some reason to refuse? The best she could do was a vague mumble, not even convincing herself as she wished she could scoop out her own traitorous eyes. 'I imagine I'll be busy for the next few days. You'd be better to ask one of the servants.'

'Ah. That's a pity. I would have appreciated your knowledge.'

That mouth curved again, as though Hester had been more gracious, and she cursed to know that she had lost the battle; but she *would not* lose the war. If Nathaniel thought his strangely courteous new manner would fool her he'd be disappointed…

She just needed to work out what he was trying to fool her *for*.

If Nathaniel hadn't known better, he might have believed he'd drowned after all. The bath drawn up before the guest room's fire was so hot, the soap so scented, that it was as close to heaven as he could imagine.

Or would have been, if his mind hadn't insisted on ticking away over the same repeated question like a broken clock.

What has really happened to Hester? It can't just be my face, surely?

He lay back, both arms resting on the sides of the vast bathtub. He should have been savouring his first real bath in five years, luxuriating in the warmth and fragranced steam, but instead it was his wife who occupied his mind as he closed his eyes and tipped his head back against the rim.

Surely she didn't still bear a grudge that he hadn't stayed behind; perhaps wounded he hadn't been taken in by the pretence of grave illness that his father had shattered with cool logic? Hester had always been so healthy that to fall ill so close to the date of his departure could never have been a coincidence. Still with eyes closed—both the green and the ruined, the leather patch sitting in a heap along with his other clothes—Nathaniel turned the question over, inspecting it from all angles.

She *had* mentioned 'running away' before she'd left the parlour, turning her back with a finality that even now he couldn't quite believe…

But, no. It couldn't be that. Such a small event in the grand scheme of things, and Hester had never given the impression of pettiness before. There had to be something else, and given time he would coax it from her.

Not for my own sake. It'll just make things easier for her if everything is brought out into the open.

Nathaniel nodded to himself, almost believing his own lie. He might have fooled himself entirely if the image of Hester's face, so intelligent and clear, hadn't passed before him at that moment, the fine turn of her profile making him sit up abruptly and sending a gout of water sloshing onto the floor.

That's of no consequence. I was merely taken by surprise at the change in her from girl to woman, that's all.

The firm set of her jaw as she'd stood in the

doorway was immaterial—as was the suspicious glint that had lent such animation to her eyes. All he intended was to set things right with Hester, now he'd been shown the value of a little kindness—a lesson learned by way of goodness shining amongst brutality—and something so pointless as pretty cheekbones would not distract him.

Consideration is what I mean to show, not useless sentiment. A man can only change so far... especially one with five years of lost business to catch up on.

Still unease writhed like an eel in his belly, and Nathaniel rose to his feet as if to escape it. Rivulets of water ran down his broad back, across taut thighs ridged with muscle, and as he brushed a hand over the thatch on his defined chest he wondered for the first time if any of his clothes had been kept—and indeed if they would still fit. He'd been far lither when he'd left—his arms would strain the sleeves and shoulders of his old shirts now, with their solid strength contained beneath tanned skin that bore the scars of hard work.

If Hester's reception so far is anything to go by she might just have burned anything I left behind.

Stepping from the bath, Nathaniel reached for one of the drying sheets left neatly folded on the bed, rubbing himself vigorously to distract from such unsettling thoughts. Before the *Celeste* had set sail he'd have assumed Hester would keep his possessions as some kind of shrine to his memory, and the notion that she might have instead done the opposite was…uncomfortable.

With an unconscious frown he sifted through the pile of dirty clothes he had removed, automatically settling the patch back over his useless eye. He'd have to hunt down some replacement clothes, and that meant making a break for his old rooms—where hopefully Hester had permitted his wardrobe to remain unharmed.

Nathaniel crossed to the door, wrapping the sheet around his waist as he went. There was nobody out on the landing, and Nathaniel moved down the corridor from the guest wing with an easy stride. Other paths led off to the left and right, but he kept straight on and round a corner until his bedchamber beckoned, its brass handle gleaming invitingly.

Only a few steps more and he'd be safely inside; and almost was, when the door beside his own jerked open and Hester materialised before him, moving far too quickly to stop herself from walking—*smack!*—directly into his bare, still-damp chest.

She gave a startled cry and he darted forward to catch her by the wrist, his strong fingers circling delicate bone to prevent her from overbalancing. The contact lasted only seconds, warm skin against skin, and yet the sensation of heat lingered in his fingertips as Hester steadied herself and pulled away, staring up at him with wordless horror.

He looked back, intently aware of how the pulse he'd felt above her lace cuff had raced— and how his own had picked up in reply at how closely she still stood, separate now but apparently unable to flee.

'Nathaniel? What are—? *Why are you wandering about the house half dressed?*'

Hester's voice was strangled, and unless Nathaniel was very much mistaken she appeared to have broken her neck. She was certainly holding her head at a very strange angle and so fixedly it might have been stuck in position with extremely strong glue, her chin high and eyes trained steadily on his face. Her own was slowly filling with colour, he noted with unexpected interest...

Until all at once he understood why.

'Not even half dressed, technically. There's only this sheet standing between me and total disgrace.'

He saw her swallow and couldn't help a swift twitch of his lips as her determination not to look down seemed to increase. Teasing would do nothing to help defrost her, but who could resist such low-hanging fruit? It was true, after all. Mercifully the sheet was still where he had tucked it but, judging by Hester's unwavering interest in the top of his head, it was clear she'd be taking no chances.

Did she like what she saw?

The rogue thought sneaked in uninvited, and Nathaniel shooed it away—although he couldn't entirely ignore it. Doubtless many women would find something to enjoy in his sculpted chest… just as most men would admire the rosy flush of Hester's cheeks, a delicate bloom he saw suited her immensely.

I seem to recall that was the first thing I ever noticed about her…how pretty her blush was. Before I determined to look the other way.

With a twinge of discomfort Nathaniel took pity on her.

Stick to the task. What have the events of seven years ago to do with anything?

'I was looking for some of my old clothes. With no valet, I'm afraid I took the matter of dressing into my own hands—although I can easily remedy that if you're agreeable to my engaging one.'

Still defiantly examining his water-slicked hair, Hester nodded. 'Of course. You might advertise at once. There seemed little point keeping Mr Eaves on without a gentleman in the house for him to wait on, but I imagine you'll find a suitable replacement.'

'I'm sure I shall. It'll be the second appointment I'll have made since my return.'

Hester frowned, for a moment meeting his one uncovered eye. 'The second appointment? What was the first?'

Nathaniel rubbed the back of his neck, just catching the fleeting and apparently involuntary snap of Hester's gaze from his face to the generous curve of his bicep as he lifted his arm. At one time her admiration had been plain, but now he wondered again at the new reluctance with which she barely tolerated his presence.

Hardly the time to be considering that. The real question is, how much do I tell Hester about who I've employed as Shardlow's new estate manager? And why I consider it a privilege to offer Jacob Morrow that place in my house now my fortunes are restored?

It was thanks to Jacob, after all, that Nathaniel had started to question his previous ways. Watching the older man make sure the sick and elderly ate first, intervening on their behalf with the foremen and tending to the injured, had shown him another perspective on those he had originally disregarded as of no use: caring for the weak rather than shunning them, the precise opposite of everything his father stood for and Nathaniel himself had believed. People didn't have to be profitable to be worth something, he'd begun to realise, and as the days had turned into weeks he had seen for himself how far a little compassion lit up otherwise grim lives.

Only the kindness of others had saved him from surrendering to his own despair, Jacob the first to give Nathaniel hope that one day their lives would improve and the British Navy would triumphantly bring them home.

But that didn't help him with his current dilemma.

How much did Hester need to know about what had transpired in Algiers, when both his body and spirit had been so nearly broken beyond repair? How could he explain to Hester how he had lived through hell, with each day filled with pain and struggle he'd much rather forget?

He couldn't—that was clear. He would never reveal his humiliation…the bowing and scraping that even now made him burn with fathomless shame. She'd never respect him if she knew how far he had strayed from the path of masculinity his father had laid out for him to follow, that example far out of reach while Nathaniel was humbled to dust.

He cleared his throat. 'I've hired an estate manager—a man I met while I was away and to whom I feel I owe a favour. I have a few ideas for improvements to make around Shardlow, and he's just the person to help me in that task. We reached an arrangement before I left Algiers— he'll be arriving any day now, I would think.'

Hester's brow clouded once more and Nathaniel steeled himself, waiting for the barrage of questions he knew would have to come.

Of course his wife would be curious, wondering when and where he had met this apparently indispensable person. He'd known he would need to think of something to explain himself—some story to conceal the weeks and months when he'd thought all was lost and despair had tried to drown him—and with a deep breath Nathaniel drew on the courage suffering had beaten into him. He would take the weight of those memories and heave them aside, never telling Hester what he had been reduced to—transformed from a selfish wealthy boy into a slave, toiling bent-backed beneath the Mediterranean sun, until he emerged as a man who had learnt from his mistakes.

But the interrogation didn't come.

'I see.'

Hester stepped backwards, finally increasing the distance between them, although her gaze still never wavered from his face. Nathaniel wondered if there was a glitter of curiosity in her sapphire glance, but if so it vanished again almost at once, replaced by cool disinterest that hit him squarely—and unexpectedly—in the gut.

She doesn't care? She doesn't want to know?

He'd prepared himself for tears and questions, sympathy and regrets; anything but the indifference written clearly across her countenance, and it was another blow to realise that it *both-ered* him.

Did she actually mourn for me, even?

The novel thought entered Nathaniel's head like an arrow, unwanted but insistent on being heard.

I always assumed she'd be beside herself, but perhaps...

'You might have consulted me before filling such an important post, but I suppose it doesn't matter much. I'll have little to do with him, any-how.'

Her words, spoken with such unconcern, were like tiny drops of ice in Nathaniel's stomach. He shouldn't care whether Hester had missed him. It was a dent in his pride, that was all...and noth-ing whatsoever to do with the dangerous flicker of respect that whispered to find she had grown some mettle in his absence. Nothing to do with the arresting curve of her waist, either, as she calmly gathered her skirts and excused herself with the smallest curtsey good manners allowed, gliding away down the corridor towards the stair-case and leaving Nathaniel to stare after her for the second time that afternoon.

A low whistle escaped between his teeth as he watched the hem of her gown whisk out of sight. 'Well, I'll be damned...'

She was certainly determined. He'd give her that. Anyone with eyes could have seen how much effort it had taken her not to look down at his chiselled form, and yet Hester had kept her head high and any curiosity to herself with a new haughtiness that intrigued him, however reluctantly.

It seems winning her over might be a challenge, Nathaniel mused, still thoughtfully studying the stairs down which his wife had escaped. He'd sworn to be a better man, and yet it seemed Hester had other ideas entirely, another prickle of wary admiration passing through him at the thought. A headstrong Hester, with her mind made up to reject him just as he had once rejected her...

The irony wasn't lost on him, and Nathaniel couldn't help a shrewd smile as he turned the handle of his bedroom and finally stepped inside.

Challenge accepted, Hester. I think we both might be surprised to find out how charming I can be.

Chapter Three

Shardlow was quiet as Hester raised the hood on her warmest cloak and crept out into the frozen garden. From there it was a straight walk round to the front of the house and away into the village, and she made sure to make as little noise as possible as she scurried across the gravel drive. It was still far too early for Nathaniel to be awake— previously never having risen much before nine— but Hester determined to take no chances as she turned in the direction of the Farleigh estate.

I must find Diana. If I don't tell someone what's happened I might just explode.

Aching eyes were her reward for a sleepless night spent tossing and turning, trying—unsuccessfully—to make sense of the past twenty-four hours. Only when the first glimmer of light filtered between her curtains had Hester finally admitted defeat, having found no reasoning to explain the man who now slept beneath her roof.

The changes in Nathaniel defied comprehension, both his temperament and his looks—not to mention the drastic alteration to his previously slim physique that made Hester's cheeks flush to recall.

Stop that.

A glistening toned chest was *not* the thing to think about when other far more important things demanded her attention, and Hester dismissed it with a scowl.

'If anything, that moment of weakness should only strengthen my resolve to eschew him with a firm hand,' she muttered to herself as she walked swiftly up Thame Magna's deserted main street. *Noticing that was a sign of things I will no longer allow. I ought to be glad it put me on my guard.*

It wasn't much of an argument, but Hester clung to it nonetheless. After all, what was the alternative? Her past feelings for her husband had led to nothing but unhappiness, and now whatever strange pretence at civility he was attempting would fall on deaf ears.

'He must think I'm stupid,' she snorted out loud, glad there was nobody around to see the curl of her lip. The chilly street ahead was empty, her footsteps muffled by a sparkling scatter of frost.

Between them surely she and her sister could solve the puzzle; once Diana had got over the shock of realising her brother-in-law was alive and well...

I don't know what his aim is, but he'll find no success with me. Thinking he can erase his disregard with a handful of pretty words when I know already how hollow they ring... Ha!

Hester lengthened her stride, aggravation giving her energy. The street climbed at a slight incline and soon her breath came quicker, little clouds escaping to hang in the icy air. At this rate she would reach Diana's in record time, and with her head down Hester ploughed on with unseeing speed.

'Good morning, Hester. In a hurry to get somewhere?'

A deep, horribly attractive voice from behind brought her up short and, closing her eyes, Hester offered a silent prayer. *Please, no. Not him. Don't let it be him.*

She turned around.

Nathaniel leaned carelessly against one of the trees that lined the street, lounging with the ease of a supremely confident man. Dressed now in an expensive coat—only slightly too small—and clean-shaven, wavy hair restrained beneath his hat, he appeared the essence of a gentleman again.

Or rather, very nearly.

The patch makes him look like a pirate. Intriguing...and dangerous.

Hester knocked the unwanted thought aside, wishing she could do the same to the leap of her pulse at his sudden presence. *Damn the man.* How was it that he managed to make her throat feel tight with fewer than ten words, sending a sudden flurry through her nerves just as he'd been able to since she was eighteen?

'Nathaniel. I didn't expect you to be out of bed at this hour.'

He smiled, the tanned skin at his uncovered eye creasing disarmingly. 'I'm an early riser these days. Where are you off to, walking with such purpose?'

It was precisely the kind of question he never would have asked before, and for a half-second Hester paused. When had Nathaniel ever shown an interest in her business? Or even stopped to notice she'd left the house, let alone wonder where she was going?

He left you to die, Hester.

Reason returned to shake its head sternly, guiding her back on course.

A smile and a few careless questions can't undo that.

She bridled a little, irritated by her own moment of wavering. This was an ideal opportunity to show her husband she would not be so easily swayed by his charm as she had been all those years ago, and she was pleased by the sharpness of her tone when she spoke.

'Do you care?'

Nathaniel shrugged, apparently unmoved by her rudeness. 'I wouldn't have asked otherwise.'

'I'm going to call on my sister.'

'Ah. The lovely…the lovely…'

Hester clenched her jaw. 'Diana.'

'Of course. But have your parents given up The Firs? This isn't the most direct route to their house.'

'My sister doesn't live with our parents any longer. She wed Lord Lavendon last year and they have taken the Farleigh estate.'

She watched the swift rise of Nathaniel's eyebrows. 'Lavendon? Impressive… A prize for any woman.'

'I believe he thinks *he* got the better end of the bargain,' Hester replied icily. It was so like Nathaniel to reduce a love match to its basest parts, focusing on the fortunes involved instead of the feelings. 'Not that it *was* a bargain. They chose each other with eyes wide open and hearts likewise.'

Unlike us, she finished silently, stubbornly returning Nathaniel's uneven gaze. *Our marriage never stood a chance at developing into anything more than a soulless transaction. You made sure of that.*

A tactful man would have sensed he wasn't wanted and left her alone. Unfortunately, Nathaniel was anything but.

'I'll come with you.'

'What?' Startled, Hester blinked at her husband. She couldn't turn up on Diana's doorstep with Nathaniel in tow—the very person who had made such an early visit necessary! 'No, no. You needn't bother.'

'But you're going. And I ought to give my respects to the newlyweds.'

She swallowed, her heart racing. How could she discuss Nathaniel with Diana when he was in the room with them? She needed time to warn her sister of his return before the two met, Diana too naïve to guard herself adequately against Nathaniel's suspicious new charm. She might believe he had really changed, and Hester couldn't allow that.

'I think…actually… I might go another day,' she improvised hastily. 'I saw her only yesterday. One doesn't like to wear out one's welcome.'

'I see.'

A glimmer of that heart-stopping smile tugged at the corners of Nathaniel's lips again and Hester hurriedly looked away, disliking the effect it had on her knees.

'So you're free now?'

'It would seem so.'

'Excellent. You can come with me to see my parents.' He shouldered himself off the tree and came towards her, his unmarked hand outstretched. 'I'm expecting my mother will cry, and frankly I'd appreciate your example as to how to deal with it.'

Hester looked down at his hand as though it were a snake ready to strike, cursing Nathaniel for outmanoeuvring her once again. If she refused to accompany him it would give the impression his presence bothered her, feeding that insufferable pride, and yet the notion of slipping her fingers into his palm made her throat contract.

'If I recall, that never was your area of expertise, was it?'

To her amazement Nathaniel's smile slid a little at the barb. 'Quite so,' he answered quietly. 'There's much I realise now I never took the time to learn.'

She hesitated, a wave of confusion rising. If she hadn't known better she might have thought he seemed contrite...regretful, even. But surely the Nathaniel she knew—the one who cared for no one but himself—would never be capable of such things. There was something going on in that cold and clever mind, and she'd never figure it out standing in Thame Magna's high street with the winter air nipping at her nose.

'Very well. As my plans have changed, I suppose I've no reason not to accompany you.'

The hand still awaited her and Hester took a deep breath. Two gloves would stand between their skin, keeping contact to a minimum, and as long as she kept her head everything would be perfectly well.

But then Nathaniel's fingers closed around hers, and Hester found herself suddenly at the mercy of a burst of stars that erupted in her stomach, setting a glittering path alight through every nerve. The feeling flared out of nowhere, leaving her to stifle a gasp as her husband gently folded her hand into the crook of one arm, holding it in place with the unyielding pressure of a bicep Hester had no choice but to notice.

He hadn't possessed such impressive strength before he left, Hester was sure, and she was distracted enough by the riot charging around her innards to allow Nathaniel to begin leading her back through the streets she had just walked. Every instinct told her to pull away but her arm wouldn't obey, locked in place by the most traitorous urge to enjoy the warmth that started in her fingertips and moved higher, despite the gloved barrier between them.

It was the first time in above five years that he had touched her; on purpose, anyway, Hester distantly recalling how he had caught her wrist the previous day. That had been over in a half-second of forbidden delight, however, and couldn't compare to *this*: able to feel taut muscle and the movement of Nathaniel's enticing frame as her step fell unconsciously into time with his, her body crying out to curve closer in spite of every reasonable thought.

Desire rose unbidden—a frightening spectre of how every fibre of her being had used to crave her husband's caress—and Hester recoiled from it as though something had bitten her. With every step she was in danger of betraying herself, of moving further and further from her vow to keep herself coldly aloof, but she would *not* allow herself to stumble when the man in question was so undeserving of the reaction he inspired with no effort at all.

Thame Magna wasn't big enough for any house to be particularly far away. The redbrick walls of Nathaniel's boyhood home, Grafton Lodge, were shortly before them—and not a moment too soon, Hester's pretence of composure worn to a thread.

Stopping to open the gate, Nathaniel loosened his grip and she finally seized the chance to slip away, her cheeks burning, raging inwardly at her stupid mistake.

Are you a naïve girl, to be led like a lapdog, or a grown woman?

Unseen beneath the cover of her hood, she set her teeth in a grimace—although it did nothing to cool the blazing of her face. She could still feel where Nathaniel's arm had pressed her hand, her fingers tingling with a ghostly warmth she hated that she enjoyed.

Do better, Hester. Don't you dare allow him that liberty again.

She followed Nathaniel up the path and climbed the iron-railed stairs that led to an imposing front door. Standing beside him on the narrow step was far too close for comfort but there was nowhere to hide as he reached for the brass knocker and rapped smartly, their arms almost touching and Hester painfully aware of every movement he made.

'You sent word, of course, to let your mother know to expect you? I can hardly bear to imagine what would happen if we'd come with no warning.'

Hester busied herself straightening her cuffs as they waited, pulling them down over her wrists to avoid having to look into Nathaniel's face. His proximity was unnerving—doubly so since that accursed constellation had bloomed in her gut to make her judgement waver—and she was barely listening for his reply until it made her head snap up sharply.

'No. Surely there's no need for such formality with my own mother?'

She stared at him. 'You didn't write to say you would be calling today? But you *have* let her know you've returned? Haven't you…?'

Nathaniel shrugged one shoulder, fanning the flames of Hester's alarm. 'I tried a few times to draft a letter, but couldn't think how to begin. Far better to explain in person where I've been—and besides, what could be a more pleasant surprise for her than for me to call unannounced?'

Astounded, Hester found she could barely speak. 'You're in earnest?'

'Of course.'

Several times her mouth moved without any words to accompany it, as she searched her husband's face for some sign he was joking and unfortunately found none.

'You have absolutely *no* idea how other people think or feel, do you?' she burst out finally, probably far too loudly. 'Absolutely no comprehension at all!'

He frowned slightly, apparently puzzled by her reaction, and Hester gestured wildly towards the house.

'Your poor mother has a weak heart! How do you think she'll cope to have *you*, her *dead son*, striding in, and with various body parts missing to add to her shock? Did it not occur to you that breaking the news of your return and your condition gently might be better than simply appearing out of the blue?'

She watched Nathaniel's frown deepen, still scarcely able to believe his recklessness—although, she considered darkly, what else should she have expected? What more proof did she need that any change in him was only superficial and not to be trusted, just as she'd already known? He was still the same old selfish Nathaniel, with no idea of how his actions affected others; or perhaps he simply didn't care, nothing on his mind but money and trade.

Nathaniel rubbed his chin slowly, apparently marshalling his thoughts. 'She'll want to know where I've been, but I've no wish for my tale to make her unwell. I won't go into detail, if you think it would distress her unduly.'

'That's for you to decide, isn't it? Only you know if your story is enough to disturb her to that extent—although by then I imagine the damage will have already been done.'

The sound of bolts being drawn from the other side of the door saved Hester from having to say anything more. Arranging her face into as pleasant a smile as she could, she nodded politely to the emerging butler, only just hearing Nathaniel's murmur at her back as they were invited inside.

'I'm no expert, but I rather suspect it is…'

Waiting for his mother to regain the ability to speak, Nathaniel reflected that perhaps Hester had been right.

Appearing in yet another woman's parlour with no warning might not have been a good idea after all—as Mrs Honeywell's current state of collapse on the sofa testified.

'Should I send for wine? Something stronger?' Nonplussed he looked to Hester, who shot him an exasperated glare and rustled across to crouch at the patient's side.

Mrs Honeywell opened one eye, seizing Hester's arm with a grip that made even Nathaniel wince.

'Have I finally gone mad, Hester?' his mother whispered faintly. 'I've so missed my son over the years that I think I see him now. Over there, by the fireplace.'

'You're quite sane, I assure you. See? He comes now to hold your hand.'

Hester glanced pointedly over her shoulder and Nathaniel stepped quickly towards the sofa, kneeling beside her on the floor. His shoulder brushed hers as he moved and he sensed her stiffen, leaning backwards a little so any contact between them was severed at once.

It was a stark contrast to her acceptance of his hand on their walk to Grafton Lodge, when the feeling of her slender fingers on his arm had shaken something inside him that had almost made him stumble. But now wasn't the time to think on it. His mother lay like a limp rag, and he became aware of a sudden warmth washing over him, starting in his chest and seeping outwards until with a jolt of surprise he realised what it was.

Happiness. At seeing Mother again.

He looked down at her, taking in the subtle changes left by the past five years. Her hair had a touch more silver at the temples, but the lines of her countenance were the same and he felt another rush run over him as he recalled her smile—the only one he could remember receiving in the whole of his severe childhood. Its sweetness had always tempted him to answer, calling to the softer part of himself he'd sought to snuff out, but his father's reproving eye had invariably been watching, and Nathaniel paused uncomfortably to think of how he'd turned his back on her affection to seek cold approval in its place.

His father had scant regard for her, and as ever Nathaniel had copied that example, burying his instinctive love so deep he might never be suspected of weak, unmanly sentiment. She might be his mother but she was still a woman—a chattering distraction—and he had far more important concerns than to waste time strengthening their bond.

Some part of him still wondered if he ought to show a little more reserve, but the lessons learned in Algiers raised their voices more loudly. With such unfamiliar emotion clouding his senses he hardly knew what he was doing as he took his mother's hand in his, feeling Hester's attention fix on him as he raised it—a little self-consciously—to his lips.

Out of the corner of his eye he saw his wife's look of amazement at his unexpected tenderness—something that shocked Nathaniel himself. His father wouldn't have liked it, but Mr Honeywell was nowhere to be seen, and Nathaniel couldn't seem to prevent himself from smiling as his mother gazed up wonderingly.

'It *is* you. You've come back!'

'I have. It's good to see you, Mother.'

Hesitantly, as if expecting him to pull away, she reached up to touch his face. When he didn't move the trembling fingers grew bolder, tracing the contours of his cheeks and lingering over the leather patch that hid his ruined eye.

'Where have you been? I thought you'd drowned when we heard the *Celeste* was lost. How can it be you're here now?'

Her questions were a little too similar to Hester's, making him recall the first moment he had beheld his wife after five long years, and Nathaniel deliberately avoided looking in her direction. *That* meeting had not gone well, only the day before but replayed in his mind so many times it already felt ingrained. The flash of defiance in her eye...that elegant upward turn of her chin... And the flicker of appreciation for the new fire in her belly that had made Nathaniel shift uneasily.

'Why didn't you write?'

Beside him he sensed Hester's attention sharpen with a barely perceptible turn of her head. Perhaps he'd been wrong, he wondered.

Perhaps Hester *did* want to know where he'd been hiding and was simply too proud to ask.

But if that was the case she wouldn't be finding out now, either.

Still holding his mother's hand in his intact one, Nathaniel used the other to rake through his hair, thinking fast. Just as with Hester, there was no possibility of telling his mother the truth: the secret shame of what he'd endured, living like a beast and breaking his back every day at the end of a whip, would never escape his lips. He'd have to say *something* but it would be nothing approaching his real fate, no persuasion strong enough to make him reveal that humiliation.

'I'm sorry.' Nathaniel gave the fingers a squeeze, feeling the bones there barely stronger than a bird's. 'I was washed ashore after the *Celeste* went down and landed in such a remote place that sending word was quite impossible. Please believe that I came home on the very first English ship I was able to board.'

Such a flimsy lie wouldn't fool anyone for a moment, Nathaniel realised, if they were thinking clearly. Which fortunately his mother was not.

She beamed tearfully, rising on one elbow to turn to Hester with eyes bright and full. 'Do you hear that, Hester? He came as soon as he could!'

'Yes. I heard.' Hester's voice was measured. 'A miraculous feat.'

'And to think I'd given up hope!' Mrs Honeywell sat up, her fainting fit entirely forgotten in her simple joy. 'Do you know, Nathaniel, it was only Hester's visits that kept me alive in my grief? She came every week to cheer me. I'm sure that without her I wouldn't be here now.'

'Is that so?'

Surprised, Nathaniel looked to his wife. In the winter light streaming through the parlour window her complexion glowed luminous as a pearl, the perfect accompaniment to the azure of her eyes so brightly illuminated by the sun, and for the first time Nathaniel wondered how he had been so blind. She was a handsome woman and he'd barely allowed himself to acknowledge it, from the delicate pallor of her cheeks to that gleam of challenge secreted among the blue, but more important than that...

She visited every week?

He sat back on his heels, aware of a new sensation stirring in the furthest recess of his mind as he studied Hester's face. She gave nothing away, with only the faintest tinge of pink creeping in at his scrutiny.

That's true kindness.

Perhaps not so cold after all.

The sensation grew stronger. Gratitude mixed with genuine admiration wound its way through Nathaniel—a combination he'd never imagined Hester would inspire after those first forbidden weeks, when he'd come so close to losing his way. Perhaps she'd always been so thoughtful, and in his self-interest and ambition he had never noticed—or valued—it before?

It was a shame it had taken being beaten half to death hundreds of miles away to open Nathaniel's eyes to her merit, that discomforting esteem for his complex wife beginning to rise again like a phoenix among ash.

'Of course.' Oblivious to the confusing turn of Nathaniel's thoughts, Hester inclined her head. 'I couldn't allow your mother to think herself abandoned by *all* her relations, could I?'

The jibe stung, but Nathaniel brushed it off. It was probably safe to say Hester felt no answering flicker of respect for *him*, and with swift unease he turned his attention back to his mother.

'Is my father here?'

'No. He's away for the rest of the month on business. I shall have to tell him of our good fortune when he comes home... He didn't tell me where he was going, so I'm afraid I cannot write to hurry his return.'

Mrs Honeywell spoke lightly enough, but Nathaniel caught a note of resignation and felt a skewer of pity lance through him—yet another novel feeling that would once have been unthinkable. His father remained unchanged, then...just about the only person who was.

If he were honest, it was difficult to summon

much disappointment their reunion would have to be delayed. There was always the chance that Mr Honeywell might sniff out his son's disgrace like a bloodhound, tracing the scent of failure and humiliation until he reached its source, and then the hard-won acceptance Nathaniel had worked for all his life would be ruined.

His father would be disgusted that his heir had been something so low as a slave—the polar opposite of everything a man should be, and not even worthy of the mud off his boots, let alone a place in the company that bore his name.

'Never mind. I'm sure I'll see him soon enough.'

'You will, but with only one eye... What happened, Nathaniel?' Mrs Honeywell reached up again, to touch his cheek softly, and he saw her lip tremble. 'To your face and your hand? Did someone hurt you?'

Her lace cap sat slightly askew after her collapse onto the sofa and Nathaniel carefully set it straight, stalling for a little more time. How to answer that question? Certainly not with the truth, but he couldn't look into her face and lie once again. Hester still knelt beside him too, and he felt her listening, keen and silent, as he simply shook his head.

'I was helping a friend to carry a heavy load and there was an accident. A case of wrong place, wrong time. Nothing more.'

It was barely half a lie this time, and Nathaniel's conscience only gave him a small pinch at how far he'd stretched the truth. He and Jacob *had* been carrying a heavy load, and it *had* been an accident that his eye was caught by the backward lash of the overseer's whip; but the agonising severance of his finger had been all too deliberate, and the memory of it sat like a fist in Nathaniel's stomach.

If he wasn't careful those excruciating days would come back to taunt him, the memories already circling like vultures as he struggled to put them away. What he needed was light to chase out the darkness, and it was holding on to that hope that he twisted to sit beside his mother.

'Let's have no more talk of that. Tell me instead what you've been about these past years. I see you have devoted no time to growing taller.'

His mother laughed, and cautiously leaned her head against his shoulder. When he didn't pull away she hesitated, then happily nestled a fraction closer as though hardly believing her luck. 'I'm too old to change now. You'll just have to take me as I am.'

He noticed Hester get quietly to her feet and stand back a little, as if to take in the scene before her. From his smile to Mrs Honeywell's sigh of absolute contentment as she rested against her son it must have made a pretty picture, and with a swift flit of his pulse Nathaniel could have sworn he saw the ghost of a curve pass over Hester's lips.

'I'll go and find a maid to bring tea. You two must have a little time alone.'

'You needn't leave, Hester.'

Mrs Honeywell half rose from the sofa, but Hester held up a hand, a tenderness in her face Nathaniel realised he'd never seen there before. It smoothed out the angles of her countenance and lent a warmth to her eyes that made him pause, swallow with difficulty, and wish he could look away.

'This moment is yours. Enjoy it. You've waited long enough.'

They walked back through the chilly streets in silence, both of Hester's hands wrapped firmly in her cloak, as though to discourage any thought of him reaching for one. With her hood up it was impossible to see her face, and Nathaniel wondered how much of a gamble he was taking as he cleared his throat.

'Thank you for looking after my mother. I think life with my father is not always easy for her, and it must have helped to have a friend.'

A dry laugh came from beneath the hood. 'Well, I know how she feels. We have certain things in common, after all.'

Nathaniel shook his head, a humourless smile stretching his lips. It was the obvious answer, and yet he couldn't help the flip of disappointment that turned his stomach. He shouldn't care so much what she thought of him, but something in him refused to let it lie.

'You've no regard left for me at all, have you, Hester? It's all disappeared like snow in sunshine…gone as if never there at all.'

'Do you think my coldness unwarranted?'

He looked down at her, this straight-backed figure walking briskly at his side. She was complicated now, with a strange mix of haughtiness and concealed compassion, and it intrigued him enough to give an honest answer.

'It's certainly regrettable.'

For a moment there was nothing but the sound of their footsteps on frost as they crossed the street. He began to wonder if she'd heard him, until suddenly the hood was lowered.

'Why now? Why decide *now* to take an interest?'

Hester shot him a sideways glance, sharp and searching. The cold had brought a touch of pink to the end of her nose, a sight so unexpectedly fascinating that Nathaniel had to think quickly for a reply.

'I learned some things while I was away. I'd

like to think I've changed for the better and am no longer quite the man I was.'

She appeared to weigh up his words, as if deciding whether or not they were wanting. There was still a glint of suspicion in her eye, but to his surprise he saw it accompanied by a cautious interest that raised the hairs on the nape of his neck. It wasn't a complete rejection of his claim; the most grace he'd been shown since his return, and enough for him to wonder whether there might be hope after all.

'I put my faith in you once and you proved with no shadow of a doubt that you didn't deserve it. Am I to trust you wouldn't do that again?'

Nathaniel hesitated. *Had* he proved that? He'd shown himself undeserving of blind adoration, certainly, but what else? She made it sound as though there was one incident in particular, and what that might have been he couldn't say.

'When? I know I wasn't a particularly warm husband, but surely being distracted isn't the same as breaking faith? A business won't run itself, Hester.'

She stared at him, turning her head so she could look straight into his face. Nathaniel watched her take the measure of him, apparently assessing something he didn't understand—and then the hood was raised and she disappeared from his sight.

'You know full well what you did.' Her voice was hard once again, any softening in it flown away like birds in winter. 'And if you can't even acknowledge it how am I to believe you've changed—or ever could?'

They weren't far from Shardlow now. There would be only another few minutes to walk until they reached its white walls, and for the duration Hester could not be prevailed upon to say another word. Her face remained in shadow, whatever crossed her countenance as much a mystery to Nathaniel as what he was supposed to have done to earn her displeasure.

He racked his mind, uncomfortably aware of how much he wanted to solve the puzzle and cursing himself for falling into this sorry mess. Making amends was one thing—realising he was in danger of desiring Hester's good opinion was another entirely, and it unsettled him more than he was willing to allow.

How has this happened?

The question surfaced and he had no power to answer. How *had* it happened that the wife he'd once thought of as a burden was now the one holding the reins and, worse, how was it that he was beginning to *respect* her for it? If he wasn't more careful the boyhood fondness for her that he'd long since thought dead might prove itself to be more alive than he liked—a thought worrying enough to make him frown harder, causing lines to cross his forehead that had nothing to do with age.

Shardlow House reared up before them and wordlessly Hester pushed open the gate, striding up the drive with Nathaniel in her wake. From the speed with which she was moving perhaps it was no wonder that her foot skidded on a patch of ice, slipping out from under her so abruptly she hadn't even the time to cry out.

'Careful!'

Nathaniel's hands fastened around Hester's waist, anchoring her upright as easily as if she weighed nothing at all. Still, gravity was not on her side, and despite his support her hand flew out of its own accord to rest against his coat, instinctively grasping his lapel and pulling them together so closely that Nathaniel could have counted her dark eyelashes.

Her face was mere inches from his, lips parted in surprise and breath coming quickly—and when she glanced up, her light blue gaze meeting his green, he felt something take hold of his chest and *squeeze*.

The shape of her beneath his palms...that gentle curve reaching upwards with such promise... She'd been his wife for two years before he went away and yet with a jolt he realised he'd all but forgotten what lay beneath those pretty dresses she wore. Youth and inexperience had made their handful of times together unmemorable, but now the desire to search his mind came sharply, the temptation to see what he could recall of her lying in his arms seizing him so hard it made him gasp.

Had he ever taken the time to see if he could make her smile, discovering what she liked and watching those smooth cheeks flame hot? If he hadn't, he'd like to make up for it now: taking his time, an experience for both of them to savour now he knew better than to rush.

Hester stood frozen in his grasp, apparently just as much a prisoner of the tension stretched between them as Nathaniel was, and he couldn't help but trace a burning line from her eyes to her lips and back again, helplessly aware that he should let go and yet unable to unlace his fingers from her spine.

What would it be like to kiss that mouth again, so soft and berry-red? *Should* he kiss her, if only to quieten the voices in his head that roared their approval?

Of course not. He'd slammed the door shut on all such thoughts the same day he'd pulled himself back onto the right path, deciding aged just eighteen that such a distraction would have no place in his heart—and besides, what woman would relish a kiss from a slave? The business was his main concern and he wouldn't forget it;

just as Nathaniel knew, with terrible irony, that
he'd never forget the moment she turned away,
cutting short the fantasy that she'd ever allow
him such an unthinkable liberty as to touch her
perfect lips.

'I'm not sure that was necessary.'

She took a careful step backwards, clearly determined not to slip and fall into his clutches
again, and loosening his grip Nathaniel clenched
his jaw. How much of the dizzying free-fall of
his thoughts had shown on his face? That half-
moment of madness, overcome by temporary in-
sanity at finding Hester so unexpectedly close;
had she felt something too? Or was he entirely
alone in this new sea he feared was deeper than
he realised?

*Don't stand around waiting to find out when
you already know the answer well enough.*

He cleared his throat, breaking the taut thread.
A minor mistake, that was all, and one he'd forget as soon as he had other things to occupy his
mind.

'Perhaps not. Forgive the intrusion. Good
morning.'

With the briefest of bows Nathaniel spun on
his heel, striding with purpose towards the house.
This time it was his turn to leave Hester staring
after *him*, but that thought didn't occur to him
until after he'd reached his rooms and poured
himself a drink.

The image of Hester's mouth stayed with him, however, all the way there, and would not leave for so much as a moment.

Chapter Four

Hester took another bite of hot toast, her eyes fixed firmly on the letter lying before her. Her parents were enjoying their wintry tour of the Lake District, and not for the first time she gave silent thanks that they weren't around to witness her discomfort. Almost a week on from Nathaniel's abrupt arrival she still didn't know what to make of it—and having the man himself seated directly across from her at the breakfast table did nothing to help order her thoughts.

'Are your parents in good health?'

She glanced up automatically at the question and immediately wished she hadn't. Nathaniel sat up to his elbows in Honeywell Trading Company ledgers and accounts books, just as he had at every breakfast time for the first two years of their marriage, but for a change his attention was trained on her, rather than the interminable lists of profit and loss, and his one green eye was more intriguing than any pair.

'Yes, thank you,' Hester muttered grudgingly.

The olive shade of that iris was more mesmerising than it had any right to be when she was so aggravated with its owner, Nathaniel still so clearly clueless as to why she'd barely spoken to him for the past six days that it made her want to scream.

But I won't. If he's too selfish to realise that leaving me on the brink of death was a bad move, I certainly won't be helping him to see it. And to think I was almost taken in by that scene with his mother, wondering if he'd truly changed after all.

She turned back to the letter. If she really concentrated maybe she could pretend Nathaniel wasn't sitting there, with that cursedly broad chest she still didn't know how he'd gained, and if she squinted *just so* she could even block the shape of him from the corner of her eye...

'Have they visited Windermere?'

Hester looked up irritably, all illusion shattered. 'What?'

'Lake Windermere. I hear it's particularly beautiful this time of year, especially if there's snow. Have they been?'

She treated him to a cold glance that he returned so innocently she had to bite down on her tongue. What was it to him whether they'd seen every lake in England? It wasn't as though he could truly be interested.

'Yes.'

'Did they enjoy themselves?'

'Yes.'

'Where do they intend to go next?'

'Kendal.'

'Do they mention their return?'

'No, Nathaniel, they don't!' Exasperated, Hester sat back in her chair so hard the legs creaked. *Now* what was he up to, interrogating her over the morning teapot and sardines? 'Why all the questions? May I not read my letter in peace?'

Across the table Nathaniel shrugged, one sculpted shoulder moving in such a way it took all her willpower not to follow it with her eyes.

'Just making conversation. I thought that was what people did at mealtimes.'

'Most people, yes. I hadn't thought you one of them.'

'Ah.' He leaned forward slightly, subtly reducing the space between them so the fine hairs on Hester's forearms prickled. 'And that bothered you? That was something you found unsatisfactory?'

Hester raised a sandy brow. So that was it. Nathaniel was trying to puzzle out her damning remark as they'd walked back to Shardlow—and he imagined his lack of conversation at the root of her displeasure? She might almost have smiled at his complete lack of judgement, although the memory of that day wiped any such thing from her lips at once.

If any other man had held her so tightly by the waist and stared down into her face with such wordless intensity she might have assumed he was about to kiss her. She and Nathaniel had certainly been close enough, with even their breath mingling in the biting air and his hands burning through layers of linen and wool to scorch her heated skin. One more step and she might have fallen into his arms completely, the strength held in those newfound muscles more than capable of lifting her off her feet. With her heart pounding and her mouth too dry for speech all the anger that had consumed her seconds earlier had vanished, leaving only bewilderment and an insistent voice that begged her, with growing urgency, to let his lips touch hers and wind back the clock to when they'd first wed...

But she hadn't waited to find out whether Nathaniel would make that final irreversible move. She'd banished the voice and pulled away, still reeling at a moment neither of them had seemed able to control, and now her reward was knowing that her pride remained intact.

Of course Nathaniel hadn't been about to kiss her. Probably she'd had a stray eyelash on her cheek, or something equally banal, and her blood ran cold at the thought she'd almost left herself open to another humiliating rejection. It was more important than ever now to be on her guard, and Hester didn't intend to let it slip for so much as a moment.

'If you think your not making polite chitchat at dinner is why I take issue with you, I'm afraid you are wrong. Or do you imagine that to be the limit of your possible flaws?'

To her surprise Nathaniel met her sharpness with a laugh. 'By no means. I'm just trying to narrow the field. You can't blame a man for asking, considering you apparently have no intention of telling me directly.'

'None whatsoever.'

'Very well, then. I see I'll have to carry the weight of conversation alone.' He settled both brawny forearms on the table in front of him, the very image of an attentive guest—albeit one far more attractive than was fair. 'I queried when your parents might return. Do they mention that in their letter?'

Hester pursed her lips, wishing she hadn't just snatched another glance at the delights that lay beneath Nathaniel's shirtsleeves.

'No, but I hope it won't be for a good while. I shan't be writing to tell them of your arrival, lest they drop everything to come home early and spoil their trip. My mother deserves this time away, and to be my father's only focus for once rather than competing with the business.' She folded her hands in her lap, glancing down to mutter more at the tablecloth than at her husband. 'Something I can well understand.'

'I beg your pardon? I didn't quite catch that.'

'I was talking to myself.'

Nathaniel rubbed his chin with his scarred hand, giving Hester a momentary respite from his undivided attention. She should have taken the opportunity to look away, but the sight of his ruined knuckles was so morbidly fascinating she only realised she'd been staring when Nathaniel's mouth quirked up at one corner.

'Did you want to ask *me* a question?'

'No.'

'You have the look of a woman with something on her mind.'

She swallowed. Avid curiosity about his wounds still simmered barely beneath the surface, but there was no chance she'd risk gratifying Nathaniel's insufferable self-importance. 'Not at all, I assure you.'

His lips curved a fraction more, and he seemed on the verge of some reply when a brisk tap at the dining room door heralded the appearance of one of the servants.

'Beg pardon, sir. There's a Mr Morrow here to see you.'

'He's arrived?' Nathaniel was on his feet at once. 'I'll come this very moment.'

Hester's brows twitched together as she watched

her husband in his unfeigned enthusiasm—a sight so unlike his lack of interest of years past that it made her wonder all over again. Who was Mr Morrow? And why was Nathaniel apparently so pleased to have him at Shardlow House?

As though reading her mind, Nathaniel paused at the door, turning back to the table. 'Jacob Morrow is the man I met in Algiers. Will you allow me to introduce you? He was a good friend to me during my time away.'

'Oh?' Hester felt another flicker of surprise. Nathaniel bothering himself to make friends? Indeed, bothering with *anything* other than the business? 'I thought you said he was a man to whom you owed a favour?'

'Can't he be both?'

'I suppose.'

Laying her napkin aside, she rose from her seat, all too aware of how close Nathaniel stood to the doorway. To pass she would have to step within a hair's breadth of him, and she found herself holding her breath as she approached.

'Allow me.'

He held the door open with a gallant sweep, and Hester was almost safely through it when she felt the light touch of fingertips at her back—a guiding hand that sent a jolt straight through to her core. It was the tiniest of touches, lasting only a moment and surely one any gentleman might offer a lady, but it set her heart to racing and she scurried rather than sailed out into the hall, cursing herself internally as she went for the fleeting desire that ran over her to turn and walk past him again.

Jacob's grip was as firm as ever when Nathaniel grasped his hand, and it was difficult to tell which man felt more relieved to see the other.

Finally. Somebody beneath this roof who's truly happy I'm here.

It was the same strong grasp that had saved Nathaniel's life, those broad fingers wrapping around his wrist to wrench him from the sea just as the churning waters closed over his head and the *Celeste* had disappeared with a final bubbling flourish. Nathaniel owed the Scotsman everything—a feeling he knew was returned, having repaid his debt in kind at the expense of his eye and hand.

'Jacob. Or is it Mr Morrow now? I feel I ought to address you more respectfully.'

He watched his friend's uneven grin widen, softening a craggy countenance just as tanned and weather-beaten as Nathaniel's own. The other man was shorter, but his stocky frame would make most think twice even without the scar that slightly lifted one lip, and Nathaniel saw Hester hesitate for a moment before coming forward.

'Hester, may I introduce Mr Jacob Morrow? Jacob, my wife, Mrs Honeywell.'

Hester nodded politely, acknowledging Jacob's surprisingly accomplished bow. She still looked a little unsure, and Nathaniel didn't blame her. Jacob was hardly the usual type for an estate manager, but looks could be deceiving. Beneath his hard exterior lay the kindness that had helped keep Nathaniel alive during their brutal captivity, and in time he was sure Hester would come to see it.

After all, she should know about hiding one's softness behind a façade. The compassion she showed my mother is so removed from the coldness she cultivates that I might not have believed it existed had I not seen it for myself.

Tempting as it was to revisit that moment when Nathaniel had seen a glint of Hester's hidden sweetness, he found he didn't quite dare. His mind might stray to what had come afterwards, when she had swayed in his hold with her upturned face like a flower seeking the sun, and the desire to kiss her had run riot through his blank mind. Only her turning away had saved them both from his making a huge mistake, and it had taken at least three days of poring over deathly dull accounts ledgers, trying to make up for five lost years, to replace the image of her parted lips.

His father would be horrified, no doubt, by his son spending so much time thinking of such unprofitable things, and Nathaniel determined again to strengthen his resolve.

I can be kind without being weak. While there's a business to run I can't afford to be distracted too far, and especially not by one who'd want none of my attention to begin with. Hopefully now Jacob's here I'll have someone to talk some sense into me.

Mercifully oblivious to the uncomfortable thoughts she inspired, Hester smiled. 'I understand you met my husband in Algiers? How was it you came to be there?'

Nathaniel cut in before Jacob could answer. 'He was a sailor. Mr Morrow expressed an interest in changing occupation, so I suggested he come here on his return to England. We left at the same time, but on different ships.'

Just as in his mother's parlour, he was stretching the truth again, and Nathaniel deliberately ignored Jacob's questioning glance. It wasn't an outright lie. The basic facts were unchanged, with only grim details left out, but he wasn't sorry when Arless appeared at Hester's elbow and his wife's presence was required elsewhere.

Both men watched her leave the hall, Nathaniel unable to stop himself from admiring Hester's figure as she walked away. Surely it hadn't been as impressive before he'd set sail for Portugal, the destination he'd never reached? It certainly hadn't in his imagination during the few times he'd thought of her, when the nights of his captivity had stretched out long and lonely for a man on his own…

'I assume you haven't told your wife what happened out there?'

Guiltily Nathaniel snatched his gaze away from Hester's retreating back, only answering Jacob when he was sure she'd disappeared.

'No. And I'd appreciate it if you didn't, either.'

'Why?'

'It's complicated.'

Jacob's brow wrinkled. 'Not delighted to have you back, I take it? No welcome with open arms?'

Nathaniel snorted. 'Not as such. She hasn't asked a single question about the time I was away—although in truth I'm glad.'

He paused to run his maimed hand through his hair, casting his mind back to the nightmare they'd left behind. Picking their way through the rubble as the British naval bombardment ripped through buildings and people alike, blood glistening on the ground and his ears ringing with the roar of cannon-fire that had drawn him and Jacob towards the English ships… The smell of smoke had hung so heavy he could almost taste it now, an acrid memory still clinging to his tongue and nothing that he wanted to revisit. The day they'd escaped had been horrific, but the existence they'd suffered for the months and years before had been terrible in a different way.

From the first moment he'd realised what fate had befallen him Nathaniel had known he would never be the same again. Something inside him had died as one dehumanising week followed the next, his sense of shame growing with each pail of filthy water he'd carried or hole dug beneath the sweltering sun.

If being a man meant standing tall and detached then he'd failed miserably, bringing disappointment and a blemish on the Honeywell family name. The only moment when he'd felt any pride had been in knocking aside the foreman who had been about to beat Jacob into an early grave and finally evening the score between them, although the agony of his maimed eye and crimson-spattered knuckles had soon eclipsed any real sense of triumph.

The fewer questions Hester asked the better, each one running the risk of exposing his secret shame.

'I'd rather not speak of it.'

Jacob shrugged. 'Fair enough. Can't say I agree, though.' He let his gaze roam around the tasteful hall for a moment, its obviously feminine décor a clear reminder of who had chosen it. 'Surely Mrs Honeywell deserves honesty? After everything she must have suffered, thinking you were dead?'

'Hester doesn't want my honesty. She doesn't want *anything* from me.'

'And that bothers you, does it?'

Was that the same question I asked Hester earlier?

The idea made Nathaniel frown, the discomfort in his stomach growing stronger. It didn't bother him. He'd decided it wouldn't, so it wouldn't. And that was the end of that.

'Of course not,' he lied. 'If that's how she feels, what can I do?'

'What indeed.'

'Meaning…?'

'Only that you're not just some spoilt rich boy any longer, as you were the day I pulled you from the sea. I thought you'd learned a thing or two from my charming influence.'

Nathaniel's eye narrowed. 'I'd defy even *you* to charm Hester. She's a more complex woman these days.'

And I find myself admiring her for it, he finished privately, hoping the thought didn't show on his face.

If he'd been in the market for a woman, and more kindly disposed to unnecessary distractions, perhaps he might have chosen Hester as she was now. But he wasn't. He didn't need her, and she was clearly determined not to need him, and there was nothing else to say on the matter other than to consider it closed.

'Enough idle talk in hallways. Come into my study for a drink.'

'That's an offer I can't refuse after three days in the saddle.'

Nathaniel found a smile. Whatever confusion Hester inspired in him would surely fade, even if his experience as a slave did not. Jacob had always managed to raise his spirits, and it seemed *that* at least was still the same, the prospect enough to slightly lighten the weight inside his chest.

He slapped his new estate manager on the back and drew him away, leaving the hall and moving down one of Shardlow's many corridors. Too distracted to notice anything more, Nathaniel remained blind to Hester behind the library door, blissfully unaware she'd caught the tail end of his conversation—concerning the need for honesty, unfortunately enough…

It wasn't until much later that evening, as he took a glass of port into the parlour, that Nathaniel finally encountered his wife again.

'There you are. I haven't seen you since this morning. Have you been avoiding me?'

Hester looked up from her desk, pen in hand and a half-finished letter lying before her. Her face was lit by a handful of candles, helpfully showing Nathaniel just how pleased—or otherwise—she was to see him.

'Of course not. Why would I?'

'It seemed like it to me. I do have *one* eye left, you know.'

'Perhaps it's faulty.'

Nathaniel felt his mouth attempting to lift, and that tiresome flicker of admiration trying once again to kindle in his chest.

Sweet as ever, dear wife.

'Who are you writing to?'

'My sister.'

'Is she unwell?'

She shot him a warning glance. 'Are we to have a repeat of this morning? A question every thirty seconds until I feel I'm going mad? Perhaps this is my life from now on—never able to have a letter in my hand without you quizzing me about it.'

Nathaniel raised an eyebrow at her tone. 'Forgive me. I'll leave you in peace.'

He strolled away to take up his usual chair beside the fire. The book he'd started a few days before lay on the arm and he picked it up, glad to hold something between himself and the irritable woman who glowered in a corner.

For a long while there was no sound but the scratch of Hester's pen and the stirring of coals in the grate, anyone peeping in through a window forgiven for thinking they'd stumbled across a scene of domestic bliss.

The truth, however, was very different.

There was an atmosphere. Nathaniel could sense it.

Hester was tetchy at the best of times but now he could almost *feel* her watching him, with something unspoken yet hostile that made him shift uncomfortably in his chair. What was her problem now? How, in sitting quietly and minding his own business, had he managed to rile her further?

Affecting not to notice Nathaniel turned the page, although the words might as well have been written in a foreign language for all he could focus.

He'd made the right decision—even if Jacob disagreed. Surely this was yet more proof. Her new coolness might intrigue him, but it also made him sure she must never know the truth. What had transpired in Algiers was too horrific to share with anyone—not least the wife who scarcely tolerated his return and might even wish him back from where he'd come. Even if Hester had been the most affectionate woman in the world he wouldn't want to put those days into words, the pain and humiliation he'd suffered something he prayed would eventually disappear into the mist.

He turned another unread page. The sensation of her eyes on him grew stronger, now seemingly only one step removed from a physical touch to his skin. It made him aware of every breath he took, absurdly unnerved by Hester noticing his slightest movement yet unable to prevent himself from sitting up straighter. Her attention did the strangest things to his stomach, making something inside it flutter like a bird in a trap.

Every man had his limit, and finally Nathaniel reached his. 'Is something the matter?'

'No.'

'Then why do you insist on staring at me?'

'Staring at you?' Hester bridled a little, although even by candlelight he saw her cheeks flush disarmingly pink. 'Don't be ridiculous.'

Nathaniel fought the urge to pinch the bridge of his nose. Hell, she was frustrating. If she had something to say, why not come out and say it, instead of gazing at him from afar and sending those accursed ripples snaking through his innards?

'I don't bite. You can share what's on your mind.'

'I might say the same to you,' she muttered, so low that Nathaniel couldn't be sure he'd heard correctly.

He leaned forward to try again. 'Pardon?'

'Nothing. Nothing of any consequence.'

Hester redoubled her grip on her pen, seeming to hold it so tightly that Nathaniel was glad he wasn't in its place, and his own fingers twitched into an irritable fist. Had any woman ever been so simultaneously provoking yet fascinating?

And, of all men, why did it have to be *him* fated to be married to her?

The tension in the room was so thick he might have spread it like butter. Any Englishman worth his salt knew there was only one sure way out of such a difficult moment, and to prevent any further disturbance to his insides Nathaniel acted at once.

Laying his book aside, he stood up from his chair. 'Would you like some tea? Allow me to ring the bell for you.'

'I can do it.'

Hester rose likewise, apparently unwilling to allow him to do her the smallest favour, and moved towards the rope hanging in an alcove. Unfortunately for her, however, Nathaniel did the same, and so he could only watch, as though from a distance, as both his hand and hers reached out for the same velvet tassel and his fingers closed— quite accidentally, as he would assure himself later—around Hester's own.

They were cold, something he only dimly registered beneath the shock of her skin on his. So slender and fragile, it could be all too easy to hurt that little hand yet he knew instinctively he never would, and what was more: he'd savage anyone who tried. Where that protective leap came from he didn't know, only that it flared up inside to take him wholly by surprise and make letting go quite impossible.

He couldn't help a swift downward glance, just long enough to see the high colour in Hester's cheeks had reached a burning crimson. She didn't look up, her eyes apparently fixed in place by his hand on hers, and the smooth line of her profile glowed in the fire's flickering light.

For the second time a disloyal voice in the back of his mind called him to move, to bend his head and seek out Hester's mouth with his, and for a second time the thread between them was cut only by Hester snatching her hand away as if it had stung her.

'I said I could do it.'

She still didn't meet his eye, instead retreating back to her desk to sit behind it as though barricading herself away. Returning to his own seat Nathaniel groaned inwardly, cursing himself for another stupid mistake.

Well, that was unfortunate.

What would it take to make him behave sensibly?

He picked up his book again and stared blindly down at the words, although they blurred before his eyes. The sensation of Hester's delicate fingers beneath his rough palm was all he could think of, tied up with the knowledge that she'd been near enough for him to smell the subtle fragrance of her hair.

It was more than any man could stand, surely,

and with a thrill of dismay Nathaniel realised he was just as fallible as any other.

'Profit over people' was taking things a bit too far, but I really ought to spend more time with my head in a ledger.

The urge to glance over at Hester's corner was strong, but thankfully this time Nathaniel's willpower and the knowledge of what his father would say were stronger.

Ridiculous to waste valuable time on a woman who doesn't want it...or me. Much better to put it to good use. Starting tomorrow, I'll make the right choice.

He turned a page, all too aware of the silent figure in the corner. But Hester had clearly come to a similar conclusion about the best way to spend her time, as presently her pen began scratching once more and she didn't look at him again for the rest of the night.

Chapter Five

Snow fell steadily as Hester clambered over a stile and kept walking, the fields in every direction already covered in a cloak of sparkling white. Glowering up at the laden sky, she pulled her coat closer around her body, although the bitter cold was only half the reason for her scowl.

Diana wasn't nearly as horrified by Nathaniel's return as I thought she'd be. If I'd known she'd be so insufferably calm I wouldn't have waited so impatiently for her reply.

Hester hadn't found the right moment to try again after Nathaniel had thwarted her earlier attempt to call on her sister, and now Diana was away visiting Lavendon's family in the West Country. That hastily scribbled letter had been the only way of reaching her and now, having read the response, Hester needed time to clear her head.

I expected Diana would share my feelings, she

thought as a freezing rush of snow invaded one boot, a wet stocking only increasing her irritation. The wind was coming stronger now than it had as she'd left Shardlow and the snowflakes fell faster, whirling across the barren fields to sting her cold cheeks. The brisk walk had been meant to help her calm down, but now Hester felt a twinge of misgiving at how quickly the weather had changed.

Perhaps it hadn't been her *best* idea to venture out in such uncertain conditions—but how else was she to escape Nathaniel for a couple of precious hours? His presence could be felt in every room, and even more so since that excruciating moment in the parlour.

Hester clenched her fist, buried deep among folds of fabric, but the feel of Nathaniel's touch still lingered. Had he done it on purpose? Winding his fingers around hers like that and wiping her mind blank of all else but the awareness of his body so close? She recalled how her breath had caught and grimly doubled her strides, although each step was more difficult now the snow drifts grew deeper with every passing minute.

'If I didn't have enough reason to dislike him already!' Hester struggled onwards, grumbling to herself as she went. 'I don't want his *honesty*? He doesn't even know the meaning of the word!'

He and his mysterious new estate manager could whisper as much as they liked. She wouldn't waste one more second wondering what exactly Nathaniel wanted to hide from her, or indeed why such a proud man would have bothered make a friend in the first place. Whatever bond existed between her husband and Mr Morrow was of no interest to her whatsoever, and Nathaniel needn't think otherwise—especially since he had admitted out loud that he wasn't bothered what she thought.

The snow really *was* getting deep...

Hester lifted the hem of her sodden skirts, eyes narrowed against the wind as she surveyed her surroundings. Had it got darker all of a sudden? The dull light that had once filtered through the thick cloud was even dimmer now, and the wind had leapt up another level, tugging at her bonnet so fiercely Hester had to grab it by the brim. Instead of being like scraps of delicate lace the snowflakes were larger, heavier, and coming down so densely it was hard to make out anything more than a few feet away.

Another prickle of unease threaded down Hester's spine. In these conditions it was no longer obvious which direction was which, or even what path she'd already walked. What had started as a mere flurry was well on its way to becoming a blizzard—something wild and dangerous in the whistle of the wind and in the way it snatched at her increasingly soaked dress.

In her surprise at Diana and her irritation

with Nathaniel she hadn't paid much attention to where she'd been walking…as she now realised far too late, suddenly disorientated and half blind from the whirl of white that surrounded her.

I need to find some shelter. I could catch my death, staying outside in this.

She turned, head down against the wind and jaw set firmly. The stockings on both feet were wet now—a horrible sensation that squelched with each step until her toes felt like ice. Blundering forward her skirts flattened against her legs, their fabric drenched and clinging and making Hester grimace with frozen disgust. Any shelter out of this weather would be a godsend, although as she dragged her legs through the deepening snow Hester had no clue where such a thing could be found.

'Can I blame Nathaniel for this misfortune too, I wonder?' Hester mumbled to herself through deadened lips. It was *his* fault she'd had to leave the house, after all—standing around so tall and ruggedly handsome, all wry smiles and secrets and 'After you, Hester…' in every doorway, making her heart leap and her palms prickle with the desire to touch…

How long would she have to bear it? How long *could* she bear it, seeing that face every day and knowing there was a part of her that still longed to rise up on her tiptoes and kiss that lying mouth?

Enough.

Scowling into the storm, Hester stumbled a little further. Indistinct trees were looming up on all sides now, their branches disappearing into the gloom and trunks bending ominously with every gust. Perhaps somewhere among them she would find shelter, Hester hoped and, groping onward, peered short-sightedly through the murk.

Thank heaven!

It was as though it had been built with this very moment in mind. Not ten feet away stood a tumbledown shack, its bowed roof heavy with snow. It didn't look fit to keep animals in any longer, let alone a human being, but Hester couldn't remember a time she'd been more glad to see a hovel as she made for the broken door.

The wood was swollen, but a hard shove sent it scraping inwards and Hester half fell inside, only stopping herself just in time with a quickly flung-out hand. At her back the wind tugged peevishly at her coat, as though trying to pull her out into the blizzard again, and with one last effort she heaved the door back into its frame, strength almost spent from her trek through the drifts.

She stood for a moment, waiting for her heart-rate to slow and her breath to even out from shallow pants. A quick look around her new shelter wasn't the most encouraging. Some snow was still managing to filter in through gaps in the roof and the dirt floor was damp, fearsomely sized spiders hanging from thick webs in each corner. Now she was standing still she felt colder than ever, in spite of being out of the wind, and she breathed a cloud onto numb fingers.

Of all the predicaments to get herself into...

'I can't really blame Nathaniel for this,' Hester admitted to the largest spider. 'It was my bad temper that made me go out walking, and now I suppose I have to pay the price.'

Her eight-legged friend didn't reply, and Hester chafed her hands. Goosebumps had risen on every inch of her skin, and her wet skirts were doing nothing to help rid her of the chill seeping rapidly into her bones. At this rate she'd be an icicle by the time the snow had passed and she could find her way home, and with apprehension growing in her stomach Hester settled down uncomfortably to wait out the storm.

'Will Mrs Honeywell be joining you for luncheon, sir?'

Seated at the head of the table, Nathaniel looked up from his pile of company books, trying his hardest to get back into the rhythm of work after such a long absence. There were some numbers that didn't make sense, and for once his mind was more on arithmetic than on Hester until he realised he hadn't seen her all morning.

'She usually does. I'm not sure what could be keeping her.'

'I don't think she's back from her walk yet, sir.' The maid peered out of the window behind Nathaniel's chair, her brow furrowed. 'She went out some hours ago and has yet to return.'

Nathaniel twisted in his seat to glance outside, his face darkening when he saw what lay beyond the glass. Brooding clouds cast a constant bombardment of snow down onto Shardlow's lawns, the wind picking up vast flakes to hurl them about—or so he assumed. The snow was too thick to see what was happening much beyond the window, although the sound of the wind moaning around the house was all too clear.

'What in seven hells—? She went walking in *this*?'

The maid looked apologetic, as though it was her fault Hester had been so foolish. 'It wasn't this bad when she set out. I don't think anyone expected the weather to take such a turn, sir.'

Nathaniel pushed himself up from the table, scattering papers onto the floor.

Damn it, Hester. Of all the stupid things to do!

'In which direction did she go?'

'Towards Drake's Hollow I think, sir. At least that's what I heard her tell Miss Arless.'

Frustration coursed through him at her poor decision-making, her lack of reason alien to his coolly rational mind. Surely everyone knew not to go walking when there was even the *chance* of a snowstorm? And yet Hester had galivanted off without a second's thought.

Nathaniel left the dining room, the poor maid leaping out of his way as though he were a charging bull. Irritation made him walk quickly, but it was something else—something much more unsettling—that made him send for his coat.

A flutter of dread stirred low down inside him as he strode towards the front door, winding a woollen scarf around his neck as he went. Had something happened to her? Why had she not yet returned? If she'd left Shardlow some hours ago she could be anywhere by now, perhaps lying frozen in a snowdrift, and the wave of dismay that washed over him at the thought almost made him pause. A measure of kindness to his neglected wife was all he'd intended; the worry for her that circled as he pulled on his hat, however, crossed that line far more than he liked. Did it stray into weakness, the most undesirable trait in a man? Or was it a sign that his newfound humanity was at war with his old detachment, something even his own mother had suffered while his father had encouraged its sting?

Why not send a servant?

The unwelcome question piped up slyly, making Nathaniel frown.

Why go yourself for a woman who wouldn't do the same in return?

The flames of his irritation climbed higher,

fanned by the shame of knowing that once he would have done just that. Because he wasn't a spoilt boy any longer—*that* was why, and he wouldn't ask a servant to do something he ought to do himself. Hester might be prickly, but she was his wife and she deserved his protection... even if a sudden recollection of the shape of her waist made him suspect he might be acting out of more than mere duty.

'Are you going out in *that*?' Jacob appeared behind the new valet who carried Nathaniel's warmest coat, looking doubtfully out through the hall window.

'Yes.' Nathaniel thrust his arms inside and fastened the buttons with unthinking speed. Where to begin his search? Drake's Hollow was at least two miles away, and what was to say she'd even made it that far? 'Hester went out walking this morning and hasn't come back. I'm going to find her.'

Jacob let out a low whistle, eyebrows raised. 'And I thought *we'd* showed fortitude. A brave woman to venture outside in a blizzard.'

'Brave or foolish?' Nathaniel shot his friend a swift glance, wondering suddenly if Jacob had a point. Perhaps it *was* impressive that Hester would sally forth into the snow rather than stay inside safe and warm, as once he'd imagined was all she *could* do... But admiration for his wife's surprising independence was not to be encouraged.

'Shall I come with you? We can cover more ground with two.'

'No.' Nathaniel shook his head, bracing himself to open the door. 'No point in three people blundering about risking frostbite. Just make sure the servants have hot baths ready on our return.'

Grasping his coat firmly closed at the neck, Nathaniel stepped outside. Immediately the wind set upon him as though it had been lying in wait, snatching at his clothes and attempting to pull the hat from his head, and Nathaniel narrowed his eye as snow whirled viciously into his face.

Thank you, Hester. Just how I was hoping to spend my afternoon.

Lowering his chin, he battled down Shardlow's front steps and crossed the wide drive, its gravel hidden beneath a rippling carpet of white. His boots sank a few inches with each footstep, and even for a man of his strength it was an effort to drag himself to the front gate, heading for the distant stand of trees he hoped would surrender his wife.

As far as he could tell there was nobody else around, the rest of Thame Magna's inhabitants probably far more sensibly occupied in front of their fires. No blurry figures appeared out of the gloom as Nathaniel trudged past the shadows of houses, struggling on until the village opened to fields that gave the wind free rein to howl its fury into his ears.

'Hester!'

He shouted into the snowy void, ploughing through the snow and straining his one good eye for any glimpse of her. All he could see was white flurries dancing around him, and yet more grabbing at his boots, dogging each step as he crossed an open expanse he barely recognised. No wonder Hester had got lost. It was so easy to feel completely disorientated when every direction looked the same and the cold dimmed the senses, neither sight nor hearing of much use with flakes flying and a gale shrieking above all other noise.

Nathaniel's worry grew with every footstep, fear replacing any irritation at Hester's recklessness.

What if I can't find her? What will happen then?

He dismissed the words at once. There was no time for hysteria—in that regard his severe schooling had been right, he admitted grimly. Sometimes emotion had to be put to one side in order to get results, and now was one of them. He would find Hester and bring her home, however long it took, and failure was not an option.

Hardening himself against any lingering doubts, Nathaniel pressed on. The cold was becoming oppressive: his hands ached and his throat hurt with each icy breath, freezing air like daggers in his lungs. He must have walked a mile already, but it was so hard to tell... Was he anywhere near the hollow, or had he inadvertently walked the wrong way entirely?

He shouted again, his voice hopelessly lost amid the sounds of the storm.

After what felt like an eternity he stopped, something catching at the very corner of his eye. Squinting through the blizzard, he could just make out the dark bulk of what looked like a clump of trees, grouped together as if to shelter something at their base. From a distance all the shapes were indistinct smudges against the white backdrop, but it was enough to draw him closer, and as he advanced his pulse quickened to see a squat stone hut emerge out of the murk. Surely if Hester had sought shelter it would be somewhere like that?

A flicker of cautious optimism stirred as he found a rough door—seemingly opened recently, if the disturbed snow nearby was any clue—and put his shoulder against the rotting wood, forcing it aside.

At first he thought he'd been mistaken. Heavy disappointment flooded him: there was nobody there—only the smell of mould and damp earth and the whine of wind through the holes in the roof. It was dark, the low ceiling and windowless walls making the space unpleasantly claustrophobic, and Nathaniel was about to turn away when a small movement in one corner captured his attention.

'Nathaniel?'

That quiet little voice darted straight to the very centre of his chest and set his heart leaping. Hester sat huddled on the floor beside a pile of old sacking, legs drawn up and arms hugging her knees as if trying to ward off the bitter cold, and as he rushed towards her he saw her lips were blue and face blanched the colour of cream. She shook violently, a few hanging curls shuddering with every breath and her eyes glazed and heavy.

'Hester!'

Nathaniel dropped to his knees beside her, all other thoughts chased away by the sight of her so pale and stiff. Without pausing to consider the wisdom of his actions, he seized her in his arms and pulled her against him, rubbing her back and chafing her hands with hardly a care for how she might react—or for how his mouth suddenly dried at the contact, her fragile body scalding to him despite the arctic chill. She looked half dead already, and a horrible picture flitted before him of what might have happened if he hadn't found her when he had.

'You're frozen. I need to warm you at once and I'm afraid there's only one way to do it.'

Swiftly he unbuttoned his coat. Holding it open, he scooped Hester closer and folded it around her, holding her to his chest so the heat of his body could begin to thaw her. He readied himself for her protests but none came—surely the only sign he needed that she was weak indeed. Instead she was quiet, cradled within the strong circle of his arms and so close he could have buried his nose in her damp hair. Her bonnet lay on the floor beside them so there was nothing to hide the lines of her face, her eyes closed now and so still that a lump rose in Nathaniel's throat.

She's lovely—and I never told her in two whole years.

A hundred different thoughts chased each other through his mind as they sat together on the ground: unease, and countless others he couldn't even name. Every nerve thrilled at the feeling of Hester so close, her heart beating next to his, rousing his protective spirit as though it were a lion. He shouldn't feel like that—shouldn't feel anything other than perhaps relief at finding her—but he could hardly help the way she made his pulse skip faster, nor the desire to hold her more tightly still.

Keep your head.

Nathaniel gritted his teeth. Things were getting out of control. If he wasn't careful he'd end up walking a path he'd had no intention of following—the same one he had dismissed so firmly when Hester had first threatened to turn him from his true purpose and he'd had to be reminded what was expected of a man. By all means he could offer Hester friendship now, after Algiers had taken its toll, but nothing else—not least because she'd surely reject him if he tried. Any feelings she might once have entertained for him were long gone, he knew for certain, and there was nobody to blame for that but himself.

She was in his lap.

Heaven help her, *she was in his lap!*

Hester lay perfectly still, praying silently that her cheeks weren't flaming crimson. With her eyes tight shut she couldn't see Nathaniel's face, but she could *feel* him watching her and it was almost more than she could bear.

A voice at the back of her mind spoke up sternly. *You ought to pull away.*

No doubt it was right, but it was just so good to finally be warm, after fearing she might freeze to death…

You're enjoying this. Far too much. And you know it.

She forced the snide little voice away. Of course the warmth of Nathaniel's chest—his broad, *impressive* chest—was the only reason she hadn't wriggled off his expansive thighs, away from his firm legs pressed against hers so closely it left little to the imagination. The fact that his hands felt so strong as they rubbed her frozen back had nothing to do with anything, and neither did the breathless havoc beneath her bodice at knowing his throat was inches from her lips. She could smell the unique scent of his skin… something unmistakably male and so enticing it raised the hairs at her nape in a way that had nothing to do with the cold.

He actually came for me.

There was no way of putting into words the relief that had swept through her as Nathaniel appeared in the doorway, his hat and shoulders covered with snow and his face grim—or the surprise. He'd come himself instead of sending a servant; or indeed, sending anyone at all? The Nathaniel she'd known five years previously wouldn't even have noticed she was missing until it was too late, and bewilderment made Hester speak before she could stop herself.

'I can't believe you came looking for me. I never would have imagined it.'

The words came out a little muffled, her lips stiff with cold, and she heard Nathaniel's dry laugh.

'Still determined to think the worst of me, Hester? You're a difficult woman to impress. Even my best efforts are doomed to failure, it would seem.'

She opened one eye—and regretted it. Nathaniel's face was even closer than she'd realised, and for half a second she lost the train of her reply, attention captured by the tanned features some wayward part of her wanted to touch. She swallowed, all too aware of the muscled arms that held her so mortifyingly in place—and even more aware that deep down, in some corner she'd tried to forget, she had always longed for them to do exactly that.

But he left me, possibly to die, and then swaggered back in again expecting a hero's welcome.

The memory of that fateful day helped a little to order her thoughts. 'You can hardly blame me for being surprised when the business has always come first for you. I remember a time when my wellbeing was not as much a consideration to you as it seems to be now.'

It was probably ridiculous to chastise a man while unwillingly cradled in his lap, and Nathaniel certainly seemed to think so as he furrowed his brow.

'What do you mean by that?'

Hester tried to sit up. Thanks to Nathaniel's body heat some of the sensation was returning to her limbs, and the niggle that called for her to move away from him grew louder. Her muscles, however, thought otherwise. They refused to co-operate, leaving her no choice but to sink back against her aggravating husband's shirt, her face flaring hotter than ever with fathomless embarrassment.

She felt Nathaniel shift a little on the cold,

hard ground. Probably the damp had already begun to seep into his breeches, but he didn't complain, instead settling himself more comfortably, like a child awaiting a bedtime story.

'You know, Hester,' he continued conversationally, for all the world as though they were at a dining table and not in the most hideous situation imaginable, 'we might be here for hours, waiting for the storm to pass. In the absence of anything else to do, you may as well finally tell me about my crimes.'

With growing alarm Hester tried another furtive wriggle. Again, sadly fruitless. She was well and truly stuck in the most mortifying prison imaginable—one carved from sinew and biceps so firm it made her blush to acknowledge it. Would Nathaniel refuse to let her go until she told him? And would he even care what she had to say if she did?

Once the answer to that last question would have been obvious, but with a start Hester realised she was no longer so sure.

'What if I don't want to?'

'That would be up to you, of course, but I'd hope you'd think better of it.'

Hester hunched slightly, trying to think despite the clenching in her gut. The nerve of him, angling to know her secrets while still concealing his own! If her limbs would obey she'd be halfway across the hut by now, but until they did the only defence she had from Nathaniel's insistence was the sharpness of her tongue.

'Do you imagine you're in a position to issue demands?'

'Probably a better one than you to refuse them.'

She gritted her teeth on rising annoyance, ignoring the hint of humour in her husband's voice. An uneasy conflict stirred inside her: reluctant gratitude for Nathaniel's rescue pitted against far less favourable feelings.

Still he has no idea what he did wrong, and now he's a hypocrite into the bargain. Why should I tell him anything when he offers nothing in return?

But that wasn't quite true, and the accusation rang hollow even to Hester's biased ears. Nathaniel had ventured out to look for her—an action worth more than whatever handful of secrets he thought she wouldn't want the 'honesty' of his telling her. The wind still whined imploringly outside and white flurries drifted down from the roof...both reminders of what Nathaniel had battled through to reach her.

'Come on, Hester. As I said before, I don't bite.'

His chest vibrated with every word, and her ear against his shirt picked up the deep cadence. The warmth of his body had long since mingled with hers, and for one disorientating second it was impossible for Hester to tell where Nathaniel ended and she began. If she was the superstitious sort she might wonder if some part of his essence had switched places with hers: her heart was harder now, where his was more open, each of them taking on some measure of the other as though to balance the scales.

She shot him one hard glance. He looked straight back, so directly that Hester felt herself swallow quite involuntarily. Laying bare her past hurt would be a big leap, but something in that serious green stare encouraged her to step a fraction closer to the edge.

'You're certainly persistent.'

Nathaniel inclined his head, as though she'd paid him a compliment. 'I'd like to know the extent of my sins. I cannot answer for them if I'm never told what they are.'

There was a certain truth in that assertion, but still it sent a current of irritation through Hester's nerves.

'It baffles me that you can be so unaware of your own failings.'

'Surely that's just another of them?'

The flicker of temper burned a little brighter. Had he really no finer feelings to consult? No clue at all that might help guide him towards an answer, even if it was wrong?

'What do you *think* lies at the root of my dislike? If you had to hazard a guess?'

'I would never presume to understand what goes on in your mind.'

Hester set her jaw, wishing Nathaniel's chiselled one wasn't still quite so close. For an intelligent man he was astoundingly dense—or perhaps merely too selfish to spend even the briefest moment considering her feelings, just as she'd always suspected.

Aggravation sharpened her voice. 'I know you lack tenderness and interest for anything other than profit. Am I to find you've no common sense either? I never took you for a simpleton, but perhaps I give you too much credit.'

Too vexed to stay close to him any longer, she tried once again to free herself from his grasp. This time she succeeded, after a fashion, and with an ungainly squirm slid from his lap, landing beside Nathaniel on the freezing ground. There was no time to celebrate, however, as in the same instant she almost keeled over, only the sudden circling of her waist by a strong arm keeping her sitting upright.

'I can do perfectly well by myself!'

'Is that right? You just wanted a closer look at the floor, did you?'

Nathaniel's face told her exactly what he thought of her unfounded confidence.

'You're still weak. Much as you resent it, I'm afraid you'll have to let me warm you a while longer if we're to reach Shardlow as soon as the weather allows.' He pondered for a moment. 'Unless, of course, you want me to carry you?'

Hester stiffened. 'You wouldn't dare!'

'Then you'll need to stay near.'

Balling her hands into fists, she said nothing as an unpleasant mixture of anger and confusion surged in her stomach. A more foolish woman might believe Nathaniel's show of gallant concern; and might not question why some part of her *wanted* to believe it, thrown off balance by his venture into the snow. The solid strength of his body pressed so close didn't help her remain aloof either, and she realised their breathing had synchronised, to bring them into an instinctive harmony that made her pulse skip.

Discomfort forced her to speak at last. 'Deceit is unbecoming, Nathaniel.'

'In what way am I being deceitful? Or is this another guessing game?'

'Pretending to care what happens to me. We both know you can't be sincere.'

Nathaniel sighed, letting out a heavy breath like a man exercising great patience. 'You're wrong. I do care.'

Hester's own patience snapped and the ire in her gut reached boiling point, her innards twisting in a hard knot. He was lying—he *had* to be! There was no way Nathaniel could claim to have any regard for her when his past actions said so clearly otherwise—even if he'd muddied the waters by his uncharacteristic actions in the present, and the arm around her waist made her feel as if her skin was aflame. For him to look into her face and lie was more than she could bear, and Hester found her lips moving before she gave them leave.

'You left me on what might have been my deathbed! Can you doubt me for wondering at your newfound concern for me when once you sailed away without knowing if I'd live or die?'

Her secret—the hidden pain she'd kept buried deep down for five years—pierced the frozen air like a burning arrow and there was nothing she could do to snatch it back.

For some unmeasurable length of time it hung there, a terrible thing that laid Hester's soul bare and left her completely exposed, and she wanted to bite out her own tongue. Where was her self-control? How could she have let it slip, dropping her guard for mere moments yet that one lapse enough for the world to come spilling from her mouth? Nathaniel would know his power now, know how much sway he had held over her unhappy life, and she felt herself turn to stone at the thought of how he would respond.

Pride, perhaps? Her subconscious twisted the knife in an already salted wound. *Knowing his abandonment hurt me so deeply?*

Surely most men would be gratified to have had such an effect—although of course Nathaniel's lack of interest in anything unprofit-able might dampen his delight. Her feelings had never been important to him after all, those first blissful weeks a lie she'd been too stupid to see, and he might greet her revelation now with dis-interest that would sting more than any gloating.

But neither of those things happened.

Instead, to her unending amazement, Nathan-iel simply laughed.

She stared at him, quite unable to process his response. Why was his mouth curved into a cyni-cal smile? Was there something amusing in her heartfelt confession that had left her nowhere to hide?

A rapid flush of heat roared up to engulf her, anger beginning to course in a steady stream that took the edge off her searing shame.

He raised an arch brow. 'Come off it, Hester. What's the *real* reason?'

'I beg your pardon?'

Nathaniel rolled his uncovered eye—and Hes-ter's ire swelled higher.

'It wasn't *really* your deathbed. My father made that quite clear.'

'Your father?'

'Yes.' He stretched his legs out, crossing ex-pensive boots at the ankles. 'Forgive me for being so blunt, but he explained at the time that you weren't truly ill. I think you and I both know your *"condition"* was just a ploy to stop me from leaving.'

Hester could hardly believe her ears, blood pounding in them loudly enough to block out everything else.

'A ploy to stop you from leaving? Is *that* your defence?'

Still captured by that blistering bicep, she twisted awkwardly so they were almost nose to nose. Looking directly at him, Hester saw confusion in her husband's face, her anger suddenly dimming—only slightly—at his complete lack of guile; and at the realisation her mouth was mere inches from his.

'Do I need another?'

'Yes! Considering you're completely and utterly wrong!'

His uncertain frown made her shake her head incredulously.

'Do you think I lay in bed for three weeks, feverish and delirious, just to stop you from getting on a boat? That the doctor telling my poor parents I might not survive another night and my skin feeling as though it was on fire was just to make you postpone your departure?'

Now Nathaniel's eye narrowed. For a moment she wondered if her fury had overstepped some mark, but then his gaze broke away from hers and he stared up at the shack's patchy roof. Eventually she saw his lips move in one low syllable, barely heard above the wind outside.

'Oh.'

She waited for him to say something more. Perhaps he'd try to make excuses, to deny any guilt, but instead he was silent.

Hester broke first. 'You honestly didn't realise?'

'No.' He still studied the ceiling, carefully following the progress of a spider along its web. 'My father told me you were affecting a far more serious illness than you actually suffered. He'd never told me a falsehood before—he had no time for something as trivial as storytelling. It never occurred to me not to believe him.'

Hester felt herself tense, even still held immovably in Nathaniel's grip, her heart racing like a hare through a field.

That can't be true.

If Nathaniel was being honest it meant her resentment had been unfounded—and unfair—for five long years, with bitterness chasing out the sweet nature she'd once possessed for no real reason. His confession didn't alter the fact that he'd been a cool and distant husband, luring her in only to break her girlish heart, but at the very least it meant he hadn't been quite so cruel as she'd believed—something difficult to accept after so long.

His father was to blame? Not Nathaniel?

It shouldn't have been such a surprise to learn he was involved, Hester thought bitterly. The way Mr Honeywell treated his own wife should surely have provided a clue as to his opinion of women, never allowing Nathaniel's poor mother to come before any money to be made. Probably he'd even be willing to sacrifice his own son…

It was a thought that caused a vivid flare of sympathy to leap in Hester's stomach, coming from nowhere to shock her with its strength. She swiftly pushed it aside, although her pulse skipped ever faster.

'Surely that can't amaze you? You must be aware he'd allow nothing to stand in the way of a voyage that could bring him profit.'

Nathaniel's reply was little more than a murmur. 'Even at the cost of a life?'

'Even that.'

Hester watched him for a moment. With his face turned to the roof the shape of his jaw was sharper than ever, dusted with the lightest covering of stubble, and she wondered—before she could stop herself—if it would be rough to trace with gentle fingertips… She wanted to look away, confusion and unease still twisting inside her, but then he dropped his chin to stare into her eyes and she was suddenly unable to move.

'I'm sorry, Hester.'

He spoke quietly, but with such steady conviction that her breath caught in her throat. His gaze, so direct and unwavering, held hers like a magnet and refused to let her go.

'Truly. I shouldn't have boarded that ship and shouldn't have called you a liar, however indirectly. I apologise sincerely.'

Now it was Hester's turn to fall silent. A slow creep of colour climbed up her neck to suffuse each cheek, and her mind stretched out blank as the snow outside.

'Well…' She hesitated, aware of the blood still pulsing in her ears.

Where now was the arrogance he'd always worn like a cloak? The self-assuredness that had seemed so impenetrable? At one time she'd longed for the chance to put him in his place, but something in his naked honesty touched her, shining a light on the softness within her she'd fought so hard to hide.

'I suppose it shows great devotion to your father to have believed him so implicitly.'

Nathaniel snorted grimly. 'Devotion may not be the right term. Blind imitation is more accurate.'

He picked up a piece of straw from the ground and crumpled it in his fist, Hester seeing his knuckles shine white.

'I don't appreciate being lied to. Not by him or anybody else. Especially given the result.'

The sour edge to his voice sent a prickle down Hester's spine. He sounded regretful, unless she was much mistaken, with an undercurrent of anger, although whether for his treatment of her or his emulation of his undeserving father she couldn't tell. Either way she couldn't think of a reply, and quiet stretched out between them until Nathaniel broke it with a turn of his head towards the door.

'I think the wind has dropped a little. We might be able to leave.'

He slackened his arm, finally releasing Hester from his grip, and she slipped away at once, cheeks still flaming as he rose easily beside her. She was much warmer now, thanks to Nathaniel, but her knees still buckled as she tried to stand, and she almost collapsed back onto the ground until he slid a strong arm around her waist.

'Careful! Are your legs still weak?'

'A little.'

She saw the ghost of a smile flit across his lips. 'Perhaps I might carry you after all? I doubt you could outrun me at the moment if you tried.'

Flustered, Hester tried to reply, but found all speech abandoned her as she stared up at Nathaniel and he stared straight back, any trace of humour gone from his face at whatever he saw in hers. Yet again he had leapt forward to save her from falling, just as on that morning on Shardlow's front lawn, but this time it wasn't anger that swept through her as he held her close.

'You always seem to be there to catch me,' she

murmured, not needing to speak any louder than that. 'Or is it your fault I fall in the first place?'

'I hope not. I don't think I'd like to have such an unbalancing effect on my wife.'

That was probably true, Hester thought vaguely as she watched Nathaniel's eye fix on her own and hold them to ransom. He wouldn't want her to feel so unsteady every time he came near. He'd made that much plain seven years ago, when he'd turned his back on her foolish affections to treat her with the coolness his father's example had instilled.

So why, then, was it she couldn't seem to help herself from arching against him like a cat wanting to be stroked, with past desire coming to life again in the delicious prison of his arms? He had no use for it…and Hester knew no good could come from allowing it any space in her mind… But hadn't she just discovered there might be less cruelty in her husband than she'd believed? And wasn't he still holding on to her so tightly she thought her bones might break, perhaps intrigued by the intimacy that could come from telling the truth?

Something was different now, some of the poison drained from the wounds each was guilty of inflicting, and as Hester felt the atmosphere between them shift she had to wonder: exactly *who* had returned from Algiers, to look down at her now with such intensity it made her lose her breath?

Afterwards, she wouldn't be able to remember who had moved first. All she knew was that one minute she was leaning against Nathaniel for support, and the next his mouth was on hers and her lips were moving as they had ached to ever since his return—and even long before that, in spite of her attempts to deny it.

In that moment nothing else mattered; not the snow that still fell outside the hut or the little voice that urged caution. Nathaniel was all there was, his arms tight around her and one hand at her back, the other moving behind her head as he deepened the kiss and only his strength stopped her from falling.

Her own hands found his shirt and clung where his heartbeat pounded so hard she could feel it mirroring hers as it fluttered like a bird in a cage with each movement of his mouth. It was dazzling, strange, unlike any sensation Hester had ever felt before, and she wanted nothing more than for him to continue as her skin sang and her breath came short and fast.

Any lingering discomfort from the cold fell away, the warmth of Nathaniel's body surrounding her on all sides. While perched on his lap she'd been mortified, knowing she ought to escape, but now she couldn't help but lean closer, feeling him redouble his grip and bear down harder still. The soft skin of his lips contrasted intoxicatingly with the rough stubble that dusted his jaw, and Hester's fingertips finally acted on their desire to skim over the sharp lines of his face and know for certain how it felt.

Lost in wave upon wave of sensation, she was deaf to all reason, acting only on instinct, until Nathaniel was the one to gently step back.

'It seems I owe you another apology.'

His face was flushed as he buttoned his coat, attempting what she assumed was a smile. It was stiff, uncertain, and she felt her own countenance burn as reality came crashing back to replace whatever daydream Nathaniel's clever mouth had woven.

How did that happen? How could I have made such a colossal mistake?

She tried to smile back, only managing a grimace as her gut twisted with shame. Which of them was to blame for that blunder? In her shock at Nathaniel's confession she had taken a wrong turn, sympathy for him clouding her judgement…and now surely any hope of a fledgling accord between them had been ruined by a foolish step too far?

Or perhaps not…

Trapped in a whirl of horror, Hester didn't notice immediately when Nathaniel reached for her hand. It took her a second to register, and her heart leapt up into her throat as he sought her eyes.

'I think we can both agree that shouldn't have

happened. I also hope we can agree on something else.'

Hester caught a sharp breath. So Nathaniel *did* regret their kiss. She'd known he must, but hearing him say it out loud caught her hard beneath the ribs.

'And what is that?'

'We try being friends. After all this time, and with my faults out in the open, perhaps we might try that.'

She hesitated. Embarrassment sat inside her like a stone, but something else crept up to join it—something that took the edge off pure humiliation.

Could I truly be friends with Nathaniel? After I loathed and mistrusted him for so long?

He was a different man from the one he'd been before he went away, that much was true, and despite herself Hester felt the embers of her previous regard for him stir anew. Years ago her esteem for him had been shallow, based only on his handsome face, but now there was a real danger of it growing into something deeper, based on the person behind the looks. Even with his scars and missing eye he was more comely than any other man she could think of, although her gratitude for his rescue and her realisation he might not be so cold after all now seemed more important than anything else.

She peeped up at him. He stood still, holding her hand as carefully as he might a piece of glass, and something inside her swelled with sudden hope. Perhaps he didn't return her misguided feelings. Perhaps she would have to redouble her efforts to set them aside. But friendship was better than nothing, and now that Nathaniel seemed determined to be a better man she might even start to enjoy having him home.

'Very well.' Hester nodded slowly, cautious but so wanting to *believe*. 'If you think it might be possible, I'm willing to try.'

Chapter Six

It was fortunate that five years of hard labour had left Nathaniel so fit. Hester was marching through the halls of Shardlow House so quickly a more sedentary man would have struggled to keep up, only pausing briefly to wave at some new painting or a rearranged room she had decorated in his lengthy absence. It was a house tour he'd wanted and apparently that was exactly what he was going to get—albeit one more rigorous than he'd expected.

Not that he was complaining. His position a few strides behind Hester afforded him an excellent view of her figure—something he found his eye insisted on wandering back to no matter how many times he looked away.

'...and in here was repapered only last year. Much fresher than the original, I think.'

Hester gestured around the airy study, where winter sunlight was streaming through floor-to-ceiling windows. Bathed in the glow she might have been one of the paintings that smiled down from each wall, her face just as pretty as any artist's creation, and the urge to tell her so suddenly balanced on the tip of Nathaniel's tongue.

Careful, now. We don't need another misstep when we're making such progress.

Unseen as Hester rearranged an errant curtain, he gave himself a small shake. Any thoughts of what had transpired out in the storm should be locked in a heavy box and buried, that heart-stopping kiss born of confusion and nothing more. With all the emotions flying about it was no wonder things had gone awry; they could hardly be blamed for making an error when the waters between them had been so muddied.

Hester really had been gravely ill, and his father had lied. Both regret and anger sat painfully in the pit of Nathaniel's stomach, although he found a smile for his wife nonetheless.

'I agree. Your taste is impeccable. Every change you've made is an undeniable improvement.'

'Oh.'

A look of uncertainty crossed Hester's face, followed—to Nathaniel's surprise—by one cautiously pleased, so far removed from the frowns of previous weeks that it made him pause.

'Thank you.'

Beneath his waistcoat Nathaniel's heart stepped

up a fraction. Was that the first time he'd paid Hester a compliment? With a nasty jolt he realised it probably was, and he felt discomfort winding through his belly as he tried to recall a time when he might have said something, *anything*, pleasant.

Wed for all those months before he went away, and never having bothered with a kind word to his own wife? Hardly surprising she'd looked so doubtful at first, but now the faintest trace of a blush was crossing her cheeks.

'It must be strange for you, coming back to find the house so altered.'

Nathaniel's mouth quirked. New wallpaper was the least of the changes to Shardlow since his time in Algiers. The difference in its mistress was far more disorientating but he could hardly tell her that, instead pretending to consider a re-upholstered chair behind his old desk.

'Perhaps a little. All for the better, however.'

That hint of pink grew deeper, and Nathaniel turned his attention to the view beyond the study windows. Hester probably had no idea how becoming she looked when she blushed, and it made it all the more difficult to remember it was only friendship they were striving for. He might regret his actions in leaving her now he knew the truth, but nothing could turn back the clock. An apology didn't mean automatic forgiveness, and it certainly didn't magic up trust. That had to be earned.

There were miles to go before he could hope Hester might place some faith in him, and once again Nathaniel's throat tightened at the knowledge he *wanted* that faith, his respect—and desire—for his complicated wife growing ever since the discovery she hadn't been faking her illness after all. She'd looked into the jaws of death and survived, all without the support of her husband, showing a strength even the hardest of men would have to admire.

It was risky to admit it, but Nathaniel had no choice. How could he not think well of Hester for showing the fortitude he'd always been taught himself until Algiers had left its foul mark on his character?

'What's that out there?'

Brushing the thought aside, he crossed closer to one window. It gave a fine view of Shardlow's gardens, still submerged in snow but the sky now a clear, piercing blue. The white lawns ran down a gentle slope to an ornamental pond near one wall where, beneath a large tree, Nathaniel could just make out what looked like a summerhouse of some kind, flanked by a couple of smaller shapes.

Intent on this, yet another new addition since his departure, he found his attention flickering a little as Hester came to stand beside him.

'Ah. I'll show you, if you like.'

She gave him a small smile—something unthinkable only a few days before and still slightly unsure even now—and the curve of her lips sent a crackle through every one of Nathaniel's nerves.

'You'll need your gloves.'

Once suitably attired, Nathaniel followed Hester down a passageway towards the side porch. The temperature dropped the closer they got to the outside, finally falling away completely as Hester pulled open the door and a swathe of snow reached for their boots.

Stepping out, Nathaniel's breath froze at once and he saw it hang before him in little clouds as Hester led the way from the house to one of the paths, hidden beneath the dazzling carpet but still guiding them down the slope towards the cluster of shapes he'd seen from the window.

'Do you see?' Hester called over her shoulder, only the tip of her nose—rosy from the cold— showing beyond her bonnet. *Even that small glimpse was endearing*, a whisper Nathaniel firmly set aside.

'Just about. A summerhouse and—' He squinted downwards. The sun was full in his face, making it hard to see, but it looked like… 'Archery butts?'

'Exactly so.'

Puzzled now, he watched Hester come to a halt beside one of the painted targets. Sheltered beneath the overhanging tree, it wasn't as deeply entrenched in snow as the rest of the garden, and Hester laid a hand on it proudly.

'I had them made to my specifications. I can come down here to shoot whenever I please— even in the depths of winter if I've a mind to.'

'And do you?' Nathaniel rubbed the back of his neck, mildly bemused. Since when had Hester been an enthusiastic archer? It was a surprise to learn she had any hobbies at all, let alone one so unlikely.

'Sometimes. Spring is my preferred season, but I like to practise now and then.'

'I had no idea you nurtured such a passion.'

Hester glanced up at him, her face suddenly clouded with something Nathaniel couldn't name.

'How would you?' she asked quietly. 'You never seemed to take much interest in what I might enjoy.'

It wasn't a rebuke, and yet Nathaniel could barely remember ever feeling so chastened as he stood there in the snow. The icy breeze might nip, but it was Hester's words that chilled him, knowing as he did that they were the truth.

Leaving when she could have died. Not even bothering to speak with her every day. Man and wife and yet I don't know her at all—I thought that was how it had to be.

Hester traced gloved fingers through the dusting of snow atop the target. The atmosphere was in danger of slipping into uncomfortable, and Nathaniel seized the first thing that came to mind.

'You must be very accomplished after all that practice. Perhaps you'd show me.'

She looked up, one cynical eyebrow raised. 'You'd like to see me shoot?'

'Of course. Unless you're embarrassed?'

Her eyes narrowed, and then he had to swallow a ragged breath at the first real laugh he'd heard from her lips. It was high and sweet, like birdsong, cutting through the biting air to warm him from within.

'Not at all. I only hope I won't disappoint.'

Hester crunched through the snow to the little summerhouse, disappearing inside for a moment before returning with a bow and handful of arrows. Selecting one and setting the rest down at her feet, she took position beside one of the targets, directly opposite the other a good distance away.

'I had them set like this to save time. This way I can shoot to one target, walk over and retrieve my arrows, then shoot back to the other at once.'

'Very efficient.'

He waited as Hester tested the string with her fingers. Apparently satisfied with what she found, she fitted her arrow and lifted the bow, moving so smoothly into an archer's stance that Nathaniel was suddenly reminded of his single experience watching a ballet.

All at once Hester might have been one of those dancers, her back perfectly straight and her arms held with graceful precision. The pose highlighted the span of her waist, its gentle curve capturing Nathaniel's attention and refusing to surrender it back to his control. For a long moment she was like a statue, perhaps Artemis carved from stone, the only movement that of her hair stirring softly in the breeze; until with her eyes locked on their target, apparently unaware that her husband's throat felt as though someone was squeezing it, Hester exhaled and let her arrow fly.

Nathaniel's mouth fell open as the arrow buried itself into the very centre of the painted target. It was in so deep only the fletching showed and, looking back at Hester, he saw quiet satisfaction in her face.

'Quite good. Not perfect, but good.'

'Not perfect?'

He could hardly keep the amazement from his voice. She was so talented and he hadn't had a clue, never suspecting such an ability lay beneath that calm exterior. Had she always been so skilled? In that moment she looked more like a huntress than a lady...

'That was extraordinary. I don't think it could have been more precise if you'd stuck it in from two inches away!'

She shrugged, although Nathaniel was sure

she was pleased. A small smile played about her lips even as she fended off his unfamiliar praise with a gloved hand, and that slight upward tick drew his eye at once.

'A fraction left of centre, I believe. I'm a little out of practice.'

Nathaniel gave a dry laugh. Perhaps his insistent murmur of admiration for her was a little too strong for comfort, but who wouldn't be impressed by such a display? It couldn't be dangerous to show his appreciation for her skill… or so he told himself.

'If that's you out of practice there's no hope for the rest of us. I'm not sure I'd be able to hit so much as a barn door.'

'Can't you shoot?' Hester cocked her head like an inquisitive bird. 'Surely you were taught? I thought all young gentlemen were instructed in such things as part of their education?'

'Ah…'

Nathaniel scratched his chin. How to explain his unusual schooling to Hester? Doubtless she wouldn't understand. Nobody would, unless they had been in his position, with serious responsibilities from a young age. Almost since birth he'd known what was expected of him, and that concentration and hard work were the only way to run an empire.

'No. My father didn't hold with anything that might distract me from the business.'

Including you.

'Distract you?'

'Yes.' Nathaniel ignored the subconscious interruption. 'I always knew I was destined to enter the trade and my father made sure I was prepared. Arithmetic and accounting were considered useful. Recreation and idle pastimes were not.'

'Oh.'

Hester's sandy brows contracted in a frown, and something fleeting passed over her face that made Nathaniel's innards clench. If he wasn't much mistaken it had been the shadow of pity, its unexpected presence a static shock to his insides.

'That must have been difficult for a child. Were you allowed no fun at all?'

The snow around Nathaniel's feet was rapidly turning to slush, and he stirred it with the toe of one boot as he considered her question. She made it sound as though it were a *bad* thing that he'd been raised with such purpose, to be single-minded and know where his duty lay. Perhaps at times he'd found it difficult, his father's emotionless striving hard to follow, although surely it had been for the best.

Hester still watched him. That look in her eyes… Was it unwelcome? The idea of anybody's pity was a knock to his pride, but Hester's hit differently. At one time her opinion had mattered less than nothing, something of no consequence, but now he found himself caring what she thought and it put him on his guard at once.

Father always said I must make sacrifices. My happiness as a child was simply one of them.

He cleared his throat. 'The business is important, Hester. It allows us to have a fine house and carriage…pays for you to have expensive clothes…' Even as he spoke Nathaniel had the uneasy feeling he didn't wholeheartedly believe his own words. 'It's the backbone of our lives and it deserves my unwavering attention. In fact, I ought to be working now. I've spent far too long away from my desk this morning already.'

Did he sound defensive? Part of him thought he must as Hester studied him for a moment, as if sifting through his reply. For some reason his pulse quickened at her silent scrutiny; he could almost sense the turning of cogs inside her busy mind, her expression thoughtful—until with a sideways glance she took him by surprise.

'Stay just a few minutes more. If nobody else taught you, perhaps I might. It won't take long, I assure you.'

'What?' He was sure he must have misheard. 'You want to teach me? Why?'

Hester's slim shoulders moved in an elegant shrug. 'Why not?'

'Well…'

Why not indeed? Nathaniel cast about for a reason but came up with none. He really *should* be working, and it was certainly risky to be spending so much time with the woman he was growing more and more fond of each day. His desk was calling... But the lure of Hester's company called louder, and with a twinge of guilt Nathaniel made his choice.

'It might be difficult.' He held up his maimed hand, using it to gesture to his eye patch. 'A half-blind archer missing a particularly important finger?'

Hester waved his objections away. 'Details. Surely you won't let a couple of trifling details get in your way?'

'Trifling details?' Nathaniel had to laugh. Who else but Hester would call a missing eye a 'detail'? If there had been pity in her face before it certainly wasn't there now, and with a pang of surprise he realised something had changed.

She's joking with me. Laughing as though we're friends.

Despite her assurances, it took Hester considerably more than a few minutes to help Nathaniel master the basics of archery. For all her confidence, his missing finger really did pose a problem. Finding the right grip was difficult for him, and she could see his frustration as yet again the arrow fell to the snowy ground.

Even removing his gloves didn't help—all it did was give Hester a better look at the brutal marks around his knuckles and the jarring stump where his index finger should have been, never less disturbing no matter how many times she saw it.

'I fear you might be wasting your time. I appreciate you trying, but I don't think this is going to work.'

He looked resignedly down at his hand, something in his furrowed brow stirring Hester's sympathy—among other things. Following his gaze, she couldn't help but wonder anew at the terrible scars he bore from his absence, and grimaced at the idea of him enduring such pain—although yet again she set aside the burning desire to ask.

He made it quite clear to Mr Morrow that he doesn't want to talk about whatever happened in Algiers. If we're doing our best to be friends I ought to respect his wishes, even if he isn't aware that I know them.

The flicker of compassion joined that feeling already sitting heavy in her chest as she picked up the arrow and rolled it between gloved palms, trying to work through what he'd told her without letting it show in her face.

His father had never let him play as a child, only allowing lesson after lesson until his son believed nothing was more important than that. It was hardly any wonder Nathaniel had turned so cold, Hester mused…something she'd reflected on countless times over the past seven years, only now—for the first time ever—she did so without the resentment that usually accompanied it.

A sad life for a little boy became a sad life for a man. I suppose it's hard to break a habit when it's all you've ever known.

She risked a glance at him. Nathaniel was struggling with the bow once again, trying to find a comfortable grasp manageable with only four fingers, and she had to admire his determination. He wasn't giving up. Perhaps that meant she shouldn't either.

'Let me try.'

Taking the bow from him, she curled her hand around the grip, leaving only her index finger free. Without it to steady the weight she felt the bow begin to droop and splayed the other three wider, shifting until at last she found a steady hold.

'Here. Like this.'

Nathaniel studied her hand for a moment. Then, carefully accepting the bow back, he moved to copy Hester's example, concentrating hard.

'This?'

'Almost. Just…' Hester gestured vaguely. He hadn't got it quite right. The placement of his fingers didn't give enough support, the bow sagging downwards once again. 'Move that one down a little…and that one up…'

'Like that?'

He still hadn't managed to find the correct grip. Much longer and he'd be even more disheartened than he had been before—a prospect Hester found she disliked. Watching him struggle made her insides twist: he was doing his best, but she could see the despondency creeping over him as nothing he tried made any difference, the bow still languishing and the arrow refusing to fit.

Before she knew what she was doing, Hester had stepped closer and reached for his hand. 'More like this.'

Standing so near she could have rested her cheek against his chest—just as she had that day in the hut, she recalled now, her face immediately growing hot—she firmly took his fingers in hers. Nathaniel said nothing, but she could sense his surprise in the way he surrendered to her control, allowing her to move him this way and that, searching for the right place. Despite the damage his hand was still so much stronger than hers, covered in calluses instead of soft skin, and yet it remained passive until Hester was finally, breathlessly, satisfied with his grasp.

Unnecessary contact, Hester. Do friends go about caressing each other's fingers?

Gritting her teeth on her discomfort, Hester waved towards the target. 'Perhaps one last try?'

The look Nathaniel sent in her direction was unreadable and raised the short hairs on the back of her neck, but he lifted the bow and, with the air of one with nothing to lose, nocked the arrow, aimed and fired.

This time he succeeded.

The arrow flew through the air to hit just below the target, burrowing into the wooden frame with a dull thud. Turning back to Nathaniel, Hester saw him smile, years suddenly falling away from his weathered face to show the young man still within.

'Did you see that?'

'I did. Very impressive.'

He laughed, his one eye creasing endearingly. 'Hardly. But a start at least—thanks to you.'

'I'm sure you're very welcome.'

Hester waded through the snow to retrieve both arrows. Nathaniel's was easy enough, but her own was so deeply embedded she had to haul to pull it free. It took her a minute to gather them, and when she turned round again she found Nathaniel watching her closely.

'It doesn't bother you, then?'

Hester frowned. 'What doesn't?'

'This.' Nathaniel held up his maimed hand—the same one she had positioned so carefully. 'The scarring, I mean. And the...what's left.'

'Oh.' Surprised, she shook her head. The only reason she might dislike it was for the agony Nathaniel must have endured, but he wouldn't want her pity. 'No. Should it?'

Inspecting the mass of scars, Nathaniel shrugged,

although Hester could tell his indifference was forced. 'I imagine it might make some people squeamish. Not a pretty sight, after all.'

It was Hester's turn to pretend unconcern. Reaching to take the bow from him, she lifted one shoulder, careful not to let her thoughts show.

Is he asking what I think? As if he actually cares?

Once such a thing would have been unimaginable. In his arrogance, the younger Nathaniel would have assumed nothing about him could be lacking, and despite the strange events of the past few weeks Hester still had to pause a moment to consider. As had happened during the storm, an opportunity had arisen for her to puncture Nathaniel's pride—and yet Hester found the prospect nowhere near as appealing as she'd always thought she would.

He appeared to be waiting for her response, seeming truly interested, and perhaps...could it be?...the smallest bit apprehensive?

'I have a strong stomach. It takes more than that to frighten me.'

Nathaniel nodded slowly, as though genuinely contemplating her answer. 'Something else I've learned about you. First your skill and now your mettle. I wonder what's next.'

He gazed down at her, so much taller that Hester had to tip her head back a little beneath the brim of her bonnet just to look into his face, and she was about to reply when she caught the change in his expression.

She watched him trace a line from her eyes to her mouth and back again, her throat drying as something passed between them that made speech suddenly quite impossible. Exactly what it was she didn't know; only that without either of them saying a word something had happened, and that whatever Nathaniel was thinking as he fixed her with his stare was nothing she could guess.

She couldn't move, pinned in place as the quiet stretched out, broken only by the sound of birds calling and the rush of blood in her ears as the two of them stood quite still among the snow. Whatever lingered in the freezing air remained unspoken, but no less intense for its silence.

Hester buckled first. 'Shall we go inside? I think we've both spent more than enough time out in the cold of late.'

Nathaniel inclined his head. By speaking she had apparently shattered the tension, and he offered his arm quite casually, in an abrupt change from the intensity of mere seconds before.

'You're right. If lessons are over for the day I ought to get to work. May I escort you back to the house?'

Hester attempted a smile, although hidden beneath her ribs her heart was jumping. What had just happened? One minute she'd been innocently teaching Nathaniel and the next something new had crackled between them like tamed lightning, catching her entirely unawares. Had he meant to look at her so seriously, with that one green eye more powerful on its own than any two together? Probably not. Probably he had no idea she'd felt anything from his stare, and surely the memory of that one heated kiss was far from his thoughts even as it haunted Hester's.

'I need to put these away.' Mind whirling, she held up the bow and arrows still in her hand. 'You go on ahead. I wouldn't want to keep you if there's work you should be doing.'

'If you're sure?'

'Quite certain.'

'Very well. I'll see you at dinner.'

Nathaniel bowed and Hester nodded as normally as she could manage. He turned away and Hester went to replace her things where she'd found them—but it was quite some time before she felt ready to return to the house.

Chapter Seven

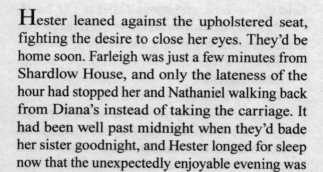

Hester leaned against the upholstered seat, fighting the desire to close her eyes. They'd be home soon. Farleigh was just a few minutes from Shardlow House, and only the lateness of the hour had stopped her and Nathaniel walking back from Diana's instead of taking the carriage. It had been well past midnight when they'd bade her sister goodnight, and Hester longed for sleep now that the unexpectedly enjoyable evening was at an end.

'Tired?'

With an effort she turned her head in Nathaniel's direction. 'Dropping. I can't recall the last time I stayed out so late.'

'Me neither. Actually, I can't recall the last time I was at a party at all.'

In the moonlight slanting through the carriage windows Hester caught Nathaniel's eye. 'And did you have a pleasant time?'

'I did. The welcome was certainly far warmer than I might have expected.'

'Diana's a good hostess. She'd never let a guest feel unwanted.'

'Even one she thought had left her sister to die?'

Hester shifted uncomfortably in her seat. A brief whisper in Diana's ear was all that had been required and then there'd been nothing but smiles, Lady Lavendon too sweet—or too calculating?—to bear a grudge.

She'll be pushing for a full and proper reconciliation now, Hester thought wryly. *If Nathaniel and I aren't holding hands in public within a twelvemonth she'll consider herself cheated indeed.*

She clenched her jaw on a yawn, feeling her face tighten with the struggle. Poor Diana. So determined to help everyone else find their own happy-ever-after, never stopping to think that perhaps friendship was all some could hope for.

And that's better than nothing. I'd take Nathaniel's friendship over his neglect any day of the week.

The carriage's wheels crunched through the remaining vestiges of snow as it climbed Shardlow's front drive, carrying Hester closer to her bed. She was almost there now, so near she could practically see it: soft pillows to cradle her head and a warm coverlet embracing her.

So set on reaching it was she that she barely felt the thrill in her fingers as Nathaniel handed her down the carriage steps. Only a short stagger up the main stairs and she'd be in her cosy rooms, the biting outside air chased away by a roaring fire and her bed beckoning to her with promises of untroubled sleep.

There was, however, a problem.

Standing in the doorway of her bedchamber, Hester uttered a groan of frustration. Instead of a leaping blaze to welcome her, only a pile of ash peered from the hearth, and the room was unpleasantly cold and dark. The new maid must have forgotten to bank up the fire and now it had smouldered down to nothing, Hester's heart sinking as she felt the chill hanging heavy in the air.

'Is something the matter?'

Turning, she saw Nathaniel on the landing, heading for the distant guest quarters she had relegated him to all those weeks before. 'My fire's gone out and the room's freezing. It's far too late to call for a servant...' Hester hugged herself, trying to muster up some warmth. 'I suppose I'm in for a very cold night.'

Nathaniel snorted. 'Is that all? I can easily help with that, if you'll allow me.'

'Can you? How?'

She watched his one uncovered eyebrow lift as if she'd asked an obvious question. 'By making you a fire.'

'Do you know how?' Hester's flagging spirits rose a fraction, tinged with no little surprise. Since when did Nathaniel get his hands dirty, or possess the knowledge of anything more useful than algebra? 'You can do that?'

Her amazement only increased with his nod. Nathaniel had hidden talents of his own, apparently, and far more practical in this instance than archery. Vaguely she wondered when he might have learned such a thing, but her attention was more on the disagreeable shiver that seized her as she walked further into the cold room. A closer inspection of the hearth showed no signs of life—something she was about to mention to Nathaniel when she noticed he still hovered just outside the door.

He looked slightly uncomfortable at her enquiring glance, hesitating on the threshold with his hat in one hand and a candle in the other. 'I have your permission to enter? I wouldn't want to intrude on your privacy.'

So tired that her mind was working at only about half its usual speed, it took Hester a moment to realise what he meant; but then her cheeks flared at once.

Of course.

Nathaniel hadn't set foot in her bedroom for years—not since that final time he'd visited her bed, a month after their wedding and only a few days before he'd cast her aside. The details were hazy now, but some fragments of that last night still remained: a vague impression of bare skin and heat that made Hester struggle suddenly to keep her heartbeat under control.

Watching him take his shirt off. Hardly daring to breathe as he came towards the bed...knowing exactly what would happen next and feeling that scandalous anticipation like a burning flood, wondering if he was as eager as I was to begin...

She checked herself hurriedly, thankful that Nathaniel couldn't read minds. 'Yes, of course. Come in.'

'Thank you.'

He cautiously stepped inside, so carefully Hester might have smiled had her skin not felt as though it might burst into flames. Maybe she didn't need a fire after all. Maybe Nathaniel could just ask to enter her bedroom every night and her ridiculous reaction would warm the entire house.

'Did you redecorate in here, too?'

Standing respectfully beside the cold fire, Nathaniel let his eye travel the shadowy room, scarcely lit by the candles each of them carried to light their way to bed. It seemed as though that sharp gaze missed nothing, despite the darkness, taking in the pretty papered walls, the thick rug and fine hangings...as well as her nightgown laid out on the bed. Something she could have sworn—with another rush of heat—his eye lingered on for longer than was strictly necessary.

She swallowed hard.

Calm yourself.

'No. My room is as it always was.'

Nathaniel nodded thoughtfully, murmuring so low that it seemed he spoke more to himself than to her, still exploring their surroundings. 'Is that right? I can hardly remember.'

Pretending not to have heard, Hester shifted her weight from foot to foot. Time was marching on and her bed still called to her—although Nathaniel's unexpected presence and her own traitorous wander down memory lane cut through her sleepiness like a knife.

'Did you make any changes to mine?'

'Your what?'

In place of a proper reply, Nathaniel gestured vaguely about the room.

Hester shook her head. 'Oh. No, I didn't.'

Nathaniel knelt down by the hearth, setting his hat and candle aside and carefully studying the grate. He seemed absorbed in examining the coals and there was a definite pause, as though he was choosing the right moment to continue.

'Would you consider allowing me to have those rooms back? The ones I have at the moment are comfortable, but not quite the same.'

Hester started, covering the instinctive movement with a cough. 'You'd like to move back into those rooms adjoining mine?'

'If you've no objection. You could keep the door between locked, naturally. That will always be under your control.'

With his back to her there was no danger of Nathaniel seeing her face, and for that at least Hester was grateful. The very last thing she needed was for him to witness the flustered opening and rapid closing of her mouth as she cast about for a reply, too tired to think quickly.

Nathaniel sleeping next door? With only a thin wall between them? The very thought made Hester burn like a torch, images of her husband preparing himself for bed flashing through her mind once again before she could stop them. Nathaniel getting undressed…unbuttoning his shirt and removing it from around that broad chest…unfastening his breeches, allowing them to slide to the floor…

Stop that at once!

It was bad enough to revisit events that had actually happened, without fantasy adding to the confusion, and Hester tried to snatch back her resolve before it was too late. Walking down that path led only to trouble; something she wished her disloyal body could understand, reacting with such *interest* she could hardly keep still.

Her voice was so high when she spoke that Hester feared she'd give herself away. 'Well, let's see how good a job you do of making up my fire. Perhaps if you succeed I might consider it.'

Nathaniel didn't turn around, still with his back to her as he sat before the fireplace, but she was sure she could hear a smile in his reply.

'A fair bargain. I accept. Now—prepare to be amazed.'

Reaching for the trug of kindling beside the mantel, Nathaniel busied himself piling and arranging in some complex pattern Hester couldn't quite follow. A paper spill touched to his bedtime candle and then transferred to the hearth was all it took for the first embers to glow, and Hester watched as flames began to spread out from the centre until the whole grate was blazing.

'There. You should be warm enough now.'

With a satisfied nod Nathaniel got to his feet, the fire now illuminating one side of his face— the unmarked side—and for a moment Hester couldn't look away. From that angle, and bathed in such flattering light, he could have been eighteen again, the illusion lasting only a split second but enough to stoke the butterflies in Hester's innards into a frenzy.

He was so handsome then. But is he more so now? Even with the scars—or perhaps because of them?

It wasn't a question she'd expected at close to two in the morning, and Hester blinked it away. She was tired, that was all, and mildly impressed by Nathaniel's newfound practicality. He'd have sent for a servant once upon a time, not particularly caring that whatever poor maid appeared had to be roused from her sleep, but now…

Another difference. Another way he's less selfish than before.

'Thank you. I'm sure I'll sleep much better.'

Hester found a tired smile. What she needed was sleep to help set her mind to rights. Come daybreak she'd be perfectly herself again and able to swerve any unhelpful notions of the changes to Nathaniel that made mere friendship so difficult, stray mumblings of appreciation for his looks and skills shoved back firmly where they belonged.

'You're very welcome. I'll take my leave of you now. Goodnight.'

Nathaniel bowed and strode from the room, Hester almost—but not quite—managing not to watch him go. Surely it didn't matter too much if she admired his purposeful walk, so long as she didn't allow it to go to her head? That same head in which dangerous fantasies waited to be given form, some of them enough to make her blush…

She rolled tired eyes at her own weakness.

Come along, now. Time for bed.

It would have been far easier to get undressed with a maid to help with the fastenings on her dress but eventually Hester laid it over the back of a chair, along with her underclothes, and reached for her nightgown, pulling it over her head with a sigh. Finally she could slip under the covers, lay her head on her pillows and seek some distance from Nathaniel in blissful sleep.

'Oh, no.'

For the second time that night Hester groaned.

Nathaniel's hat was still beside the fire, its tall black shape gleaming in the undulating light. If she didn't know better she might have thought it was taunting her, catching her attention just as she was getting into bed and now watching as she hesitated, one hand grasping her richly embroidered blankets.

She could just leave it there until the morning. Nathaniel wouldn't need a hat while he was sleeping—what difference would it make whether it spent the night in his rooms or hers?

No difference at all. By the time I'm tucked up I'll have forgotten all about it.

He was an early riser, though, Hester thought uneasily as she frowned at her unexpected guest. What if Nathaniel wanted to go walking before she was even awake, intending to slip out but unable to find his hat? He'd be irritated, and she'd be disturbed, and it might be a disagreeable incident for both of them.

She wondered briefly about returning it, before dismissing the thought out of hand. Wandering the halls of Shardlow in the middle of the night, trying to remember exactly which guest room she'd banished Nathaniel to… No. It could wait very well until the morning, and that was all there was to it.

Hester firmly pulled back the covers and slid beneath them, dragging them up to her chin as she settled against her pillows. They welcomed her with open arms, pulling her deeper and enveloping her comfortably from all sides.

This was not the time to be fretting about someone else's headwear, of all things—not while the prospect of sweet oblivion beckoned. The sheets were cold but would soon warm with the heat of her body, she was sure, and with a contented sigh she finally closed her eyes to sleep.

For all of about five seconds.

She sat up, throwing the covers off again. The wretched hat seemed to watch her come towards it, and perhaps it even smiled as she snatched it up and made for the door.

Sitting on the edge of his bed, Nathaniel flexed his right hand, grimacing at the dull ache in what was left of his index finger. The stump throbbed damnably sometimes, usually when he was tired, and with an irritable grunt he began to unbutton his shirt.

Doubtless he should have retired earlier, but the evening hadn't been anywhere near as tedious as he'd imagined a night of idle chatter would be, and Hester's sister a far more forgiving hostess than he knew he deserved. If only he could be as sure of how Hester herself felt about him, in some ways almost friendly, and yet still holding herself apart.

He reached the final button and let the shirt hang loose as he crossed wearily to the fire to stoke up the flames. In the mirror hanging above the mantel he studied his shadowy face, and was just about to reach up to remove his eye patch when a soft knock at the door made him pause.

'Is someone there?'

He waited for a moment. If there was somebody outside they were keeping very quiet… With a frown he moved to open the door—a frown that turned rapidly to surprise as he saw who hesitated on the landing.

'Hester?'

In the light of her single candle he watched her eyes dart first to his bare chest and then sharply up to his face, understandably flustered at his state of undress. It took less than a single heartbeat for him to realise she was none too formally attired either, wearing only a thin nightgown that hinted delicately at what lay beneath—and then the heartbeat in question stepped up a notch, accompanied by a distinctly *ungentlemanly* stirring lower down.

'You left your hat in my room.'

Hester held out the offending article—something Nathaniel hadn't even noticed she carried.

'I thought you might want it tomorrow morning and be annoyed when you couldn't find it. I know you're an early riser now.'

'Ah.' He took it from her, careful not to brush her hand. The sight of her in her nightgown was rousing enough; touching her in this state might be more than he could stand. 'I hadn't yet missed it. Thank you.'

She nodded, her eyes dropping from his to look away down the corridor. The flame of her candle wavered a little, and Nathaniel realised her hand was shaking. 'You're shivering. Are you cold?'

'I underestimated the walk from my quarters to yours and didn't think to throw on a shawl. It seems much further away at night.'

Nathaniel turned the hat over in his hands. Probably he should send her directly on her way, ignoring the pitiful quaking of her fingers and the goosebumps he could see rising on her wrists... But the unexpectedly strong temptation of Hester in a nightgown clouded his better judgement, and he heard himself speaking before he even knew what he was saying.

'Come in for a moment. Let me lend you a blanket for the long trek back.'

Hester glanced at him uncertainly. 'I couldn't. You'll be cold yourself.'

'I only use one. All the rest are spare.'

She hesitated, still lingering out on the chilly

landing, and he wondered if she might refuse. Part of him suddenly wished she would: what was he thinking, inviting Hester into his bedroom at this hour of the night? It was a dangerous move, and perhaps only her good sense would save them—but then she cautiously stepped inside, and the time for second-guessing himself was gone.

Nathaniel moved away quickly, busying himself with the tangle of blankets at the foot of his bed. He only realised Hester had crept further into the room, perhaps making for the fire, when she spoke directly from behind him and made him jump.

'You sleep on the floor? What—? Why?'

Turning, he followed her puzzled gaze to the pile of pillows and coverlet laid out between the bed and the fireplace. From the doorway she wouldn't have been able to see, but her vantage point beside the hearth gave a clear view now, and he bit back a sigh at the confusion and curiosity in her eyes.

Now is the time she finally chooses to ask a question? When I'm too tired to think up a convincing lie?

He shrugged, hoping it looked casual enough to dampen Hester's interest. 'A habit I picked up in Algiers. It's a difficult one to shake after five years.'

Her brow creased and Nathaniel held his

breath, dreading what might come next. Would she press further?

She was still examining the heap of bedding piled on the floor, no doubt wondering why it was preferable to a mattress—a question Nathaniel hardly knew the answer to himself. After so many months sleeping on straw-strewn ground a proper bed should have been wonderful, but the softness hurt his back and confused him when he woke, and the only respite he could find was in curling up beside the hearth.

Perhaps Hester might be kinder if he told her now than she would have been previously, but he'd rather pluck out his remaining eye than admit to such a strong-willed woman how low he had been brought. He needed to change the subject, and he had to do it fast.

'Have you given any thought to my request?'

Still with a faint frown, Hester turned her attention back to Nathaniel. 'To return to your old rooms?'

'That's the one.'

She folded her arms across her narrow chest. Defensive? he wondered. Or just cold? 'If you really want them, I suppose that would be acceptable.'

Nathaniel forced a smile. Hester didn't sound entirely sure, but he was grateful nonetheless. Perhaps in his old rooms he'd be better able to outrun the past; his own bed might be more com-

forting, the familiar paintings and furniture a
balm for his troubled soul.

*Although I'll be next door to Hester. That
might bring problems of its own.*

'Thank you.' He attempted to make the curve
of his lips more natural, trying to stretch the
creases beside his uncovered eye. 'I'll endeav-
our not to disturb you too much.'

At random, he plucked one of the blankets
from his unused mattress and shook it out. 'Here.
Take this and you can finally get to bed.'

He held it out to her, relief washing over him
as she swung it around herself and that tantalis-
ing glimpse of her figure disappeared from his
sight. She'd be horrified if she knew the direction of his thoughts, Nathaniel mused grimly. It
was about time he collected himself and remembered it was friendship Hester had agreed to—
and nothing else. Any minute now she'd walk
back through the door and go off to her separate
bed, leaving him alone in his rooms with no one
to blame but himself for allowing such a woman
to slip through his fingers.

'I'll bid you goodnight, then.'

Clutching the blanket to her chest, Hester gave
him a sleepy half-smile that hit him square beneath the ribs. Surely she had no idea how lovely
she looked, with her curls falling like spun gold
about her shoulders and her face free of the suspicion she'd worn only a few weeks ago, when

she'd been so much more guarded in his presence and a moment like this would have been impossible. Now there was barely any uncertainty as she turned to leave, stumbling slightly on the trailing tail of the blanket that dragged along the floor.

'Let me help. The last thing we need is you taking a fall at this hour.'

Nathaniel stepped forward. Unwinding Hester from her wrappings, he averted his eye as once again that enticing nightgown flitted into view, quickly making sure to pull the blanket around her so not even so much as an inch of lace cuff showed. Fastidious as any lady's maid, he arranged the hem about her neck, tucking it in so no cold night air could wend its way underneath—and only realised when it was far too late that it brought them face to face, with nowhere to hide from the sudden knife-edge Nathaniel knew they were balanced upon.

Perhaps it was the heady warmth of the room and the vague invitation in Hester's eyes that made him lose his head. Looking down at her all thoughts of restraint and cool logic melted away, only awareness of her quiet breaths and how prettily her hair shone in the firelight left to circle his blank mind.

Gently, as slowly as if she were a wild fawn he didn't want to scare away, he reached to trace the glowing line of her jaw. The skin there was so soft… The only thing that could ever be softer was Hester's gasp as his fingertips strayed beneath her chin, carefully tilted her head up—and guided her into his kiss.

She reacted at once, allowing the blanket to fall away and curving against him like a reed in a storm, fitting her slight body against his and flooding Nathaniel's every nerve with the desire to pull her closer still. Fragile yet stronger than he could have guessed he felt her arms come around him and her hands explore the tight muscles of his back, roaming over him until he shuddered with the longing for them to search further. His own hand dropped from Hester's face to the swell of her hips, feeling the smooth curve beneath thin linen enough to make him groan.

When had her lips grown so skilled? They danced with his, moving in a heated rhythm that stole every breath and left him struggling to stand. Perhaps it was animal instinct; Nathaniel certainly felt something feral mutter to him as his palms slid upwards across Hester's ribs, counting each slim ridge until they reached her collar and lingered on the ribbons at her neck.

'Can I?' He could hardly speak, breaking their kiss only for the barest moment to murmur into Hester's ear.

Apparently she struggled likewise, as with eyes shut a fevered nod was her only answer, turning at once to a shiver as he nipped at her lobe.

His fingers shook as they drew the ribbons

free, untying the neat bows to leave Hester's throat exposed. With the sound of blood thumping in his ears Nathaniel dropped his head to her neck, ducking beneath her jaw to tease the spot where he could feel her pulse leaping with hopeless speed. One hand cradling her lower back, the other parted her nightgown further, revealing the delicate sharpness of her collarbone and the entrancing hollow at the base of her throat that cried out for his tongue to explore.

It was close to the sensation of drunkenness: every inch of Hester's body was intoxicating, the warm scent of her and the velvet feel of her skin overwhelming, driving out all other thought. Any notion of their entanglement being a bad idea disappeared as Hester tipped her head back to invite him closer, baring her throat for his lips and wilting in his hold as if only his arms could sustain her.

The only danger Nathaniel could see was her falling to the ground completely and, barely noticing in which direction they moved, he backed them nearer to the wall. Trapped between his body and solid stone, Hester raised her arms to twine about his neck, seeking his mouth with hers and once again stealing his every breath with the urgent movement of her lips.

With his eye closed, it was Nathaniel's other senses that took control. His fingers felt every thread of Hester's flimsy nightgown and ears heard each ragged sigh, his nose filled with the scent of her hair and the fresh aroma of rosewater soap…as well as something else…

'Hester, you're burning.'

He looked down into her face, a pulse of helpless want jolting through him as he took in her flushed cheeks and her eyes dazed and heavy.

'I know…'

'No, not like that. I think—I think it's your nightgown.'

The dreaminess in Hester's unsteady blue gaze vanished instantly. 'What? Oh, hellfire!'

She leaped away from him, hurriedly slapping at the smouldering hem of her nightdress. The flames hadn't taken hold properly, but they'd left an ugly scorch mark nonetheless.

Hester held the ruined material away from her in dismay. 'What happened?'

'In the heat of the moment we must have strayed too close to the fire.'

Nathaniel rubbed the back of his neck, suddenly unsure what else to say. All the good sense that had abandoned him only minutes before was beginning to trickle back. *Had* it only been minutes? He could have sworn he'd been kissing Hester for hours, and now the heat pulsing below his skin felt more like shame than passion.

Why on earth did you do that? What were you thinking?

Hester still fussed with the hem of her nightgown, the only glimpse of her face visible beneath her curtain of curls glowing a bright scarlet. She looked every bit as mortified as Nathaniel felt, and just as confused, too, when she finally peered up at him again.

'I thought you wanted us to be friends.'

'I did. I do.'

Cheeks still flaring, Hester clutched her nightgown at the neck. The ribbons hung loose where he had untied them and Nathaniel averted his eye at once, determined not to let his gaze linger where his lips had mere moments previously.

'And yet...?'

'I know. I'm sorry.' Nathaniel gritted his teeth, fighting the urge to bury his head in his hands. Him and his stupid, cursed lack of control. Would he never learn? 'I must have had too much to drink with Lord Lavendon. He's a very attentive host.'

Hester shot him a sideways glance that did nothing to settle his racing mind. 'Is that right? Perhaps you took too much port with him after dinner?'

'That must have been it. Strong stuff, as I recall.'

She nodded, but only slightly, her attention shifting from him to fix on the floor. There was something in her downturned face he couldn't quite make out, although staring at her was the last thing he ought to be doing as regret circled inside him like a bird of prey.

You idiot.

As if she'd return any kind of feeling warmer than friendship when in her estimation he still had so much ground to make up, he thought wretchedly. His previous treatment of her had been so poor, as he was only just starting to discover; no wonder she looked troubled, the fancy Hester had once held for him ruined by his neglect and now his advances doubtless unwanted…

As well as bold.

What business had he in putting his lips on a woman far too good for their soiled touch, his kiss polluted by the secret shame of what he'd endured? He had to make amends.

'Truly, Hester, I apologise. I shouldn't have imposed upon you. Again.'

A split-second memory of their snowstorm shelter flitted through his mind but he shooed it away, steeling himself against the recollection of Hester nestling in his arms.

'I have no excuse but to plead the combination of drink and my own weakness. I am entirely to blame.'

This time Hester didn't even nod. She'd clearly heard him though, judging by the barely noticeable tic of her mouth as though she was about to say something—a twitch Nathaniel caught despite its subtlety, so aware was he of every move she made. He watched as she retrieved the blanket lying forgotten at her feet and drew it around herself, putting a barrier between them that suddenly seemed impenetrable.

'Apology accepted.'

At last Hester spared him a swift cut of her sapphire eyes. He hadn't been wrong. There truly was something there he couldn't name—a shadow only she understood.

'I'll be going to bed now. Probably best that I leave before anything else is damaged.'

Nathaniel inclined his head in a polite approximation of a bow, despite the chaos of thoughts running through it.

Before anything else was damaged?

Was she referring simply to her nightgown, or to the emerging accord between them that he had just thrown into disarray?

'Of course. Goodnight. And thank you for returning my hat.'

She shuffled away from him, her slight figure made bulky by the blanket as she stepped out onto the landing and pulled the door closed behind her. The handle made a loud, definitive click, and only once he was sure he was alone did Nathaniel allow a growl of pure frustration to escape.

Chapter Eight

Hester flipped over the printed card, running her fingers across an expensively embossed crest. Too absorbed by the invitation, she almost walked headlong into Nathaniel coming the opposite way through the hall, his own attention likewise captured by what had arrived for him on the post tray that morning.

'Oh!' She pulled up short, catching a similar startled look from Nathaniel at her unexpected presence. 'Sorry. I wasn't paying attention.'

'Neither was I. Distracted by this.' Nathaniel held up the paper in his hand, a single sheet covered in small, neat writing. 'I should have watched where I was going.'

'No, no. It was quite my fault.'

'Not at all. I ought to be more careful.'

Hester mustered a smile, although fresh discomfort twisted low in her belly. Ever since that scene beside Nathaniel's fire things had been strained, different, the two of them now painfully polite as though to make up for what had transpired. They might almost be strangers again—albeit strangers who had passionately explored each other's lips, the mere thought of it making heat flare beneath the bodice of Hester's gown.

There was a horrible pause during which neither looked directly at the other. It only lasted a moment, but Hester felt every second stretch out unbearably, until both cracked at the same time.

'Your letter—?'

'Who is your—?'

Nathaniel smiled—a stiff, forced thing that matched Hester's own grimace. 'Sorry. I was just going to ask who your letter was from.'

'Not a letter but an invitation.' Hester studied the card once again, relieved to have somewhere to look other than at her husband. 'From Diana. She invited me weeks ago to a ball next Saturday, to celebrate her first wedding anniversary, and has just sent an amendment to include you too.'

'A ball? Well, I look forward to it.'

'You'll come?'

Hester glanced up in surprise. Nathaniel had spent every day since their encounter locked away with his books and ledgers—and every night, too. The light of his candle crept beneath the door separating her rooms from his now he had taken back his own quarters, and it flickered until the early hours, Hester barely able to sleep knowing Nathaniel sat scribbling at his desk mere metres away.

'I assumed you'd be working. Can you spare the time?'

She saw something flit over Nathaniel's face, quick as a blink. 'Would you rather go alone? I wouldn't want to intrude.'

'By no means. I only meant you don't have to come if there are other demands on your schedule.'

'I thought perhaps it might please you for me to attend.'

Caught off guard, Hester hesitated. *Would* it please her? *Yes*, was the undeniable, instinctive answer. The thought of an evening with Nathaniel was more appealing than she'd ever admit, even if the confusion between them meant she had no idea what to expect from such a thing. At the very least there would be dancing: another chance to revel in the strength of Nathaniel's arms and feel his body close to hers, the mere idea of it more exciting than any ladylike sensibilities should allow.

'It would.'

Nathaniel nodded, although more to the wall behind Hester's head than at her directly. 'Then nothing would give me greater pleasure.'

Hester swallowed, her throat suddenly and mysteriously dry. Probably he was just trying to make amends for what had happened four nights before, when the effects of Lavendon's potent port had made him forget—for that brief, wonderful moment—it was only friendship he desired. If her flaming nightgown hadn't decided to cut their entanglement short, who knew what might have happened next?

Hester certainly didn't, and now the prospect of attending the ball with Nathaniel only added to the whirl of bewilderment that was her constant companion whenever he was near.

Another excruciating pause threatened to settle, but this time Hester acted swiftly. 'And who is your letter from?'

'Ah.' Nathaniel held up the paper again, skimming the fluid writing with his one eye. 'My mother. Asking whether we'd join her for luncheon today.'

A perfect opportunity to change the subject. 'Of course. I haven't yet paid my weekly visit.'

'I'll let her know to expect us, then. The last thing I want is to catch her unawares like the first time, even if I've tried to make up for it since.'

A slightly more real curve lifted Nathaniel's mouth, triggering a corresponding skip of Hester's pulse. He was so handsome when he smiled. It sharpened the line of his jaw and rolled back some of the years his absence had imprinted on his face, the difference so stark it always made Hester want to stare.

She was in danger of doing just that right now.

With a small start she dragged her eyes away. 'Shall we ride over? The snow is almost gone and I haven't ridden in a while.'

'Good idea. I have a meeting with Mr Morrow this morning, but I'll have the horses readied for afterwards.'

A question teetered on the tip of Hester's tongue, but she stopped herself just in time from asking how the estate manager had settled at Shardlow. He certainly seemed popular, despite his somewhat alarming appearance, but Hester couldn't help but feel he avoided her as much as possible. Perhaps he wanted to be sure none of Nathaniel's secrets escaped…secrets Hester could only guess at.

Unseen as she carefully folded the card in half, Hester frowned. Apparently it was yet to dawn on Nathaniel that sometimes telling the truth helped unburden the soul. If she hadn't snapped that day in the storm, and let the hidden past spill from her mouth, she might still believe him to be as cruel and thoughtless as ever, rather than learning that his father bore most of the blame. Any friendship between them would have died before it had even begun to live—but that was Nathaniel's choice. If he didn't want to share she wouldn't make him. The peace they were building was too fragile to bear much pressure.

Blessedly unaware of what his wife was thinking, Nathaniel gave a quick bow. 'Shall we say we'll meet outside at half-past eleven? I'm looking forward to the exercise.'

The quickest flash of how good Nathaniel looked in the saddle darted before Hester's eyes, and she turned away before he noticed the vague discomfort in her face. Appreciating a man's form was one thing. Doing it in front of him was quite another, and not something that ought to be encouraged.

'As am I. I hope we'll have a pleasant afternoon.'

A 'pleasant afternoon' was not *quite* what Hester was having as Nathaniel helped her into the saddle of her gentle black mare—she didn't know what word would accurately describe the feelings that coursed through her: a combination of awkwardness and scandalised delight as he stood so close. With both of his hands locked around her waist she barely knew where to look as Nathaniel prepared to lift her, throwing her up as effortlessly as though she was a sack of feathers.

'Are you settled?'

Reaching up he kept one hand on her lower back to steady her, the sensation of it all Hester could focus on, and she had to admit to taking a little longer than strictly necessary to modestly arrange her skirts.

Finally she nodded. 'I'm ready now.'

Nathaniel withdrew—leaving a somewhat

cold, bereft patch where his hand had been—and swung himself onto his own horse, gathering the reins in one smooth motion. He turned the grey gelding's head and together they trotted down the drive, hearing the gravel crunch beneath two sets of hooves as they made for the gate and Thame Magna beyond.

From her position slightly behind Nathaniel's horse, Hester was at perfect liberty to admire the cut of his figure. Seated upright, with impressive shoulders squared, his bearing was enviable, and Hester noticed more than one lady cast an appraising eye over him as they rode down the main street.

'It's sunny today. But for the chill it might almost be spring.'

Nathaniel reined his horse back to come level with Hester's mare. 'Discussing the weather, Hester? It's a sad state of events when that's the best you can come up with.'

Slightly nettled, she was about to reply when she caught the gleam of humour in that one wicked green eye. In the wintry sunshine it glowed emerald, the fair hair visible below the brim of his hat shining likewise.

'What would you suggest as an alternative?'

'Anything. Anything is preferable to conversing about the *weather*.'

Possibly it was being out in the crisp air that made the difference. Now the shadow of Shardlow had receded her feeling of strain had shrunk too, perhaps being trapped within four walls allowing no space to escape her own thoughts. A little of the weight of confusion seemed to have lifted from Hester's chest, at the very least, and she felt the corners of her mouth rise.

'I see. Well… How about…?' She cast about for a suitable topic, but anything of interest evaded her until with a triumphant nod she came up victorious. 'How are you finding being back in your old rooms?'

'I like it very well indeed, thank you,' Nathaniel answered, briefly touching his hat at some passing acquaintance. 'Far more comfortable than the ones I was consigned to when I first arrived. About as far from your own as it was possible to get, weren't they?'

It wasn't a complaint, his tone still joking, and Hester raised one brow. 'And whose fault was that?' she asked dryly. 'Bursting in unannounced and expecting all to be exactly as it was before? Frankly, you're lucky I didn't make you sleep in the cellar.'

Nathaniel groaned. 'Please don't remind me. When I think how that must have been for you… No wonder you weren't dancing for joy. I can still remember the look on your face—and, let me tell you, it was not one of delight.'

With a flicker of surprise Hester redoubled her grip on the reins, hoping Nathaniel wouldn't see.

It never would have occurred to her that he'd notice her reaction to his return, let alone be able to recall it so long afterwards.

'I'm not sure either of us behaved at our best that day.'

'You needn't reproach yourself. I'm sure there's nothing you said or did that I didn't deserve, considering how poorly you believed I'd treated you before I left.'

They rode on for a moment in silence. What Nathaniel was thinking Hester couldn't say, but her own thoughts moved so swiftly through her mind that it made her dizzy. Did he want to talk about what she'd told him out in the storm? They hadn't touched on it since, but was there more to say—more they might have spoken of at the time, had that heart-stopping kiss not thrown all into disarray?

'Don't dwell on that. There was misunderstanding on both sides.'

'Even so…' Nathaniel leaned down to pat his horse's glossy neck, his face conveniently hidden for a second by the brim of his hat. 'There was more to it than one single instance. Leaving in the way that I did was unforgivable, but we can't pretend I didn't let you down long before that.'

The carousel of Hester's thoughts whirled faster as she watched her husband straighten up again, any glint of humour in his countenance fading fast. He glanced across, meeting her eyes only briefly, but enough to stoke the embers in her stomach.

'Surely it's for me to choose what I find forgivable?'

'That's true,' Nathaniel agreed, his attention fixed firmly now on the road ahead. 'It's up to you whether you want to extend to me your grace…but it's for me to decide if I can ever forgive *myself*.'

Looking down at her gloved hands, Hester hardly knew what to say. Probably the safest option was nothing; with her mind spinning uncontrollably, something might spill out that she didn't intend. And then what would happen?

I might tell Nathaniel even more secrets, she cautioned herself, watching her mare's ears flick at the whinny of a passing horse. *I might reveal how I feel at this moment, wondering that he has finally realised how poor a husband he was—or, worse, how it moves me to know he regrets it.*

Which would not be welcome.

If Nathaniel was coming to repent of his coldness, it meant only that—a small measure of shame, not the desire for anything more from her, and certainly not her sentiment. He might be kinder, but the Honeywell Trading Company still had him by the throat, leaving no room for anything else and she would be foolish indeed to think otherwise. A lifetime of ambition was unlikely ever to be replaced just because he had found some compassion. It made him more pleasant to live with, that was all; something she ought to be grateful for, instead of wasting time wondering if…

Out of the corner of her eye she saw Nathaniel suddenly sit a little higher in the saddle.

'I think… Is that my father's carriage?'

Hester's head snapped up. 'Where?'

She followed Nathaniel's pointing finger. To her swift dismay it seemed he was right. Mr Honeywell's grand carriage moved in the distance, instantly recognisable by the smart pair of chestnut mares.

'It certainly looks like it. Do you want to catch him up?'

'Would you be able to ride that fast?'

Despite the growing knot in her stomach, Hester couldn't help a small smile. She was in no rush to meet Mr Honeywell again now she knew of his malign influence, and yet the earnest—if misguided—concern on the face of his son was sweet indeed.

Without a word of warning Hester shook her horse's reins, urging the mare onwards so abruptly she had to call over her shoulder to Nathaniel as she left him behind.

'Why don't you decide? *If* you can catch me!'

Nathaniel and Hester were flushed and laughing as they entered Grafton Lodge's drive just behind the carriage, neck and neck, with barely a whisker to tell the winner.

Leaning back in the saddle, Nathaniel pulled his horse to a stop, looking across to see Hester's eyes shining. 'I believe the victory is mine.'

'Absolutely not! Anyone could see I was miles ahead!'

'I'd hesitate to call a lady a cheat, but...'

The faux outraged wrinkling of Hester's nose probably wasn't fit for a lady either, but it made Nathaniel's grin widen. With some of her hair threatening to fall loose and her colour high she wasn't quite her usual proper self, different but still just as alluring as he slid from his horse and held out a hand to help her do the same.

Standing together on the gravel, they waited for the carriage door to open, a hint of uncertainty that hadn't been there before beginning to circle in Nathaniel's gut.

I haven't seen Father in above five years, and the last time I did he lied to my face. What will our first meeting be like now I know the truth?

Glancing down, he caught Hester biting her lip, the same unease he felt written clearly across her face, and a jolt of understanding crackled through him. How horrible it would be for her to see the man who had placed so little value on her life. He should have thought more quickly, Nathaniel admonished himself harshly, realising far too late that she was left with nowhere to hide—but then he watched as her head came up and her shoulders straightened, and the composure nobody but he knew she was forcing took his breath away.

He leaned down to mutter into her ear...a pink, pretty ear that reminded him of a delicate shell. 'Hester. If you'd rather not—'

'I would absolutely rather not.' She kept her eyes unwaveringly on the carriage, standing quite still as the door handle turned. 'But that doesn't mean I won't. I'll need to see your father sooner or later, and I'd prefer to jump before I'm pushed.'

There was no time for him to reply. The carriage door swung open and a passenger stepped out: Mr Honeywell, looking every bit as austere and unsmiling as Nathaniel remembered. He leaned on a cane now, a difference from five years ago, but the expression was the same and so was the measured voice that addressed Nathaniel by name.

'Nathaniel.'

Mr Honeywell didn't come any closer, or show any sign of surprise to see his long-lost heir standing large as life in front of him. Instead he inspected his son coolly, starting at the top of his hat and working downwards, lingering briefly on the patch and weather-beaten face before giving one curt, apparently satisfied nod at what he found.

'I see your mother spoke true. She told me you'd returned when I arrived home this morning.'

Nathaniel nodded back, the vague discomfort in his belly growing worse. A servant approached to take his horse's reins and he handed them over, glad for a chance to look away as he ordered his thoughts. Shouldn't a father show a little more reaction when meeting a son back from the dead? To hear Mr Honeywell speak they might as well be indifferent acquaintances, the lack of emotion that had once seemed so normal now feeling anything but.

'Yes. She invited us for luncheon, but I don't know whether that was before or after she knew you were back.'

'After, probably. Some damn fool notion of a reunion, in all likelihood.'

Beside him, he felt Hester stir. Mr Honeywell hadn't so much as looked at her. Perhaps he thought her below his notice? A spark of irritation kindled behind Nathaniel's breastbone at the thought, joining unhappily with the other sensations already holding court there.

He gestured towards her, hoping his voice would remain steady. 'You'll have seen Hester regularly, of course, on her weekly visits with Mother. No need for a touching reunion there.'

Mr Honeywell finally spared her a glance. 'Hester.'

'Good afternoon, sir.'

Her curtsey was far more elegant than his father's brusqueness deserved—but then, Nathaniel thought, elegance came as naturally to his wife as breathing. A snatched glimpse down at her showed the first signs of strain, however, and he held out his arm.

'Shall we go in? It's too cold to be standing about, and I imagine my mother will be anxious to see us.'

Hester took hold of him at once, small fingers resting lightly on his forearm but still somehow managing to affect his insides, and Nathaniel had to take a moment to wonder at how far they'd come. Not so very long ago she'd shied away at the offer of his hand, and yet now there was no hesitation in her touch, or in the way she drew closer to him, perhaps for reassurance as his father frowned.

'Yes. Come inside. My bones mislike this cold air.'

All three made for the grand ivy-strewn house, Mr Honeywell leading the way in spite of the cane. His father walked with a pronounced limp now, Nathaniel saw, with interest as well as a fleeting glimmer of sympathy—something he was quite sure would never have occurred to him before Jacob's actions in Algiers had set him on a different and infinitely kinder course. Now he might almost have found some patience for his irascible papa, had the man not ridden roughshod over Hester's heart and done more damage than Nathaniel feared he could mend.

'It's as well you've returned,' Mr Honeywell huffed. 'It was a blow when the *Celeste* went down and to believe I'd lost my heir—and a damned nuisance to think how to replace you. The business is growing more quickly than ever, and another steady pair of hands is just what's required.'

Unseen by either of his companions as he followed them up the front steps, Nathaniel tightened his jaw. That was the extent of his father's happiness to see him home. No mention of having missed him, or feeling any pleasure to know he was safe: only the potential for profit, as if he was more machine than man, and the avoidance of tedious paperwork.

'I know. I've been studying the past few years' books while you were away and noticed the upward trend. It seems I'm to congratulate you on your success.'

The front door opened and the little procession stepped inside. Servants materialised to help with hats and coats, and some of the darkness in Nathaniel's thoughts was chased away by the brilliance of his mother's smile as she emerged into the hall.

'Nathaniel! Hester! I'm so glad you came.'

She hurried towards them, pressing a fond kiss

first to Hester's cold cheek and then reaching up on tiptoe to reach Nathaniel's. He stooped to embrace her, catching the surprised disapproval on his father's face to see such newfound sentiment—and in his own house, no less. In the old days Nathaniel wouldn't have dreamed of such a thing, and some relic of that time sat uncomfortably within him as the four seated themselves in the best parlour.

'Aren't we a merry set? The whole family together again!' Mrs Honeywell beamed around the room, although her gaze didn't linger on her husband for long. He had produced a notebook from his pocket as soon as he'd sat down and now ignored his wife completely as he looked through it with a stern frown.

Hester could always be relied on to find a tactful reply. She leaned towards her mother-in-law, seated beside her on an overstuffed sofa, and squeezed her hand. 'It's a day I'm sure none of us ever imagined. How good it is to see you smile again after so long.'

His mother patted Hester's arm. 'Dear Hester. Always so kind.' She took a teacup from the tray proffered by a smartly uniformed maid, thanking her pleasantly before turning back. 'We were lucky indeed to find such a wife for our Nathaniel—were we not, Mr Honeywell?'

Nathaniel's stomach dropped even more at his

father's indifference, not even deigning to glance up from his little book of figures.

'There was no luck involved. One of Townsend's daughters was the best match from a business standpoint, and as the other was too young to wed, Hester was the most logical option.'

A hot dart of anger lanced between Nathaniel's ribs and instinctively he looked across at Hester, cursing his father's unkindness. She was carefully studying a painting on the opposite wall, her face determinedly blank, but there was a tinge of colour in her cheeks that made him want to shake his father by the lapels.

Had he always been so objectionable? Nathaniel already knew the answer, but for some reason that bluntness rankled in a way it hadn't before Algiers had altered more than just Nathaniel's face. There was no excuse to embarrass Hester, and he felt that quick flash of temper burn brighter as he saw her blink rapidly, as though fighting to remain calm.

A snide little voice lifted its head to mutter into his ear. *He's only saying out loud what you used to think privately*, it murmured quietly, not needing volume to make its point. *You can't deny that once upon a time you viewed Hester in exactly the same way: as a business proposition, and an inconvenient one at that.*

Nathaniel clenched his teeth so tightly it hurt. As much as he'd have liked to reject the charges his subconscious brought, he knew that they were fair. Once he'd thought of Hester just as his father did now, and shame tore through him like wildfire.

He cleared his throat, trying to hide the churn of anger and regret that gripped his chest like a vice. 'I'm thankful Diana *was* too young. Hester could have had her choice of men, I've no doubt, but I know I would never have found a better wife.'

The maid handed him a cup and he took a sip of tea far too hot to enjoy. It burned his tongue, but saved him from having to meet anybody's eyes—not his mother's surprised but delighted grey, nor his father's sharply disapproving green, and certainly not Hester's sapphire, behind which he had no idea what she could be thinking. All he knew for sure was the way his heart had stepped up a notch, and he wondered now at the wisdom of allowing such a dangerous truth to escape.

There was no choice but to power on through what might be an awkward silence, and with another more cautious sip he affected a shrug. 'Anyway, Diana has subsequently made an excellent match of her own. Hester and I are attending a ball to celebrate her first year wed to Lord Lavendon.'

'Oh, how wonderful.' Thankfully Mrs Honeywell took her cue from his unease. 'She was good enough to invite us to the wedding, you know, although as your father was too busy to accompany me I went alone. A year already! How does she settle to married life, Hester?'

'Very well indeed. You'd think she'd been born into her title if you were to see her about Farleigh, and her husband is besotted.'

'I can well imagine. She was a beautiful bride—and her dress! Such exquisite beading at the hem!'

'Did you notice the lace? Lavendon had it imported from Italy just for her.'

With the conversation turning to gowns Nathaniel breathed a sigh of relief, wishing he hadn't when his mother slid him one quick glance. There was something in it he didn't *quite* like: something a bit too knowing, as though for the first time in his life the two of them shared a secret, and Nathaniel rose not entirely casually to cross to the parlour window.

He stood looking out, glad to turn his back to the scene behind. The gentle hum of female voices continued as both silks and satins were considered, although the words washed over Nathaniel like a wave as he allowed his mind to cover past ground.

I ought to be more careful.

Many more mistakes like that and the whole world would know how he felt about his wife, putting Hester in the excruciating position of having to reject him straight out. Their fledgling friendship would lie in tatters—and for what? His mother already wondered. He could tell from that single searching look. And his father would soon harbour suspicions of his own at the change anyone could see in his son.

If he concentrated, Nathaniel could just make out their reflections in the window's glass, and for a moment he watched the tableau behind him without the players' knowing. The pale form of his father was still engrossed in his lists of profit and loss, while Mrs Honeywell and Hester sat close together, the intimacy between them raising an unexpected lump in Nathaniel's throat.

It's as though Father doesn't even see them. No wonder Mother looked to Hester for comfort while I was away, and no wonder Hester was so quick to give it.

He passed a hand across tired eyes. Sooner or later he'd challenge Mr Honeywell on his unforgivable lies, but not today. Hester had already been humiliated once this visit, and with another surge of ire Nathaniel swore she wouldn't be again.

To think I ever followed his example of how to be a man—and still might, had Jacob not shown me it's possible to be strong while also kind.

'And will you be having a new gown? For the ball?'

His mother's earnest voice cut through the disquiet that held Nathaniel in its grip. Her ghostly reflection was animated, and even Hester's seemed happier as she shook her transparent head.

'I have so many pretty ones already. I'm ashamed to admit there's probably a couple I've never worn more than once.'

'A woman's prerogative, my dear. I'm sure everybody, including Nathaniel, will think you look well in whatever you decide. Don't you agree, Mr Honeywell?'

Bless Mother for trying, Nathaniel thought wryly as his father looked up, clearly irritated by the interruption. He hadn't been taking the least bit of notice, and kept his notebook open as if intending to return to it at any moment.

'Don't I agree with what?'

'That Nathaniel will appreciate Hester in whatever gown she chooses on Saturday.'

Mr Honeywell grunted. 'A pointless question, considering he won't be here to see her. I'm riding down to London on Friday to visit the warehouses and Nathaniel is coming with me.'

Nathaniel turned at once. 'What was that, sir? This is the first I've heard of any such trip.'

'You've been away for five years and you need breaking back in.' His father flipped another page, either oblivious to Nathaniel's tone or—more likely—entirely unmoved by it. 'Business doesn't sleep. Perhaps you need reminding.'

As if a lit match had been dropped into a pile

of leaves, the embers of Nathaniel's anger began to smoulder anew. He didn't look at Hester, instead directing the full force of his uneven gaze to his father's impassive face.

'I'm afraid I cannot consent. I have a prior engagement.'

'You have an invitation to a ball. A waste of time when there's so much else of importance to occupy you.'

'But this occasion is important to Hester. Does that deserve no consideration?'

Mild surprise swam through Mr Honeywell's expression, rapidly consumed by displeasure. He looked as though he was about to speak when Hester broke in, calmly enough, but with the pink tinge of her cheeks burning brighter.

'I understand, Nathaniel. Of course your work must come before something as trivial as a ball.'

Nathaniel lowered his voice a little, although there was no hope of not being overheard. 'I told you I'd attend.'

'I know you did. But I also know you have other responsibilities.'

He frowned, his aggravation gaining ground as conflict began to stir inside him. The business *was* important, and despite his anger at his father he couldn't deny it. It took vigilance and concentration to build success, his work ethic an inheritance passed down through his family to rest on Nathaniel's shoulders, and in truth some part of him hesitated at the idea of neglecting his duty. There was always something to be done, and relaxing for so much as a moment could be enough to allow competitors an edge.

But Hester. Surely I can't disappoint her again when I've done so countless times already?

Mr Honeywell's example of how to be a good husband was non-existent, with his abandoning Nathaniel's mother for untold lengths of time and all but ignoring her on the rare instances he was in her presence. Wouldn't Nathaniel be almost as bad if he broke his word to Hester, proving his unfeeling father's influence still held him in its grip? It had been a slow awakening, but now the scales were falling from Nathaniel's eyes surely there was no excuse to continue to behave with such blind ignorance as before.

However, it seemed the decision had been made for him.

With a proud lift of her chin—clearly more for Mr Honeywell's benefit than for his—Hester slipped him a small smile. 'Really, Nathaniel. Do what you must. You're under no obligation to me.'

'Hester—' he began, not really knowing how to finish.

It was probably just as well that his father interrupted, his cold nod at Hester as close to approval as he'd ever show. 'You see. She appreciates the proper order of things. We'll leave on Friday as planned.'

Nathaniel felt the muscles in his neck flex with strain but said nothing to argue back. What was there to say, after all? He wouldn't get into some war of words like a petulant child—and besides, that niggle of uncertainty, still a kernel but threatening to grow, muttered to him that the Honeywell Trading Company had always come first. Money wouldn't make itself—something Hester clearly understood—and if she gave him leave to break their arrangement then he should take her at her word.

But as he turned back to the window, Nathaniel couldn't quite find the will to be pleased.

Chapter Nine

Hester hadn't counted the hours until Nathaniel's departure the following Friday, but she couldn't deny that when she woke the morning after he'd left it was with a heavier heart than she'd like. He'd be gone for a week, and the prospect of Shardlow without him seemed strange, somehow—ironically enough, considering how many times since his return she'd wished for exactly that.

With a languid stretch of sleepy muscles Hester sat up in bed and surveyed her empty bedroom, attempting to ignore the niggle that gnawed immediately beneath her ribs. If Nathaniel had to miss this evening's gathering, so be it. The only alternative would have been to beg him to stay, and she'd rather bear a night of disappointment than risk her pride. Whatever his newfound humanity, the business still came first—as she was well aware—and she wasn't such a fool as to hope anything different.

Leaning back against her pillows, Hester twisted her disordered curls up in one hand, feeling their soft weight. Should she perform her toilette at Farleigh? she wondered. It would be far more pleasant to dress her hair and herself with Diana for company, and her sister would surely chase away any lingering disappointment Nathaniel's absence had left at the back of her mind. Time with Diana might be just what she needed, and as she heard a soft knock at the door Hester made her decision.

'Good morning, ma'am.'

'Good morning, Arless. I've been thinking about this evening. Would you please have my gown and things for later packed and sent over to Lady Lavendon? I'll do my toilette at Farleigh, I think, before the ball.'

'Of course, ma'am. I'll see to it at once.'

Watching the maid bustle to open the curtains, Hester nodded to herself. It was always a pleasure to see her sister, her sweet nature the perfect foil for whatever disagreeable sensations twined through Hester's gut. Maybe she'd even be able to forget about Nathaniel for a short while beneath Diana's roof, some part of her considered—even as the rest of her knew it was as likely as learning to fly.

* * *

If it was a distraction Hester wanted later that evening, Diana seemed more than happy to oblige.

'Now, Hester, you're nearly finished…' Lady Lavendon held her head to one side, inspecting her sister as a scholar might a rare book, her French lady's maid hovering at her shoulder.

It seemed something was wanting, and Hester stood as patiently as she could manage as she waited for the verdict.

'Yes. *Very* nearly. If you'd allow Brigitte to apply just the tiniest hint of rouge…'

'No, thank you.' Hester ducked away, only narrowly escaping an attack on her cheek. 'I've been primped and prodded quite enough. I didn't realise what sharing a titled lady's toilette entailed—getting you ready is an event in itself.'

Studying her reflection in the grand dressing mirror of her equally grand rooms, Diana adjusted a stray feather. In her soft green gown she looked like a wood nymph, willowy and lovely as a classical statuette.

'It's expected of me these days, I'm afraid. Lavendon has influence and therefore so do I— whether I want it or not. People look to me to set an example, and that includes in how to dress.'

'I'm not sure I envy you that. I wouldn't know where to begin in setting myself up as a fashion plate.'

'Nonsense. You look beautiful tonight. It's a shame Nathaniel isn't here to see you.'

Smoothing down the front of her pale blue gown, Hester carefully avoided her sister's eye. It was the first time he'd been mentioned all day, and the mere sound of his name brought colour to her face with no need for rouge. 'Well, his father couldn't spare him. The business, you know…'

'Oh, I know. That Mr Honeywell.' Diana pursed her lips, teasing an already perfect curl between two fingers. 'Can't allow anything to distract his son from making money, can he?'

'I don't know that I'm much of a distraction.'

'You shouldn't be so sure. I saw how Nathaniel looked at you last time you were here. I was half afraid he was going to eat you.'

Hester's head jerked up. A swift glance showed Brigitte busy arranging a vast box of ribbons, mercifully not listening to her mistress's conversation, but Hester flashed Diana a warning look.

'He did no such thing. Don't be absurd.'

'It's true.' Finally satisfied with the set of each ringlet, Diana shifted her attention to Hester, not repentant in the least. 'You couldn't move an inch without him noticing, and I'm quite sure at one point he was openly staring. You needn't believe me if you'd rather not. Lavendon saw it too, however, and he quite agreed.'

'You discuss my marriage with Lavendon?'

Hester almost choked. It was uncomfortable to know her own sister harboured such dangerous opinions, but dragging her brother-in-law into it too… 'He knows your thoughts?'

'Of course. He's my friend as well as my husband. Something I'd love you to discover for yourself.'

It was Hester's turn to examine herself in the mirror and she did so now, although she hardly saw what lay before her as she stared into the glass. Surely Diana couldn't be right? Nathaniel would never have watched her so hungrily, calling to mind a picture of a child with a cake. It was just wishful thinking on her sister's part—the romantic side of Diana's nature crying out for everyone to feel the same magic of young love that she lived daily.

As much as Hester might desire it that would never be the truth, and it was with a hint of sadness that she affected a shrug. 'Nathaniel and I *are* friends. Just…not anything more.'

'If you say so.'

Diana smiled, her tone so indulgent it made Hester feel about six years old. Clearly nothing would change Diana's mind now she had made it up—including the cold truth—and, resigned to her fate, Hester took her sister's arm.

'Ought we be going down? Your guests will be arriving soon, and they'll be desperate to see what you're wearing.'

A raised eyebrow met her feigned concern. 'If I didn't know better, Hess, I might think you were teasing me.'

'Teasing the famous, trendsetting Lady Lavendon? I wouldn't dare.'

Together the sisters descended the stairs, two birds of paradise glittering beneath Farleigh's enormous crystal chandeliers. Hester had been right. Diana's guests began to appear almost at once, and Lady Lavendon turned on the full power of her gracious hostess charm.

'I'll see you in a little while,' Hester murmured as yet another well-dressed couple made a bee-line for Diana. 'I know you have work to do.'

'Just don't stray too far. You may need to come to the rescue if Sir Neville starts telling me about Waterloo. Again.'

Leaving Diana to her duties, Hester withdrew further into the ballroom. It was filling fast, and everywhere she looked showed the highest of high society crowding in: men proud of shapely calves and women hoping to display a new gown—and the figure inside it—to its best advantage.

There were many faces she recognised, but just as many she didn't, doubtless belonging to titled individuals she'd never met, and Hester couldn't help but wonder at how far her sister's star had risen. A merchant's daughter married to a lord... Many of the ton's young ladies were resentful that Diana had taken the biggest prize, but as Hester watched Lord Lavendon move to stand proudly beside his wife she knew that for him there could never have been anyone else.

The sight of Diana's happiness lifted some of the despondency lurking at the back of Hester's mind; but not all of it, and with a concealed sigh she looked away.

Where was her own husband at that moment? Hidden away in his London office, lost in a world of taxes and insurance and debts owing to the firm. Something as inconsequential as a ball would be far from his thoughts and her along with it, more important concerns occupying the space she would never inhabit.

It was a fact she had to accept, and she tried to force resignation as she straightened her skirts. Anyone could have seen how Nathaniel hesitated when given the choice between the ball and visiting his warehouses, obviously torn between his promise and his true desires, and she'd known at once that she would release him.

Going to a party on her own was uncomfortably reminiscent of five years prior, when Nathaniel had never been able to spare an evening from his work, but there was little to be done about that. Her growing feelings could bring nothing good, clearly, so she would ignore them, placing them back in their box as a bittersweet reminder of when she'd harboured hopes for the future that would never bear fruit.

Another scan of the room helped cheer her, however. Several friendly faces were turned in her direction and Hester moved to join the nearest group, wending her way through the chattering throng until she was taken by a welcoming hand.

'Hess! How well you look tonight!'

Mrs Agnes Grey, a friend since their days in short gowns, kissed Hester's cheek. Her husband gave Hester a grateful nod and left at once for the siren call of the card room, evidently relieved to have escaped as the band began its first few tenuous notes and the lines for dancing began to form.

Agnes slipped a hand through Hester's arm. 'We old married ladies must sit out the dancing, I suppose. Come and take a glass of punch with me instead.'

They retreated to one side of the room, where refreshments beckoned. When both were furnished with a full glass, Agnes laughed.

'Did you notice how quickly Grey left for the gaming tables? Apparently Lord Finton is here tonight. By all accounts he's a terrible whist player and throws money around like water. Quite a sight to be seen, apparently.'

'I can well imagine.' Hester grimaced. 'What a fine thing to have more money than sense.'

Agnes smiled, although it struck Hester as a little uncertain. 'Did Nathaniel feel the lure of the tables too? I haven't seen him.'

'No.' Hester pretended to watch the dancing for a moment, hoping to hide the sudden drop in her stomach at the mention of his name. 'He's in London on business.'

'Ah.' Agnes peered down into her glass. When she spoke her voice was soft, and Hester had to lean in to catch it. 'I confess, dearest, I was a little surprised you didn't mention his return. I heard it in passing, and was more amazed than I can say.'

The twist in Hester's stomach increased. Agnes didn't sound indignant, more confused if anything, and Hester could have kicked herself. She should have told Agnes herself. Instead the rumour mill had got there first, and now her oldest friend was probably hurt to be excluded.

'In truth, I hardly knew how to speak of it. It's been the most…unusual time. I'm sorry if my silence upset you.'

Agnes took Hester's hand with a gentle squeeze. 'You don't owe me an apology of any kind. I was worried, not offended. I hoped you weren't distressed, that's all—'

She broke off, suddenly looking over Hester's shoulder.

Her face fell. 'Oh, dear. My sister-in-law is coming our way. Be on your guard—she's desperate for the full tale of Nathaniel's return, and I'm afraid her motives are less genuine than your friends'. The faintest hint of gossip and she descends like a hound on a fox, and a husband back from the dead is the best thing she's heard of in many a year.'

Hester steeled herself at once. 'Then I fear she'll have to be disappointed. I don't even know any details of Nathaniel's miraculous reappearance myself.'

'No?' Agnes frowned briefly. 'Even so… You may not want to share the information you *do* have with Ellen. Not unless you want your private affairs all around town by tomorrow morning.'

A presence loomed at Hester's elbow and she closed her eyes for a half-second before turning round. 'Good evening, Miss Grey.'

'Mrs Honeywell.'

Agnes's sister-in-law dropped a short curtsey and came up alight with avid interest. It radiated from her in an almost tangible force, making Hester want to take a step back.

There was no preamble to her eagerness, not even any pretence at polite chatter to help pave the way to the main event. 'Your husband's return is all anyone can talk of. It's just too thrilling!'

Miss Grey craned her neck to peer among the crowd. It was obvious who she was looking for—

or at least it was to Hester, who took a sip of punch before making a carefully measured reply.

'Mr Honeywell isn't here. He has business in London that needs attending to most urgently.'

She could sense Agnes's discomfort, but had no time to do anything about it as Miss Grey leaned closer, lowering her voice to a whisper that invited confidence while offering none in return.

'Avoiding having to be seen in public? It's true, then, that he staggered back to Shardlow with half his face gone and missing one hand entirely?'

'Ellen!'

Poor Agnes looked agonised at her sister-in-law's complete lack of grace, and Hester could barely control a flare of irritation. Was that what people were saying? Exaggerating Nathaniel's injuries for their own ghoulish entertainment?

'No,' Hester answered shortly. 'One eye and one finger is the extent of his loss, and I'd appreciate it if you could correct anybody who says otherwise.'

'Oh.' For a moment Miss Grey's enthusiasm ebbed, but in the next breath she bounced back. 'May I ask how it happened?'

'You may ask, but it's not in my power to tell you.'

It seemed her lack of insight was disappointing. Hester saw Miss Grey's brow crease, evidently at a loss as to how one could fail to know every minute detail of such a fascinatingly morbid event and then selfishly deny everyone else the tale.

She gave it one last try. 'It must have been a huge shock to find Mr Honeywell altered to such a degree. How was it to see him so changed from before?'

Hester hesitated. Such a tactless question didn't deserve any consideration, and yet it hit home, forcing her to take another sip from her glass to cover the pause. Nathaniel *was* altered and she couldn't deny it—although not only in the shallow way Miss Grey implied. His face was marked and his right hand maimed, but it was the transformation to his character that was the most striking—and, she thought with sudden warmth beneath the bodice of her gown, the most important.

He could have come back with no face whatsoever and his new nature would still have called to her. A perfect countenance was a pale substitute for the better man she was getting to know.

'He is indeed changed from before he went away. There may be differences—but I can't say they are for the worse. In fact, I might even say in some ways he's improved.'

Miss Grey's eyes lit up with fresh curiosity, but her chance to dig further was stolen by a voice from behind them.

'I'm sure that's praise I don't deserve.' Nathaniel stepped forward, offering a gentlemanly bow to each surprised woman in turn. 'But I'll accept it nonetheless. Good evening, Hester. I'm sorry I'm late.'

Hidden by his waistcoat, Nathaniel's heart raced as he took in every detail of the vision before him. He knew he shouldn't stare, but Hester captured every last fibre of his attention and there was nothing on earth that could distract him.

The powder-blue of her gown shimmered slightly in the candlelight, its cut hinting delicately at what might lie beneath. It was the perfect colour to set off her dark blonde curls and they gleamed almost gold, the ringlets at each ear accented by a stylish arrangement of white feathers that only added to the angelic impression.

But it was her face that eclipsed all else. Shock was turning rapidly to wonder—and then came a smile so blindingly beautiful it made everything and everyone around him dull by comparison. If he'd harboured any doubts about his rash decision to ride through the night, apparently abandoning good sense entirely, just one look at Hester convinced him he'd made the right choice.

'Nathaniel!' She gazed up at him, cornflower eyes full of questions. 'But...why aren't you in London? How is it you're here?'

It was an effort to think of an adequate reply while his pulse still leaped and the rapt stares of all three women were fixed on him. Thankfully, however, Agnes Grey seemed to understand.

'Come with me, Ellen.' She linked her sister-in-law's arm and began to gently guide her away. 'I see Mrs Stokes standing alone, and I'm sure she'd be glad of some company.'

Miss Grey didn't look delighted to be leaving at such an interesting juncture, but there was little she could do as Agnes plunged them both back into the crowd, Nathaniel and Hester watching the two retreat until they found themselves alone.

'Well...'

Hester's mouth was still lifted in the prettiest curve he'd ever seen. She looked genuinely pleased to see him; all the reward he could possibly desire for taking such an enormous risk.

'I certainly wasn't expecting this. I thought you had great heaps of work to plough through and wouldn't see the light of day for a week. Did you manage to finish earlier than planned?'

'Not exactly.'

At her inquisitive glance Nathaniel took a breath. During the whole long ride from the city to Thame Magna he'd rehearsed this moment, wondering what he might say, but as Hester waited he realised the best reply was the truth. Or at least something close to it.

Casting his mind back to the unpleasant scene earlier that evening, Nathaniel hid a grimace. In all likelihood his father was still angry—coldly and quietly, but angry nonetheless. It would take a long time for any forgiveness to come Nathaniel's way, if at all, although that hardly seemed to matter now, in the heady warmth of Hester's smile.

'Oh! Nathaniel! You came after all?'

A flurry of feathers made them both turn. Diana stood looking delightedly from one to the other, her colour high and her eyes sparkling, and he noticed a strange unspoken exchange pass between the two sisters. It seemed to require only the subtle movement of eyebrows but they appeared to understand each other implicitly, Diana's raised and Hester's furrowed—even more severely when Lady Lavendon seized his arm.

'I must have you and Hester dance. I know it's not considered terribly fashionable to dance with one's own wife, but you'll indulge me, won't you? You look so well together tonight.'

He bowed, feeling a touch of heat beginning to rise. What man *wouldn't* want to dance with the goddess that was Hester that evening, her slim back and lifted chin surely raising pulses all over the room?

'I wouldn't want to disappoint my hostess. If Hester will have me, I'd be honoured.'

He caught a wordless flash of Hester's eyes in Diana's direction, but when she faced him she seemed perfectly composed. 'Of course. If my sister commands us.'

Even with a glove separating her skin from his, Nathaniel's still prickled as he took her hand and together they found their places in the set. The band struck up and the couples nearer the top began to move, Nathaniel and Hester standing opposite each other while they waited their turn.

'So, will you tell me how you're here?' Hester had to raise her voice a little to be heard above the surrounding din of voices and music. 'I thought you were to tour the warehouses all week?'

'I decided on a change of plan.'

'That much is evident. What happened?'

Nathaniel surveyed the couples on his left and right. Nobody was paying him any mind. The men only had eyes for their partners and vice versa, their attention fixed elsewhere.

'I'd agreed to be here with you tonight before my father raised the notion of going to London. I realised I was in the wrong place, so I came back to rectify my mistake.'

'But…won't he be displeased?'

A brief picture of Mr Honeywell's tight, furious face flickered in Nathaniel's memory. 'He can be if he likes. I'm not a child, to be ordered by anybody but myself.'

Hester shook her head, candlelight glancing

off her curls. 'I can't believe you'd choose a ball over working. I feel I hardly know you at all!'

Nathaniel looked down at his boots, suddenly unsure. The truth balanced on the tip of his tongue, one he hardly knew how she would receive, and yet he couldn't quite manage to restrain it.

'It wasn't the ball I chose. It was you.'

It was as though all the air had been sucked from the room. Hester's gaze clouded with uncertainty, searching his face like one suspecting a joke at her expense.

'Me?'

'I didn't want to let you down again. It seems I did that enough five years ago.'

Her lips parted in surprise but nothing came, leaving Nathaniel with no idea what his wife was thinking—and no immediate way of finding out, as the couple to his left stepped forward and there was nothing to do but follow them, cutting off any hope of conversation until the end of the dance.

Talking might be out of the question but perhaps words weren't needed. He almost *felt* Hester's eyes fix on him, and the expression in their depths stole every breath from his burning lungs. Looking into the azure shadows, he saw a hundred unspoken questions, one chasing after the next but none able to hide the beautiful confusion in her glowing face.

There might as well have been no one else in the room for all Nathaniel could look away, he and Hester joined together by an invisible thread that stretched from one leaping heart to the other and tightened with each step. All the soul-searching and uncertainty seemed worth it just to see her move, and now Nathaniel couldn't imagine why he'd ever doubted himself.

Sitting behind his London desk, he had found his thoughts refusing to fix on his work, constantly drifting back to Hester and the disappointment he feared his actions had caused until he hadn't been able to stand any more. It was the choice he should have made from the very beginning—his wife's feelings over faceless profit, although the frightening novelty of such a thing still shook him to the core.

Coming together in the centre of the set Nathaniel took Hester's hand. They touched for the briefest of moments and yet a streak of lightning lanced the length of his arm, settling in his chest to make him wonder if he was suffocating. She came closer still, the searing connection now joined by an unbearable urge to abandon all sense and seize her in his arms. Circling each other like a pair of hungry wolves the air felt static, something in it brooding and *waiting*, somehow, like the calm before the breaking of a storm; the band must still be playing, and the other dancers moving, but for Nathaniel there was nothing in the world but that sapphire gaze and the heat of one gloved hand.

His mind seemed to have gone curiously blank. He moved in a daze as all thought fled to be replaced by sensation: Hester's delicate fingers in his, slight dizziness as she rose and fell with perfect timing, but all the while holding his unwavering attention without a single word.

Perhaps he'd said too much. Perhaps he shouldn't have told her the conclusion he'd come to as he'd sat at his lonely desk. But surely no man alive could have looked at her and not felt the same weakness Nathaniel did as she spun gracefully, skirts floating out and catching the light to make her shine brighter still.

The dance might have lasted minutes or hours. He couldn't tell for how long Hester skipped in and out of arm's reach, the temptation to capture her growing with every beat until the music finished and he had no excuse to lay claim to her any longer—something it seemed Lord Lavendon had been waiting for.

'Honeywell! Diana told me you were here.' Their host broke in, unwittingly shattering the tension that held both Nathaniel and Hester in its thrall. 'Just the man I need, if Hess can spare you.'

Hester stepped back demurely, although her cheeks were suffused with a flush that only increased her prettiness—and Nathaniel's pulse.

'Of course. I was thinking of going out for some air anyway.'

'Excellent.' Lord Lavendon leaned down to mutter closer to Hester's ear. 'You'll find your sister hiding on the terrace. She's doing a fine job, but even the best hostess needs a break occasionally.'

'I'll go to find her. If you'll excuse me?'

She dipped a vague curtsey and moved away, Nathaniel's heart sinking slightly as he watched her slip through the dense crowd. He didn't want her to go. While they were dancing she'd almost been in his arms, although the unreadable glance she shot him over her shoulder now, just before she disappeared, was enough to make him pause.

Lavendon clapped him on the shoulder. 'Come into the card room. Finton is gambling away half his fortune and I need a man of good financial sense to talk him down.'

'And you came to me? Was the selection really that poor?' Nathaniel forced a smile, although his innards felt like a writhing bag of snakes. What was that connection? Hester *must* have felt it too. It was more than a dance, surely, and yet with Hester it was always so difficult to be sure...

Mercifully Lord Lavendon remained oblivious to his brother-in-law's turmoil. 'Don't be an ass, Honeywell. Everybody knows you have the best head for business this side of London.' He stopped for a moment, a slow grin unfurling.

'Although perhaps that's changing. Diana mentioned you should be working at this very minute, only something—or perhaps some*one*—made you return early.'

Nathaniel only realised he must look as flustered as he felt when Lavendon barked a laugh. 'I see. Well, there's no shame in it. My wife is my main concern, and I don't mind who knows it. From what Diana tells me, it's about time you started feeling that way about your own.'

It would be bad manners to flee from one's host, Nathaniel imagined, although the temptation to do just that was strong. The conversation was getting a little too close to the bone for comfort, and with another forced smile he attempted a diversion before it was too late.

'Lord Finton, then. How much has he lost?'

The rest of the evening was far less eventful than the start—at least concerning Hester. Nathaniel hardly laid eyes on her again until it was time to leave, and only when he was helping her down the carriage steps on their return to Shardlow did he feel her hand in his once again. She hadn't spoken at all on the journey, instead sitting with her gaze fixed on something beyond the darkened window that Nathaniel hadn't been able to see, whatever she was thinking hidden from him behind determinedly averted eyes.

Reaching his room, he sank wearily down

onto the bed and sat for a moment in silence, staring unseeing at the floor. The house was quiet, cloaked in the deep silence of the night, the gentle crackle of flames in the fireplace the only sound and their orange glow lighting Nathaniel's face as he buried it in his hands.

What had possessed him to speak out loud of the feelings that had grown so slowly since his return? The regard for Hester that now threatened everything he'd thought he believed? For all their determination to be friends he still had a long way to go before he could consider himself forgiven, and with a low groan Nathaniel tightened his fingers.

Would things be strained between them? Had he ventured too far at last, revealing the gradual but terrifying truth that Hester meant more to him now than profit and ambition ever could?

Nathaniel sat for a while, still cradling his head as a storm clashed inside it. He might have stayed like that all night if a faint scratch hadn't caught his ear, soon joined by another sound that made his head jerk up sharply.

There was no mistaking it, although it was so unlikely that for a moment he was sure he must be dreaming: the distinctive rasp of a key turning in a stiff lock, followed after a breathless pause by the tentative creak of unoiled hinges.

From the side of the bed Nathaniel could only watch in stunned silence as the unused door between his room and Hester's opened slowly—so slowly that time seemed to stand still—and then she was before him, wearing only her nightgown and the set face of a woman who had made up her mind.

Chapter Ten

Hester wondered if Nathaniel could hear the wild leaping of her heart from the other side of the bedroom. To her it was unnaturally loud, cutting through the taut stillness and beating so hard she could feel it hammering right down to her toes. She was completely exposed, standing with nothing to shield her, but the conclusion she'd come to during the carriage ride from Farleigh drove her on—even if the thought of what she was about to do made her tremble from head to foot.

'Hester? What…?'

Nathaniel rose from the bed, but checked as she held up a hand. He didn't come any closer although his eye raked over her, its intensity making her shiver, and, screwing up all her courage, Hester asked the question she half dreaded him answering.

'Was it really me you came back for tonight? You were telling the truth?'

Relief flooded her at his single nod—along with a nameless rush that stirred sparks in her belly. His expression was inscrutable and yet with that one dip of his head Nathaniel told her all she needed to know, the atmosphere suddenly airless as each watched the other's every move.

'Is that why you're here? To ask me that?'

Nathaniel's voice was steady, but a thrill ran through Hester at the strained undercurrent only one hoping for it would have heard. There was a definite note of careful restraint, and it lit a taper beneath the thin fabric of her gown, increasing the temperature that was already scalding.

She swallowed. The speech she'd rehearsed seemed so foolish now: as if she ever could have hoped to put something that defied description into words. Nathaniel's revelation that evening and the repeating of it now pushed her closer to the edge until there was nothing to do but jump—out into a void where the only thing she could be sure of was the dizzying whirl of her own feelings…at last.

All the confusion and soul-searching and the denial of what she couldn't fight had fallen away at his simple confession. Now she was just a woman standing before a man, hoping he had come to feel the same.

'Hester?' Nathaniel prompted her quietly, still

sounding as if he were under tight control. 'Is that the only reason you came to see me? It's getting late and you must be tired. We can talk about it in the morning if you'd like.'

'No,' Hester managed to croak, hearing the parched anxiety in her voice but unable to stop it. 'There's something else. Something else that I… I want to…'

She couldn't bring herself to finish. The sentence faded, tailing away into nothingness, and Nathaniel allowed it to die with a patience that belied the tension pulled painfully taut across the room.

'Something else? Something else you want?'

Hester shook her head. She couldn't make herself say it out loud: the desire for him that held her so unescapably in its grip, tightening each day until tonight her defences had finally snapped. The last time she'd been this nervous in a bedroom alone with her husband had been on their wedding night, so long ago she could barely remember what had transpired. She only knew how it had made her feel—alive in every sinew, burning with an inner fire she hadn't understood.

Everything was different now, however. So much had changed since then that they might be two other people entirely—although Hester's newfound mettle abandoned her as she tried to find the nerve to do as she'd planned. Rooted to the spot, she wavered, unable to go forward or back, hesitating on the threshold between her room and Nathaniel's and cursing herself for the indecision she feared would make her look weak.

But then—terrifyingly, delightfully—Nathaniel acted first.

Slowly, as if to give her plenty of time to run, he came towards her, Hester having to raise her chin to look up into his face and what she saw there making her throat clench with strangling force. She didn't move a muscle, standing perfectly still until Nathaniel's hands reached for her and with one smooth movement lifted her from the ground.

Her legs came up immediately to encircle his waist, matching the swift twining of her arms around his neck. Supporting her with effortless strength, Nathaniel ducked his head to capture her mouth, a hand beneath each of her legs pinning Hester against him with nowhere to hide even if she'd wanted to.

It was as if her blood had turned to something hot and fierce, surging inside her and spurring her on. Clinging to Nathaniel, she wound her fingers through his hair, pressing his lips down harder onto hers and feeling every last nerve crackle at his low groan. Her nightgown was rucked up scandalously high but she couldn't break away to arrange it in any semblance of modesty, a gasp escaping her as she felt Nathaniel skim the bared flesh of her thigh. His palm was scalding, blistering heat following its progress higher until his fingers slid beneath the hem of her nightgown to cup the generous curve they discovered. Hester's breathing grew ragged, each snatched breath mirroring the sharpness of Nathaniel's own.

He turned for the bed, stumbling blindly as Hester bit down on his lower lip. Still carrying her pressed tightly to the front of his body, he sank onto the mattress, Hester kneeling astride his lap but neither willing to break the blazing contact of their searching mouths.

Acting on the basest of instincts, Hester let her hands stray down to Nathaniel's chest, only managing to surface when her fingers found the buttons on his untucked shirt. 'Can I—?'

It was the same question he'd asked her that night in her bedroom, when their kiss hadn't been the only thing on fire, and the answering glint in Nathaniel's eye told her he recalled it too. The hungry gleam sent a shudder skittering the length of Hester's spine, and her eyes fluttered closed again as Nathaniel leaned forward to nip the sensitive place beneath her jaw.

'Yes. If you'll allow me the same liberty.'

She nodded briefly, somewhere in the back of her mind admiring his restraint. Her own sense of propriety had fled, only animal impulse and long-denied desire surging to carry her along a path she'd never known existed as with trembling fingers she freed the first button. The next one followed, and then another, and another, until Nathaniel's shirt hung free and she ran questing fingertips over the warm ridges of his muscled stomach, revelling in his harsh sigh.

A vague, indistinct memory of their very first time together flitted through her otherwise blank mind: as a lad of eighteen his physique had been nowhere near as impressive, and she couldn't help but wonder anew exactly how the intervening years had brought about such a change.

But then Nathaniel's hand moved to the ribbons at her neck, and nothing else seemed to matter but the heat of his palms moving downwards across her shoulders, slipping her nightgown away as they went, until it pooled, soft and white, around her waist. Hester saw Nathaniel's jaw tighten, a tendon in his neck working furiously as his gaze swept across her with molten need, and she found the nerve to smile instead of cover herself as a prim voice somewhere deep in her subconscious insisted she do at once.

'Are you well?'

'I'm not sure…'

Nathaniel's voice was like gravel, the dark want in it enough to make Hester's skin blaze.

'All of a sudden I'm finding it hard to breathe.'

'Perhaps you're too warm. Let me help you.'

Copying his movements, Hester traced the firm shape of Nathaniel's shoulders, sliding her hands beneath his shirt to peel it away. Allowing herself a long look at his bare chest, she drank in the line of hair stretching down to his breeches, guiding her like an arrow to places unknown. Exactly what lay below that waistband she couldn't remember, although with a hot flush of sudden shame she realised just how much she wanted to find out.

Her flicker of hesitation must have been obvious. At once Nathaniel slackened his hold on her hips and drew back, his eye still hazy, but clouded by concern that touched her heart.

'Hester? Is something amiss?'

He searched her face so earnestly Hester had to fight the urge to take his in her hands and kiss him again.

'Do you want to stop?'

'No.' She shook her head firmly, setting the unwanted sensation aside. 'Not unless you do?'

A glance down at the front of Nathaniel's breeches answered that question without a shadow of a doubt, and Hester's smile returned as he took one fallen ringlet between two unsteady fingers.

'Forgive me...'

He sounded hoarse, the ripple his voice sent through Hester's stomach only growing as his hand strayed from her hair to the back of her neck, to gently stroke the nape.

'I shouldn't have rushed. For some things a man ought to take his time.'

Hester tried to reply but found she'd forgotten how. Nathaniel's fingers, so warm and skilled, drifted from her nape to her collarbone and—with the briefest of searing glances to gauge her reaction—moved down, skimming over one soft peak and stealing every coherent thought Hester had ever had. Her eyes closed in an instinctive desire to feel every sensation to the fullest, and when she opened them again the helpless longing in Nathaniel's face was more than she could bear.

She stood up. Her nightgown fell to her feet and she stepped out of it, hardly believing her own daring as she watched Nathaniel's lips part on a hungry intake of breath. Hester stood before him, goosebumps rising on every inch of her skin that had nothing to do with the night air, and she felt herself almost come apart at the seams as he looked up, hers to do with as she wished. The very idea made her knees buckle—something Nathaniel must have seen as a slow smile unfurled itself across his face.

'Or perhaps time is of the essence... What would you decide?'

In place of an answer Hester leaned down to press her lips to his. Immediately his hands were on her, drawing her closer, until with one deft move she found herself on the mattress, looking up at the canopy above. Turning her head, she saw Nathaniel by the bed, their positions suddenly reversed but the feeling of power still singing in Hester's blood.

Watching him unfasten his breeches, her heart railed against her ribs as if trying to break free. His fingers shook with what she knew to be yearning, and her own hands were no steadier as his breeches finally slid to the ground, revealing the full glory of the man she had married with no idea of the journey their lives would take. Another fleeting fragment of their wedding night tried to emerge, but it flickered out again as Nathaniel came closer, kneeling beside her on the bed, and the sight of him was too mesmerising to allow any other thought.

He lay along her side, the vast expanse of him so hot to the touch that Hester wondered if he'd burned her and she reached out to pull him closer still, feeling the delicious friction of rough hair on soft skin as his weight came down on top of her. Bracing himself on his elbows, he took her lips once again, a growl issuing from his throat when she gently ran neat nails down the broad landscape of his back and then ventured further, the mystery of what his breeches had concealed a mystery no longer and enough to make her gasp.

'Hester…' With what seemed like great difficulty Nathaniel broke the kiss to stare down into her glazed eyes, his own eye growing darker as her fingers continued their exploration of his un-mapped skin. 'Are you sure you want to do this?'

She looked back, breath coming hard and fast and finding it difficult to think. Nathaniel's face, so close to hers and handsome enough to make her sigh, obliterated all reason, feelings seeming so much more important than thoughts—until she forced her brain to work.

'Are you sure you want to do this?'

Even almost at the moment of no return, Nathaniel had stopped to ask the one question he must be praying she'd answer with *yes*, and Hester marvelled yet again at how much he had changed. The passionate man who now waited for her reply was worlds away from the cold stranger she'd married, and he had proved tonight that he was capable of putting her first—even before the business she'd feared would always be his only concern. He might not love her, ex-actly, but it was enough to build on until—who knew?—they might even find something close. He had given her hope where once there had been none at all, and Hester felt the last of her doubts fall away as she stretched up to reclaim Nathaniel's mouth.

'I've never been so sure of anything in my life.'

Faint birdsong roused Nathaniel from a deep and dreamless sleep. It was hard to tell exactly what time it was but his best guess would be near dawn, the room still dark but those first few tentative chirps signalling the start of a new day. Slowly emerging from unconsciousness his mind felt sluggish—until with a jolt he sat up sharply.

The other side of the bed was empty, the rumpled sheets still warm, and a horrible sinking feeling gripped him at once.

Where's Hester?

Throwing off the coverlet, he was about to stand when a voice came from the other side of the room.

'Are you going somewhere?'

Peering through the gloom, Nathaniel made out a shape crouched beside the cold hearth, and felt his sudden tension bleeding away at once.

'To look for you. I thought you'd run away from me.'

He caught what might have been the shake of a blonde head. 'I woke to see the fire had gone out. I wanted to see if I could light it again, as you did for me, but I'm not sure how to begin.'

Nathaniel leaned back against the pillows, feeling a welcome surge of relief. She hadn't fled from him, then, in a fit of regret for their night together—the thought of which made a particularly *interested* part of his anatomy sit up and take notice. Hester's nightgown still lay in a pale puddle beside the bed, and the question of what she was wearing as she knelt by the fire made his pulse tick faster.

A further look proved disappointing, however. By the pallid gleam it seemed she had wrapped herself in one of the sheets from his makeshift bed on the floor, and with more than a flicker of regret Nathaniel likewise folded one around his waist as he got up and went towards her.

'Can I help?'

'Unless you want us to freeze to death before breakfast, please do.'

She didn't sound the least bit hesitant or reserved; *something to be grateful for*, he thought as he felt along the dark mantel for his tinderbox, all too aware of the barely dressed form of his wife mere inches away. It would seem there was little danger of her lamenting what had happened in the early hours and Nathaniel blessed her for it. The single most wonderful experience of his life had been bearing down upon Hester and hearing her sigh of delight, and if she had felt ashamed afterwards it would have broken his heart.

He crouched beside her, still hardly able to see, but sure she was watching. Her quiet breathing was close to his ear and his skin prickled at the sensation, stirring the hairs at the nape of his neck and making his hand shake slightly as he struck the flint and sent a spark dancing out into the gloom. It settled among the heap of kindling Hester had so helpfully arranged and began to smoulder, the flames growing stronger as he blew onto the burgeoning fire.

In the soft light he could at last see Hester's face, and for a second he feared his chest might burst at the smile he found there.

'Good morning.'

'Good morning to you, too.'

Her colour deepened a little, but still there was nothing more than the natural, sweet shyness anyone might show under the circumstances.

'Did you sleep well?'

'Yes, thank you. When I eventually got round to it.'

Hester's lips twitched—but then her gaze shifted to fix on something Nathaniel realised far too late he hadn't meant her to see.

'Your patch… It must have come off while you slept.'

Instinctively he reached up, his chest tightening when his fingers met ruined flesh instead of leather. Pressing his hand over the vivid scar, he turned away, determined to spare Hester the sight of something he didn't relish himself.

'Damn it. I never meant for you to see me like this.'

He tried to get up from his crouch beside the hearth, but warm fingers on his arm made him stop.

'Don't,' Hester said quietly, her voice firm but soft. 'Let me look at you.'

Still kneeling on the ground, wrapped in the white sheet with her dark golden hair spilling over her shoulders, she looked like a Greek goddess, so powerful in her beauty that Nathaniel had no choice but to obey.

Reluctantly he sat down again, although he didn't move his hand. 'You don't need to see this. It'll give you nightmares.'

She shrugged, the pale moon of her face glowing in the firelight. 'As I told you before, I have a strong stomach.'

Hester moved a little closer and Nathaniel readied himself, although his heart still leapt as she took his hand and lowered it to her own lap. He forced himself to meet her eyes as in silence she studied his missing one, feeling himself tense as he waited for the verdict.

'I suppose I disgust you now.'

He tried to speak lightly, but failed. How could she *not* be repulsed by the mess left behind by the foreman's whip? Nobody could see that and remain unmoved—and Hester, although extraordinary in many ways, was human like any other.

But she was also surprising.

'You suppose wrong.'

Taking his face in her hands, she drew his head down until Nathaniel could have counted each sweeping lash, and gently—so gently it felt more like a summer breeze than a kiss—

she touched her lips to the red welt where his
eye should have been.

'I'm glad you finally shared that with me. I'd
very much like it if there were no secrets between us now.'

Caught between warring emotions, Nathaniel
said nothing—although that didn't stop his mind
from whirling. The feel of Hester's velvet lips on
his marked face, their perfection a jarring contrast to his flaws, made his innards burn with
the desire to catch her up and kiss her back. But
something else—a creeping shadow of uncertainty and guilt—cautioned him to think twice.

There was still one secret left, and he had no
wish to share it with the woman who had stolen
his heart.

Returning Hester's gaze, he admired its clarity, intelligence and honesty combined beneath
a blue more lovely than any other. To tell her the
truth of how he had lost his eye would reveal
how far from grace he'd fallen, and how would
Hester ever be able to look at him the same way
once she knew how low he'd crawled?

'Of course.' He managed a pale imitation of
a normal reply, although at the questioning tilt
of Hester's head he could have sworn she knew
more than he cared to imagine. 'I would like
that too.'

His hand still lay in her lap, and Nathaniel
took a sharp breath as she traced each finger,

skimming over the missing index as though she'd done it all her life.

'With that said, are you ever going to tell me what happened while you were away?'

The unease in his stomach circled faster. 'I thought you were determined not to ask?'

'That was when I thought... Well, it doesn't matter what I thought then. I'm asking now—is there anything else I ought to know?'

Her fingertips crossed his palm—something that might have tickled if Nathaniel hadn't been so distracted by the twist of his insides. Two rival voices murmured in his ear, each tempting him to follow, but damning him whichever way he chose.

If I tell Hester how I really spent the last five years, won't she see me differently?

The idea of putting his nightmare into words, describing how as a slave he had been treated little better than an animal, made Nathaniel recoil. Once he had kept the truth from Hester out of mere pride, but now everything was different. Her good opinion mattered more than ever, and seeing pity in her face—or worse—would be more than he could stand. She was a strong woman who deserved a strong man, and surely learning that he had been kept as a beast of burden would tarnish him for ever in her mind.

Then again...

If I lie, I'll be no better than the selfish boy I was before. Putting my thoughts and feelings above Hester's and keeping her in the dark.

He swallowed hard, feeling as if his throat was filled with broken glass. Neither option was one he wanted, and yet they were the only ones he had. Backed into a corner, he had to choose: turn away from all the progress he'd made, both as a husband and as a man, or risk Hester thinking as badly of him for his humiliating servitude as he did of himself.

He would have to find the lesser of two evils, but nothing could be more difficult—especially now they were closer than ever to forming a connection he'd never dreamed possible.

Nathaniel made his choice.

'No.' Looking down at Hester's fingers, intertwined so prettily with his own, he forced himself to finish what he'd started. 'There's nothing else.'

With his attention fixed on her hand Nathaniel couldn't see Hester's expression, although judging by her continuing silence he feared she wasn't fooled.

The room was growing slowly lighter as weak sunlight bled beneath the curtains and soon there would be nowhere to hide from the all-seeing sharpness of those periwinkle eyes. Guilt and uncertainty sat heavy like a stone, but Nathaniel sought to ignore it as he cast about swiftly for a way to divert her from his lie.

'I ought to go back to London. I thought perhaps tomorrow.'

'Oh?' Carefully Hester disengaged her hand from his, the movement clearly to disguise a disappointment he hardly dared believe. 'So soon?'

'I'm afraid so. But I've been thinking… Why don't you come with me?'

Her head came up at once. 'What? Really?'

Despite his self-inflicted discomfort, Nathaniel couldn't help but smile at her surprise. 'Yes, *really*. Have you ever seen the warehouses? I'm sure you'd find them interesting.'

'In truth, I've always wanted to. It's never seemed right to me that I know so little about how the company is run. I'd jump at the chance to learn more.'

Hester returned his smile, sending a river of relief through Nathaniel that his distraction had worked. But then her lips turned down instead of up, and his unease returned with a vengeance.

'But what about your father? Won't he mind my being there?'

Nathaniel set his jaw. His father was the very last person he wanted to think of while wearing nothing but a sheet, Hester's enticingly similar state of undress never far from his mind.

'I can't say I care if he does.'

Unwelcome as they were, however, thoughts of his father came regardless. They found a way in to stir a fresh pang of guilt, holding a harsh mirror up to his conduct and casting doubts that gnawed like hungry rats.

I have lied to Hester as my father lied to me. How can I claim to want to be a better man when I still take him as an example?

The question repeated itself in a taunting echo as he knelt beside the fire, Hester still close but suddenly seeming out of his reach. She was the kind of woman a man might search for his whole life and never find, and the fact it had taken him so long to realise only increased the shame that held him in its fist.

The spectre of his father's influence loomed larger the more Nathaniel sought to pull away, chasing him down as though he were prey. Hester ought to have the world, but he couldn't even manage to give her honesty, Nathaniel realised, angry at the similarity that tied him so cruelly to the one person he no longer wanted to imitate in any form.

'Was I very much like him before I went away?'

The words came out as a blurted mess he wished he could have phrased better, but with Mr Honeywell's presence like a ghost at his shoulder Nathaniel couldn't think clearly.

'My father, I mean. Was I really the kind of husband to you that he is to my mother?'

To her credit Hester met his eye without flinching, although her flame-lit face clouded. 'Why do you ask?'

Nathaniel shrugged helplessly. Why *had* he asked, when he already knew what the answer would be? Perhaps some masochistic part of him craved punishment for his dishonesty—confirmation that his sudden wretchedness was his just reward.

'Because I need to know.'

'Then, yes,' she answered simply. 'And, yes.'

It was exactly what he'd been expecting, but to hear it out loud hit him squarely in the gut and made it hard not to look away.

'I'd like to change.'

'You already have.'

The flare of guilt grew hotter. He *had* changed, but not enough. In a horribly ironic twist, the prospect of losing Hester's regard had caused him to shut her out—the very thing she'd detested in him to begin with—and Nathaniel felt desperation rise.

'Even more. I'd like to be the kind of man who deserves a woman like you.'

Hester's lips parted, drawing his focus at once. In the feeble morning light her skin shone like a pearl, smooth and beautiful and tempting him to touch. When she smiled it dropped a lit match

into Nathaniel's stomach, setting fire to his regret, and the flames leapt higher with her reply.

'You can work on that. Starting with taking
me back to bed.'

Chapter Eleven

Hester ran a hand over yet another length of silk, marvelling at its sheen. All about her bolts of material lay stacked neatly on long shelves, line after line of satins and muslin in every colour imaginable. They gleamed like jewels as she looked around the warehouse, from floor to ceiling piled high with the spoils of the Honeywell Trading Company.

'I've never seen anything like it. There must be miles of fabric in here.'

'Most likely. Worth thousands of pounds, too.'

There was a touch of quiet pride in Nathaniel's voice, and she turned to see him surveying his domain with a satisfaction that made her smile.

'I can well imagine. It's certainly an impressive display.'

'Our customers think so, at least. We supply almost every dressmaker from here to Aberdeen, including those in service to the palace.'

Hester's lips curved. 'My gowns are made from the same cloth as Maria Fitzherbert's? A worthy claim indeed.'

Nathaniel raised a brow, although a glint of humour sparkled. 'Princess Charlotte's, you mean. Royalty is a *slightly* more fitting comparison for you than an infamous mistress.'

Hester snorted. The unladylike sound was muffled by the countless rolls of expensive brocade and silk, and she wondered again how many filled the warehouse in which she now stood— the first of three the company owned. Since their arrival in London that morning Nathaniel had been her guide to the world of business, shedding light on things that had been a mystery and answering questions that at one time she would never have dared ask.

She spun slowly, drinking in the dazzling scene like a child in a confectioner's shop. 'It's wonderful. The colours are so beautiful—I could tarry in here all day.'

Nathaniel had the grace to look modest, but Hester could tell he was pleased. His great-grandfather's trading empire was the Honeywell inheritance, after all. He might be coming to feel something for her now, but there could be no mistake: the business was still important to him and a shadow of the unease she'd felt as they knelt before his bedroom fire returned, reminding her not to forget it.

And he still hasn't been entirely honest with me, Hester thought reluctantly as she watched Nathaniel inspect a heavy roll of damask. *Even after our night together he still hasn't told me the truth of what he and Mr Morrow were discussing that day in the hall. If he still has secrets, how am I to completely give him my trust?*

It was an uncomfortable question, and one she tried to lay aside. Surely by now Nathaniel had done enough to earn her faith, something she wanted so badly to give him? He'd shown her he could be kind, and now that they shared a bed she ached to allow him the full keeping of her heart—almost, but not quite, ready to take that final leap.

'I'd like to say we can stay here that long, but I'm afraid I need to visit the office.' Nathaniel slid the damask onto a shelf and leaned back to approve its placement. 'There are some papers that require my signature, and frankly I'm not sure I'd trust you left in here alone.'

Pretending offence, Hester lifted her chin. 'And why not?'

'Because you seem to be even more of a magpie than I realised. I've seen how you admire all those satins, and I'm very much afraid I might return to find you wearing half of next year's profits.' The glitter in Nathaniel's eye grew brighter and Hester's narrowed in response. 'I hope you'll leave your newfound treasure without a scene. I'd hate to have to chase you back to the carriage...'

She was on her guard at once. 'Are you saying that if I wanted to stay a while longer, perhaps until I had inspected every single silk, I couldn't? And that if I ran you would chase me?'

'That's exactly what I'm saying.'

'I see...' Hester frowned as if seriously contemplating her next move. 'I foresee a problem.'

'Oh? What is that?'

'I'm significantly faster than you.'

She darted away, slipping like an eel down one of the shelf-lined aisles, her spirits lifting at Nathaniel's laugh. The sound of quick footsteps at her back spurred her on, and Hester picked up her skirts to outpace her hunter.

There was nobody else in the warehouse. If there had been, there was no way she would have behaved so childishly. Probably it was unbecoming for a well-bred young lady to be flitting about with her hem flapping about her ankles, but all Hester could feel was the sudden lightness that came with being truly alive—and what was more, she had Nathaniel to thank for it.

'You're only making things more difficult for yourself, Hester.'

Ducking round a corner, Hester tried to catch her breath. Nathaniel didn't sound tired in the slightest, whereas her heart fluttered and her shoulders rose and fell with effort. She couldn't recall the last time she'd run *anywhere* and, being in such poor condition, it was no surprise when she felt an arm come around her waist.

'Well? What will you do now?'

Nathaniel's low murmur in her ear made Hester's legs weaken at once. His lips almost touched her skin, each word sending a shiver through her as she turned in his grasp to look up into his face.

'I don't know. Negotiate for my release, I suppose.'

A slow grin spread across Nathaniel's face—slightly wolfish—and Hester felt herself stir.

'As victor, I believe I should set the terms.'

'What would you suggest?'

He didn't answer. Instead Hester swallowed a gasp as Nathaniel leaned down to find her mouth, leading her into a kiss more gentle than his wicked smile threatened. His arm tightened at her waist, drawing her closer until she could feel the hard lines of his body pressed against hers, his desire for her shamelessly obvious.

With commendable effort Hester drew back, although still she swayed in the circle of Nathaniel's arms. 'You don't mean…? Not *here*?'

He met her gaze, something in it so hungry that her blood burned until he breathed a shaky sigh.

'No. One of the men could walk in at any moment…more's the pity.'

To Hester's disappointment he slackened his

grip, although some measure of that animal longing remained as he held out his hand.

'Perhaps we could call in at Areton Street before I return to work. I think those papers might
be able to wait a little while longer.'

Hester's throat dried at the implication, but
she merely nodded, taking Nathaniel's elbow as
though he hadn't just set her pulse alight and
allowing him to lead the way to the door. Outside in the bleak February mist their carriage
stood waiting, the horses tossing their heads impatiently as Nathaniel handed Hester inside and
she settled herself against the comfortably upholstered seat.

Nathaniel climbed in behind her and seated
himself likewise, standing briefly to knock on
the roof in a signal to the driver. The horses
lunged forward eagerly, throwing Hester back
roughly in her seat as the carriage lurched into
motion—all the flimsy excuse Nathaniel needed,
it would seem, to move to sit beside her.

Hester smiled down at her lap as she felt a
strong arm snake along the back of her seat.
'If I didn't know better I'd think you paid the
horses to do that. How many sugar lumps was
the bribe?'

'I beg your pardon? Can't a man want to prevent his wife from taking a fall without being
accused of an ulterior motive?'

'Some men, yes. I'm not so sure about you specifically.'

Anything else she might have said was cut off by the delightful sensation of a hand at the nape of her neck. It crept beneath her bonnet, finding an unwary curl and winding it round gentle fingers.

'Always so suspicious…' Nathaniel toyed with the ringlet, his lips once again close to her ear. With one casual move he reached for the window, Hester's heart leaping as he drew down the blind.

'Although in this case, with good reason.'

Only when the carriage rolled to a halt did Hester come up for air, cheeks flushed and bonnet askew in the most telling manner possible. Nathaniel's kisses had made her dizzy, and he looked a little dazed himself as he ran a hand through his hair and retrieved his hat from where it had rolled beneath the seat.

'We're here.'

Hester smoothed down her gown and pulled her red cloak closer about her shoulders. Her hands were less than steady, and she didn't resist when Nathaniel carefully straightened her bonnet for her, tweaking the ribbons under her chin like a nursemaid with an unruly charge.

'Will I do?'

'Perfectly. The image of a respectable lady.'

'Despite your best efforts.'

She heard Nathaniel's dark chuckle behind her as the carriage door opened and she alighted onto the pavement, hoping her lips didn't look as scalded as they felt. Her breath still came shorter than she liked and one look at Nathaniel only made things worse, the air between them charged and crackling as he took her arm to help her up the steps.

Nathaniel's house in Areton Street was smaller than Shardlow but situated in one of the most fashionable parts of London, its pristine frontage and tall, gleaming windows echoing the tasteful interior. Hester had only visited once before, a few months after her wedding, but so unhappily the place had done little to recommend itself. Now, however, everything was different. Her opinion of the elegant house had improved along with her regard for its master, and as they stood in the hall Hester already felt quite at home.

Arless came forward to take her cloak and bonnet and Hester thanked her with a smile, although she had barely an ounce of attention to spare from Nathaniel's presence at her back. Even without touching she could feel him on her skin, the desire to curve towards him a magnetic pull that only the entrance of the butler made waver.

'Good afternoon, ma'am.' He offered Hester a handsome bow before turning to Nathaniel, arm outstretched for his coat. 'Allow me to take that. I wonder if you know, sir, that Mr Honeywell is waiting for you in the parlour. He has been for some time.'

Hester's stomach plummeted. Mr Honeywell was in this house? His timing could hardly have been worse. It was something it seemed Nathaniel felt likewise, as he muttered a quiet curse Hester was glad she couldn't quite hear.

'Did you expect your father today?'

'No. It seems he has decided to call on us unannounced.'

Fighting the temptation to point out that Nathaniel had been known to commit the same crime himself, Hester gathered her nerve. Seeing her dour father-in-law was never a prospect she relished, and after Nathaniel's rash action the night of the ball she feared a scene even more awkward than normal.

But she wasn't to be cowed by a man's displeasure—and most definitely not by one who had interfered in her marriage.

'Never mind. Let's go in. We shouldn't keep a guest waiting.'

Leaving Nathaniel no time to reply—or for her courage to fail—Hester straightened her shoulders and sailed down the corridor to the parlour. Opening the door, she saw Mr Honeywell standing at one window, and caught the instantaneous tightening of his face as he turned and watched her enter the room.

'Good afternoon, sir. I hope you haven't been

kept too long.' She dipped a curtsey in civil greeting, perversely amused to see his annoyance increase at being forced to respond.

'Hester. I wasn't aware you were here.'

Mr Honeywell's disapproving eye fell on his son as Nathaniel appeared on the threshold behind her, and she was sure she felt both men tense. Trapped in the middle, there was only one way for her to go, and Hester seized it with both hands.

She waved towards the comfortable-looking sofas as though she'd lived in the house all her life rather than having arrived only that morning. 'Won't you sit down? Tea will be along shortly.'

To set an example Hester took a seat, a glimmer of relief passing through as Mr Honeywell and Nathaniel did the same—albeit on opposite sides of the room and with the wariness of two circling lions. A taut atmosphere descended, some unspoken tension between father and son that neither seemed willing to break.

'Nathaniel invited me to accompany him here to London and I was delighted to accept,' Hester cut in smoothly, affecting not to have noticed that the temperature of the room seemed to have dropped below freezing. 'I've had a tour of the first warehouse already this morning and enjoyed myself immensely.'

Mr Honeywell's already forbidding frown grew deeper. 'The warehouses are not intended as entertainment,' he replied coldly, making Hester feel as though icy water dripped down her spine. 'Especially when Nathaniel ought to be working hard to catch up on what he missed two nights ago.'

Beside her on the sofa Nathaniel bristled, and only just in time Hester managed to stop herself from laying a hand on his arm. 'Entertainment was not the intention,' she countered mildly. 'I was interested to better understand what the company trades in, and now I know.'

Her father-in-law's lips thinned. Clearly he wasn't keen on something—either the idea of Hester invading his kingdom or the fact that she spoke against him, but Nathaniel stole any chance for her to find out which caused the most offence.

'Was there something you wished to speak with me about, sir?' Nathaniel rested one expensive boot on the opposite knee, so carefully casual Hester knew he felt anything but. 'Something specific that couldn't wait until I had returned to the office?'

'Yes.'

Mr Honeywell ventured that far and no further, pausing to flick Hester a cool glance. It was clearly her cue to leave; instead of meekly exiting her own parlour as she would have once, however, she politely averted her eyes, gazing out of the window to give Nathaniel and his father the illusion of privacy.

If Mr Honeywell wanted to call in with no warning that was his choice—but he wouldn't chase her out with his bad temper...something he seemed to realise when she didn't move.

'I've had word from one of our suppliers in Spain. They have a new variety of fine lace that I think will suit very well for next season, provided we can fetch it back to England in time.'

Out of the corner of her eye Hester saw Nathaniel nod. 'I read the letter. Is there a problem?'

'No. The voyage is mostly arranged already. The only thing to settle on is the exact date you and the crew will depart. I want that decided today.'

It took a second for Nathaniel to realise what his father had said. The sharp turn of Hester's head was the first warning sign, and it helped the pieces fall into place.

'I'm sorry. Did you say when *I* will depart?'

At Mr Honeywell's curt nod Nathaniel sat forward. 'I've only been back for two months. Surely you wouldn't expect me to go to sea again so soon—or indeed at all, given what happened last time?'

He watched his father's expression darken, sure his own must be following suit. He had no way of knowing how similar they looked at that moment—two faces set and each man determined not to be bested by the other. On the very edge of his field of vision he could just make out Hester, sitting very still, no doubt waiting with bated breath to hear what would come next.

Nathaniel pressed on. 'No other company sends a partner on every voyage. I don't feel it's necessary for me to be present on this one.'

'Someone needs to keep a close eye on the goods. That much is essential.' Mr Honeywell's countenance didn't soften and his chilly stare held no emotion at all. 'I'd go myself, as I always did, but with this cursed cane I'm too unsteady on my feet to weather the rough seas. I confess to some disappointment that you appear afraid to take my place.'

Impatience flooded Nathaniel's entire body, alongside a hit to his pride at his father's barb. 'It was never *essential*. You only insisted it was. You never really had to go away for all those months that added up to years. Nothing and nobody made you, and the company wouldn't have fallen apart if you'd stayed at home.'

Sitting across from his father, Nathaniel felt the anger he had held on to ever since that day in the snowy shack rise all over again. A list of Mr Honeywell's sins flashed through his mind— none of them ever atoned for or even acknowledged in any way. By following his father's example Nathaniel had hurt Hester beyond endurance, and now it seemed history was beckoning him to repeat it.

'Mother is left alone so often I think she has become numb to it. But I don't imagine it was easy for her, especially when you could so easily have stayed.'

He felt Hester draw a little further into the sofa at his side, but he didn't take his eye from his father's rigid face. The cool detachment he saw there was fading fast, replaced by growing temper like the sky clouding before a storm.

'Why are you bringing your mother into this? What relevance does she have to this conversation?'

Mr Honeywell's voice crackled with restrained ire, the lash of it making Hester visibly uneasy. Nathaniel's fingers itched to reach for her hand, but he resisted, unwilling to pull her into his father's line of fire.

'I seek merely to illustrate a point. You are gone for long stretches at a time, and have never stopped to consider the consequences or whether it was even worthwhile. I've given the same thing much thought since my return, and I have decided I won't sail again.'

He sat back, resolutely refusing to let his aggravation show even as his heart leapt savagely. Once he would have agreed to his father's demands without question, but with Hester within touching distance for the first time Nathaniel felt he had something to lose. They were just starting to discover each other, finally setting out together in a marriage that might turn out to be more than a practicality…perhaps even something more precious than the finest Spanish lace.

Still, he couldn't pretend it was an easy choice. It went against his every instinct, and the tiniest thread of doubt wended its way through the tapestry of his decision, tainting his certainty. For years the Honeywell Trading Company had been the love of his life and it was difficult to think otherwise—even if it seemed that title might now be claimed by Hester, the only rival for his heart the business had ever had.

The air in the parlour grew heavy with oppressive silence. The clock on the mantel ticked away and a fire curled in the grate, but none of the three people moved until Mr Honeywell rose stiffly.

'It seems you are not yourself this morning. Another disappointment.' He looked down at Nathaniel, the knuckles at the handle of his cane shining white with strain. 'I have meetings now, and more again later. Call on me tomorrow to conclude the business we should have finished today.'

'There's no need. I've made my feelings plain.'

'Your *feelings*? Yes.'

Mr Honeywell glanced at Hester with distaste, Nathaniel's hackles rising in response.

'As I said. Call tomorrow. I would talk with you alone.'

Nathaniel got to his feet, but his father was already moving for the door. It opened as he reached it and a maid carrying a laden tray entered, shrinking back against the wall as Mr Honeywell barged past as though she wasn't even there.

Standing in the middle of the parlour, Nathaniel watched his father's retreating back, an unhappy mix of emotions welling up inside him. The young maid hesitated in the doorway, only coming forward when he forced a smile.

'I apologise. My father can be careless at times.'

She set the tray down and left, leaving Nathaniel and Hester alone. Still fixed on the open door, he didn't see Hester get up, and the soft brush of her hand against his made him start.

'Nathaniel?'

Turning, he saw concern in her pale face that made him run a weary hand over his own. 'I rather wish you hadn't seen that.'

'I'm sorry. Perhaps I should have left the room when it was clear your father wanted me to, but in truth I didn't care to give him the satisfaction.'

'No. You did well. He's far too used to people jumping to obey his every whim.'

Including me, Nathaniel finished grimly as he returned to the sofa and dropped heavily onto it.

He'd won this skirmish but worse was to come, their meeting tomorrow sure to be unpleasant whether his father got his way or not. Already a weight had begun to settle in his gut, only growing as Hester came to sit beside him.

She looked down at her hands, clasped neatly on her lap, apparently searching for the right way to begin. He knew what was coming, although that didn't make it any more welcome when the inevitable question arrived.

'Have you really decided not to sail?'

Somewhere deep inside he felt a twinge at the faint hope in her voice, but Nathaniel nodded slowly. 'As I said, it was never really necessary. My father's obsessive desire for control over every aspect of the business meant he supervised every voyage and then expected the same from me. I suppose it should have occurred to me much earlier that there was no real need for it, but at the time the company overshadowed everything else in my life and I had no reason to ask questions.'

He rubbed his forehead. A slight ache was gathering behind it—perhaps the pressure of too many thoughts inside his skull. On the one hand the Honeywell Trading Company demanded his unwavering devotion, while on the other hand sat Hester, and it was a novel thing, once unthinkable, to acknowledge which way he wanted to lean.

'I don't want to be the kind of person he is. I'm not sure it reflects well on a man to be leaving his wife alone so much and for so little reason.'

'I see.' Hester still examined her fingers, only the slightest hint of colour in her cheeks betraying whatever she was feeling. 'An admirable sentiment, but I wouldn't want to be the cause of any rift with your father. I don't ask you to choose.'

'I'm aware of that. Any choice is mine alone.'

'And the one you've made is to stay at home? With me?'

'Yes. I promise.'

There could be no going back now he'd said it out loud. The die had been cast and any hesitations and torn loyalties would have to be swallowed or denied, no matter how they sat heavy as a stone in Nathaniel's stomach. He'd declared his feelings for Hester as clearly as he dared while the spectre of his secrets still hovered, casting an invisible barrier between them that meant he could never truly let her in.

She might not be so keen for me to stay if she knew how badly I was tainted, but I owe her my active presence in our marriage, and to make the effort to heal the damage I did before.

The vow wasn't quite enough to completely chase away his unease, but it was the best Nathaniel could do. With Hester sitting so close it was difficult to concentrate, anyway, and he found himself reaching for her before he even knew he'd moved.

'I hope you won't mind my hanging around Shardlow, getting under your feet. When will you go back? I need to stay in London a while longer, but you're welcome to return home if you'd like.'

'Tired of my company already?'

Hester raised an eyebrow, although Nathaniel caught a whisper-soft sigh as his fingers traced the veins at her wrist.

'Trying to get rid of me when I've only just arrived?'

'Never. I just thought…given my father's proximity…'

'He doesn't frighten me. Perhaps once I wasn't so brave, but I find now things are different.'

Nathaniel could well believe it. 'So I've realised. I almost feel sorry for him if you've made up your mind to stand your ground.'

She met his eye, the quiet determination he saw there more admirable than she knew.

'The very last thing I want in all the world is more conflict. I understand how important the company is to him, and to you, and I never want to come in between—but I won't allow him to make me feel the way I did five years ago ever again. I'm not a young girl any longer and your father holds no sway over me now.'

Beneath his fingertips Nathaniel felt the unhurried beat of Hester's pulse and wondered if she could tell how his had stepped up. It was almost a declaration of war and he had to question, if the worst were to happen and his father decided to cross her again, which side would be victorious.

It was impossible to call.

Chapter Twelve

'Where are we going?'

Nathaniel sounded slightly wary as Hester guided him down Grosvenor Street, the air once again bitingly cold and snapping at her fingertips. All around them the impatient bustle of London stretched as far as the eye could see, fashionable couples parading slowly in expensive clothes and the rattle of phaetons making it difficult for Hester to hear herself think.

'And, while I consider, what's in the bag?'

Hester swallowed a smile at her husband's suspicion, holding the bag in question more tightly. 'You'll see soon enough. We're almost there.'

He gave her a narrow look, although the skin around his eye creased. 'Should I be worried?'

'It's difficult to say. I suppose you'll have to wait to find out.'

They walked on, admiring the elegant houses that reared up on either side, until the wall surrounding one of the Royal Parks grew closer. Hester made directly for the gate, the grass beyond it sparkling with frost beneath hard, bright sunshine.

'A promenade, Hester? A bit cold for pointless walking to and fro, isn't it?'

Despite his mild objections Nathaniel turned in the direction of Kensington Gardens, the place where London's best and brightest gathered to peacock and preen, only to look surprised when Hester instead tugged him in the opposite direction.

'Not a promenade. Something altogether more exciting.'

'I thought showing off to strangers was the pinnacle of amusement for young ladies?'

'And gentlemen, I'll thank you to remember. It has its place, but not this morning.'

Nathaniel allowed her to lead him across the grass and onwards, until at last Hester felt him stop dead.

'Surely you're not serious?'

The Serpentine stretched out ahead, its usually rippling surface glassy with ice so thick it glowed milky in the sun. Skaters moved effortlessly over the frozen waters, some skilled and some less so but all with faces pink with enjoyment, and the air was filled with shouts and laughter that echoed in Hester's ears.

'I most certainly am. Why else would I have brought these with us?'

Reaching into the bag, she pulled out a set of new metal skates and with a flourish handed them to a bewildered-looking Nathaniel. He took them without a word, turning them over as if he'd never seen anything like them before, and shot a confused glance at Hester as she retrieved a pair of her own.

'Where did you get these? And how did you know the Serpentine was frozen?'

'Arless told me this morning. She and a couple of the other maids went sliding on their half-day yesterday, so I crept out while you were working after breakfast to buy some skates. It took some time to track these down, but I'm glad I found them eventually.'

'But…why? Why go to all that bother?'

Hester wrinkled her nose. 'What do you mean, why? Because skating is fun! Don't tell me you've never been before?'

Nathaniel ran his fingers over the gleaming blades, saying nothing, and Hester could have kicked herself. Of course he'd never skated. It was an entertaining but ultimately useless pastime, and the very kind of thing his father would never have allowed. As an adult it wouldn't have occurred to Nathaniel to leave his desk and venture onto the ice, and Hester cursed herself for drawing attention to all the happiness Nathaniel had been taught to forgo.

'I'm sorry. I thought…after what happened yesterday…perhaps you might appreciate something to take your mind off your troubles. I know you have a meeting with your father and might not be looking forward to it.'

He looked up, any sign of his misgivings fading quickly. 'That's very considerate of you. I appreciate the thought.'

Hester hitched her smile back into place, although she couldn't help another twinge of guilt. Distracting Nathaniel from whatever feelings his father conjured *was* a prominent reason for why she had dragged him out, but not the only one. Her own thoughts were jangled and uncertain, and anything to push them from the forefront of her mind was most welcome.

The unpleasant confrontation in the parlour yesterday had left a sour taste in her mouth that even Nathaniel's promise not to sail couldn't completely wash away. Instead, it was that very thing which made her hesitate: try as she might, she couldn't shake a niggling doubt that wondered if he might regret his decision, his devotion to the Honeywell Trading Company something so ingrained she feared nothing else could ever compete.

But she had to trust his word. He'd made a vow, of sorts, and she had no choice but to hold him to it and place her faith in the changes that had won him her heart—even if he wasn't yet fully aware that he held it in his keeping.

'So, shall we go out on the ice? I don't pretend to be particularly good, but I feel sometimes that's the point.'

A bench stood nearby, and Hester sat down to strap the skates to her sturdiest pair of boots. After only a breath of hesitation Nathaniel did the same, watching his wife's example until both were balanced on thin metal blades.

'Is this not dangerous?'

'It can be, if the ice isn't thick enough, but don't worry. Diana and I skated around Thame Magna's duck pond often as children, and I can count the number of times we fell through on one hand.'

Trying not to laugh at Nathaniel's fleeting look of alarm, Hester took his arm and together they approached the frozen lake, moving like ungainly ducks on their skates. At the water's edge Hester took a breath, feeling it burn in her lungs as she took first one careful step, and then another, until she stood away from the bank with nothing to reach for if she fell.

'Are you coming?' she called over her shoulder to Nathaniel, who was eyeing the ice dubiously. 'The first step is the hardest, but after that I'm sure you'll be a natural.'

She heard him mutter something under his

breath, but he followed her all the same, placing his skates down gingerly like an infant learning to walk. Almost immediately he wobbled, and Hester glided back to take his hand, helping him slip away from the bank and out towards the centre of the lake.

Nathaniel's fingers gripped hers like a vice, and in a sudden reversal of their usual dynamic he clung to her for support. The face below the brim of his hat was uncertain and Hester patted his arm. 'Don't worry. I won't let go.'

'I'm not worried.' Nathaniel sniffed dismissively although any onlooker might be forgiven for not quite believing him. 'I'm just finding my feet.'

With admirable determination he pushed forward, moving unsteadily, but moving all the same. A group of younger men, barely more than boys, came speeding past in a graceful curve and Nathaniel watched them go, the light of competition finally kindling in his uncovered eye.

'Do people race on here?'

'Sometimes. Why? Do you want to try?'

Regretfully he shook his head. 'I think perhaps I ought to practise first. No point in trying to run before I can walk.'

'A wise decision. Shall we start gently, with a slow lap of the lake?'

Together Hester and Nathaniel slid onwards, cutting a glittering path across the ice. The soft hiss of their skates was pleasant, and the sun illuminated the park's beauty with brilliant clarity, but it was the feel of Nathaniel's hand in hers that set Hester's heart skipping like a leaf in a breeze. It felt so natural now to have him close—something she'd never dared to dream—and a cold shadow fell over her at the idea he might still change his mind and leave her alone.

Trust him, Hester. That's all you can do.

'What do you think? Am I a fast learner?'

Nathaniel's grin pulled her from her fretting at once. 'Oh, absolutely. I felt sure you'd spend all morning on the seat of your breeches, but it seems I was wrong.'

His chin lifted a little. 'I have my suspicions that you may be humouring me.'

'Not at all.' Hester hid her mouth behind her hand so Nathaniel couldn't see. 'How can you say such a thing?'

'Because you said that in exactly the same sort of tone my nurse used to use when I'd eaten all my vegetables.'

This time there was no hope of concealing her amusement. 'Did I? I can only apologise. I do hope you don't feel slighted.'

'Slighted? No.' Nathaniel raised a brow, and then the gleam returned to his eye to make Hester immediately on her guard. 'Issued with a challenge? Yes.'

Before she could utter any kind of warning he

let go of her hand and darted away, moving over the ice with a speed that made up for his complete lack of technique. His posture was wrong, for a start, leaning so far back Hester knew what was coming before it even happened.

'Nathaniel! Not so quickly!'

She skated after him, drawing alongside at the precise moment he overbalanced and began to topple, grabbing wildly for something to save him as he fell—which, unfortunately for Hester, turned out to be her cloak.

They collapsed in a heap of skirts, skates and tangled limbs, mercifully accompanied by a dull thud rather than the sharp crack of breaking ice. With unintentional gallantry Nathaniel cushioned Hester's fall, although the wheeze that escaped as she landed on his chest, knocking the air out of him, was less gentlemanly.

'Hester…when did you get so heavy?'

She rolled to one side, freeing him, and lay for a moment to catch her breath. The ice beneath her back was hard and flat, but the sky above reached out soft periwinkle-blue, the occasional wisp of cloud like a newborn lamb frisking towards the horizon. Out of the corner of her eye Hester could see fellow skaters peering over in concern, and from somewhere inside she felt a laugh bubble up to the surface.

Turning her head, she caught sight of Nathaniel's winded face, and the dam holding back her laughter broke completely. It rang out over the frozen water, uncontrollable despite the chill rapidly seeping in from her wet dress. She just couldn't help it, and when Nathaniel joined in Hester wondered—vaguely, above the aching muscles in her stomach—if they would ever stop.

Eventually she managed to snatch enough air to speak. 'What is it they say about pride coming before a fall?'

Nathaniel sat up, his chest still heaving, finally back in control. 'Yes, but I could tell you were impressed. Don't try to deny it.'

'I couldn't even if I wanted to.'

'That's all I wanted to hear. Let me help you up.'

He leaned over her, his shadow falling between Hester and the endless sky. His hat had come off in their tumble and her bonnet had come loose, so there would be nothing to prevent him from bending to capture her lips—something that seemed to have occurred to Nathaniel, too, as Hester saw his jaw tighten suddenly and a thrill crept down her spine that was worlds apart from the cold touch of the ice.

She watched his gaze travel from her eyes to her mouth in a scalding track that chased away the February chill. Lying on her back with Nathaniel so close conjured up memories of other occasions when they had been in just such a situation, and Hester felt heat come roaring up from her neck to colour each cheek.

But he knew the rules. Nathaniel was as well versed in stiff social etiquette as Hester, even if there was reluctance on both sides as he took her hand and helped her to her feet.

'Your dress is soaked. You'll catch your death out here in the cold like that.'

Still a little dazed, Hester glanced down at her damp and dirtied skirts. 'I think you might be right. I'll have to return home to change.'

Nathaniel nodded, brushing a few specks of ice off the brim of his hat before replacing it neatly on his head. 'As much as I'd like to accompany you, it's probably about time I called on my father. Let me find you a cab to take you back to Areton Street.'

At the mention of Mr Honeywell Hester's insides clenched, although she fought hard to keep her expression clear. 'Thank you, but I can manage. You go to see your father.'

'Are you sure?'

Forcing a brittle smile, Hester nodded. The knot buried low in her innards twisted tighter, but there was nothing she could do to unpick it while Nathaniel stood before her, and even less when together they left the ice and removed their skates. Somehow, as Hester put them back into their bag, she felt as though she was packing away something else as well, signalling the end of something she couldn't quite put her finger on.

She watched him go in silence, his broad shoulders unmistakable even from behind. As he reached the edge of the park and disappeared from view Hester swallowed down unease, the taste of it bitter and unwanted but clinging to her tongue.

It would be so easy for him to go back on his word. For all his promises, the man who had so wounded her all those years ago might still lurk beneath the surface, ready to replace this new Nathaniel she was growing to love. He'd given her little reason to worry so far, but there was always the chance that his father's influence might prevail—and then everything they were building would lie in ruins at the feet of Nathaniel's ambition, and her heart in pieces along with it.

The offices of the Honeywell Trading Company were just as stern and austere-looking as their owner, and Nathaniel felt himself tense as he climbed the steps. Despite the sunshine outside, the corridor that greeted him was dark, its unenthusiastic welcome mirroring the one he had come to expect from the man he was there to meet.

He tapped on a door that bore his father's name on a grand brass plaque and waited with rising impatience to be received. The sooner their showdown began the sooner it would end and he could put it behind him, moving onwards with the new life he and Hester were carving out together.

'Enter.'

Mr Honeywell's dry voice came from the other side of the door, and Nathaniel took a second to ready himself before turning the handle and stepping inside.

'Nathaniel. At last.'

Seated behind his vast desk like a king on a throne, his father put down his pen and sat back in his chair. He flicked a hand towards a matching one on the other side of the desk and watched as Nathaniel dropped into it, his sharp eyes missing nothing while simultaneously seeing little of which to approve.

'Your sleeve is dirty.'

Resisting the urge to stand straight up again, Nathaniel shrugged. 'I took a fall while I was skating this morning.'

'While you were *what*?'

'Skating. On the Serpentine. It's frozen over.'

Mr Honeywell's face contorted briefly, as though he was trying to understand a foreign language, before settling into weary disgust. 'I see. It seems I have called you to meet with me just in time.'

A flicker of irritation stirred in Nathaniel's chest but his father pushed on.

'I imagine you know why I want to see you. You can't be ignorant of my thoughts.'

'No, sir. I'm well aware of what you'll want to discuss. My only question is why you think it necessary, given there's no possibility of me changing my mind.'

It was as though he hadn't spoken at all. Mr Honeywell brushed off his son's words like flies, lacing his fingers together and studying Nathaniel over the top of them.

'The voyage to Spain is fixed for a week from now. That will give you plenty of time to prepare yourself for travel.'

The irritation beneath Nathaniel's breastbone glowed hotter, becoming close to anger now at his father's cool condescension, but he forced himself to remain calm.

'I've made my stance perfectly clear. I won't be going on any more unnecessary sailings and I won't be leaving Hester alone for months at a time. My mind is made up and there's nothing else to be said on the matter.'

Mr Honeywell's jaw tightened visibly, his cold demeanour under threat. 'You've already spent far more time with her than you ought. I've poured everything into this business, and I won't allow it to be squandered because you've had your head turned—once again—by some pretty chit of a wife.'

'Don't speak of Hester that way.' Nathaniel's

anger leapt immediately higher, curling around him like a flame. 'I still care about the business. I just seek a balance this time, rather than to lose myself entirely in the trade as you do. I'm not choosing one to the exclusion of the other— there's room enough for both, if only you'd see it.'

'Of course there isn't.' His father's eyes were narrowed, fixing Nathaniel with an icy, unwavering stare. 'Did you learn nothing from my example? From that of your grandfather, even? Ever since your return you've spent half your time mooning around after Hester. Sooner or later she'll grow tired of you—and then what will you have that was worth sacrificing your duty to both the company and yourself?'

Nathaniel shook his head at once, although the faintest whisper began to unfurl, as thin but as permeating as smoke, to remind him that he'd had a similar thought himself. If Hester ever learned the truth of his time in Algiers her feelings for him would *have* to change—perhaps not reverting back to contempt, but almost certainly marring her affection... How could they not? One so tainted as himself wasn't worthy of her regard, only her ignorance standing between him and ruin.

'She will not,' Nathaniel growled, attempting to ignore the sly murmur in the back of his mind. 'I have no cause to think it.'

'No? You're certain of that, are you?' Mr Honeywell's mouth thinned. 'You forget I'm not an easily fooled man. You're not the only one who has seen the world. I know what happens in some of the places we've visited, and I have a good idea of what happened to you.'

Nathaniel's throat dried instantly. He sat up straighter in his chair, suddenly conscious of the rapid beat of his heart. 'I don't know what you mean.'

'I think you do. I think you know exactly what conclusion I came to when you arrived home with a labourer's muscles and the mark of a foreman's whip on your face.'

Watching for a reaction, Mr Honeywell settled his forearms more comfortably on the desk's leather top. He looked exactly as he did when thrashing out a difficult contract, Nathaniel realised distantly, only it was his son in the firing line and not some supplier.

'Yours wasn't some feeble love match, Nathaniel. It was all business. How can any silly infatuation of Hester's survive once the cold reality of your time away is revealed to her? Her romantic notions of a returning hero will be dashed once she has learned the unsavoury truth of what she is married to, and I believe you know it.'

His father's mouth twisted into a sneer that Nathaniel wanted, with sudden violence, to strike from his face.

'I can't pretend I'm not disappointed, either,'

he went on. 'To think my own son could sink so low, and after everything I taught you of how to be a man…'

Nathaniel's eye glowed hot and bright. At one time his father's contempt would have cut him to the quick, but now he barely felt the rake of its claws. 'Fortunate for me, then, that I'm no longer a boy scrabbling for your approval,' he ground out. 'It's Hester's respect I want now, above anyone else's—even yours.'

'That much is clear from your behaviour these past months. A shame, then, that such a thing could be shattered with but a few words. Women are so easily convinced…'

Nathaniel hesitated, pulled up short by the threat. His blood felt hotter than ever before and his jaw ached where he clenched it, the tendons of his neck stretched tight. It was as though he'd been struck squarely in that soft place only Hester knew about, his vulnerable underbelly sliced open by his father's cruel words.

'You don't know Hester. If you did you'd see how wrong you are. And how would she find out? Are you suggesting you might be the one to tell her?'

Still with his arms on the desktop, Mr Honeywell examined his hands. All of a sudden he looked tired in a way Nathaniel hadn't noticed before—doubtless from untold hours poring over his books, and if circumstances had been different Nathaniel might have felt sympathy. Instead he could think of nothing but Hester's face as it had been that morning out on the ice, flushed pink with cold and her eyes bright with life and humour.

How differently would those eyes look at him if all was revealed? It was the fear that had haunted him ever since his feelings for her had started to blossom into something more than mere tolerance, and his father was seeing straight through him as though he had a window into Nathaniel's soul.

'I'm advising you to review your priorities before it's too late.'

Like someone playing a game of cards, Mr Honeywell had an ace up his sleeve, and now he laid it before Nathaniel with cruel finality.

'Do your job properly or I'll find someone else who can. I was considering making your cousin Stephen my heir before you returned. He's a young man with promise, and I very much doubt he would allow some foolish fancy to distract him from his duty.'

'You would disinherit me?' Still reeling from his father's previous jab, Nathaniel felt as if he'd been punched all over again, his head ringing with too many voices arguing among themselves. 'If I refuse to go to Spain, leaving Hester alone again for absolutely no real reason after I have sworn I'd stay, you would strip me of my place in the company?'

'I would seriously consider it.'

Beneath his still-damp coat Nathaniel's skin prickled, gooseflesh rising on every inch. For most of his life the business had been the only thing of any importance to him, even during his captivity, and to be cut away from it would be like losing a limb. Part of him could scarcely believe his father would stoop so low, and yet another part knew there could be no mistake.

'I've given you no reason to do that. All my work is done, and more. The only thing I refuse to do is sail, when there's no call for my being aboard.'

Mr Honeywell flexed arthritic fingers spotted with ink from his pen. 'Your loyalty to your wife is misplaced as well as unnecessary. She was a merry enough widow while you were away for five years. I imagine she could spare you for a few weeks now with very little trouble.'

Nathaniel passed a hand across his face, the desire to wipe the sneer from his father's still overwhelmingly strong. When he'd walked into this office he had imagined an argument—not this merciless spotlight on all his insecurities that made him feel exposed and raw.

As wrenching as it was to admit, his father was right. Of course Hester could do without him—and for considerably longer than a few weeks. He thought again of her that very morning, her lips parted on that beautiful laugh, and his stomach dropped like a stone. She was so free and vibrant, and what was he in comparison?

Dirty. Humbled. A disappointment, and hardly what I know a man should be at all.

Sooner or later Hester would come to see him for what he was, even without his father's interference, and then what would happen? How could he inspire her respect when for years he'd known none, so soiled and unworthy he had hardly been able to call himself a man when once he'd been so unbending?

Perhaps Mr Honeywell sensed his son's indecision. Nathaniel had read once that sharks could smell blood in the water and home in to finish off an injured seal and his father struck him as doing just the same—a predator taking down its wounded prey.

'People are fickle, Nathaniel. Money and duty are not.' He spoke more levelly now, that edge of anger smoothed out into his usual flatness. 'Don't abandon both for something that won't last. Go to Spain and forget all this nonsense.'

Nathaniel looked up, sure the pain in his innards must be blazing from his eye. 'What of last time you sent me off on a pointless voyage? You lied to me about Hester's condition to get me on that boat. What have you to say about that?'

Serenely unmoved, Mr Honeywell lifted one

shoulder. 'Only that you have no place to lecture me about honesty when you're the one keeping secrets from your wife. You've no intention of telling Hester about your time in Algiers and we both know it. Unless you'd rather I did you the favour of hinting at it myself?'

A skewer of agony impaled Nathaniel, lancing through his chest directly over the place where his heart leapt with hopeless speed. There was no running from it or turning away, and in that moment he felt true despair at the unavoidable choice in front of him.

If he left for Spain he would disappoint Hester—but for how long would her hurt truly last? She'd survived without him for five years, and he couldn't deny she had become far more independent before his return. She didn't *need* him, as she'd been quick to point out, but she seemed to *want* him—and that alone was enough to make his uncertainty a hundred times worse.

But Father has just said out loud what I've suspected all along. Not that his word means much to me any longer.

His relationship with Hester would change once she knew his secrets, and the notion of falling in her esteem was more than he could bear. If he chose to leave she would be stung, but either way her affection for him would one day wither—or, worse, turn to the kind of pity one might feel for a wounded animal rather than a proud man.

And don't forget his threat of disinheritance. Once Hester is finished with me the company will be all I have left, and not even that if I refuse to sail.

He glanced at his father, who met his eye with a face so expressionless Nathaniel wanted to shake him, shout at him—anything to make him realise the suffering he was causing his only son. But Mr Honeywell would never understand. He had never loved anything or anyone as much as money and power, and to try to explain why Nathaniel felt torn in two would be like trying to explain to the dead.

'It seems I have little choice.'

Nathaniel could hardly bring himself to speak, the bile in his throat so bitter it choked him. There was no way out of the position he found himself in other than to hurt both Hester and himself—although surely any pain on Hester's part would be far shorter-lived than his own? She was everything a woman could be and more, and he should count himself lucky that he'd been allowed even such a short time basking in the warmth of her good graces.

'I'm not the one who put you in this situation. That was entirely your fault. I didn't raise you to forget your responsibilities and devote yourself quite pointlessly to a woman only yours by previous arrangement.'

Nathaniel's eye burned with emotion, but he determined not to let it show. At the very least he wouldn't give his father the satisfaction of knowing how complete a victory he had won, in less than an hour shattering all of Nathaniel's dreams for the future and scattering their remnants to the four winds.

'Of course. Nobody could ever say you are anything but a shining example of ruthless ambition. If I came to care for Hester it was never learned from you.'

Mr Honeywell blinked in the same slow, reptilian manner that had always made Nathaniel wonder if he was entirely human.

'I imagine you intend that as a rebuke. But I'll never be sorry for training you for a profitable future and to ensure the success of the family trade as your great-grandfather and grandfather would have desired.' He picked up his pen, and as abruptly as his brutal attack had started, it was over. 'Now we've reached an accord perhaps you'd take your leave? I have other appointments.'

But Nathaniel didn't move.

I'll have to tell Hester. I'll have to return to Areton Street, to the woman I love, and tell her that I'm leaving all over again when I promised I wouldn't. My word will mean even less to her

than it did before, and the cruellest part will be
knowing that she'll think I wanted it this way.

Sick unhappiness roiled within him like a churning sea, tossing Nathaniel on savage waves. He knew what had to be done, but there was nothing he wanted less than to look into Hester's face and destroy her trust, along with it the new respect she'd had for him which he had held so precious.

'Nathaniel? I said I have other appointments.'

His father didn't even lift his head, fixed on whatever he was writing in one of his interminable ledgers. It occurred to Nathaniel that he ought to resent the snub, but he was barely aware of anything but the pounding of both his head and his heart as he finally got to his feet.

'I'll stay in London another couple of days, to settle my affairs here, but I'll suggest Hester goes back to Shardlow ahead of me. I don't imagine she'll feel inclined to stay with me once I've told her I'm breaking my word.'

'Whatever you think best.'

Mr Honeywell sounded almost bored—bored by the misery of his only son, and completely unable to empathise with any finer feelings at all.

'Close the door on your way out.'

Chapter Thirteen

Diana's face was blank with confusion, bewilderment making her look even younger than usual in the early sunlight. 'I don't understand. How can Nathaniel be going away again? He's only just returned!'

Hester continued to stare out of Farleigh's morning room window at the gardens beyond, laid out in a patchwork of greens and browns. Her eyes stung with unshed tears but she held them back, determined not to break her vow to never let them fall.

'A buying trip to Spain. It appears his presence is now essential, despite his assuring me of exactly the opposite only the day before last. He's stayed behind in London until tomorrow to make arrangements, and then he'll come back to Shardlow until the ship sails next week.'

She could sense Diana's concern without even looking in her direction. Her sister had still been in her nightgown when Hester had arrived just after dawn, not having slept a wink after the journey home from Areton Street, but Diana had rallied at once, with maids coming from all directions to dress her at the first sight of Hester's tight and pale face.

Now the two sat in silence, neither sure what to say to such a turn of events that had blindsided them both.

'But he came to the ball specifically to please you, leaving all else behind. I saw with my own eyes how he could look at nothing but you all evening. How can it be he does this now?'

Slowly Hester shook her head. It hurt to move: her neck and shoulders ached from being held stiff all night, even her own muscles turning against her. Deep in the black hollow of her chest her heart beat with the solemn rhythm of a funeral march, wretchedness so all-encompassing there was no way round it. It was like the first days of her marriage all over again—hopes dashed and promises broken and knowing herself to be a fool for believing in the affection of an inconstant man.

'We must have been mistaken, thinking we saw some partiality on his side that wasn't there after all.'

'I refuse to believe that. Nobody could have watched you together that night and failed to see he was in love with you.'

'Don't.' Finally Hester tore her eyes from the window, and Diana flinched a little at the powerful suffering written plain across her sister's countenance. 'Please. Don't say that word.'

Those four little letters were like daggers between Hester's ribs, and she almost bent double with the pain of hearing them. No matter how hard she tried to think of anything other than the conversation of the night before her mind returned to it so endlessly she feared she was losing her wits, playing over and over again in a merry-go-round of misery.

The instant she'd seen Nathaniel's face she had been able to tell something was different. He hadn't needed to make a sound: his eye refused to meet hers and she had known, with the instinctive dread of one fearing the worst, that he had changed his mind.

His explanation, when it came, was almost inconsequential, no feeble excuse even half as painful as when he'd entered the room and she'd seen he'd rather have been *anywhere* else but there.

Dimly, she wondered again exactly when he had decided to grind her hopes into dust— although it hardly mattered now. At which particular moment had he realised the call of adventure and profit was so much more appealing than keeping his promise to a wife he hadn't even chosen for himself? Now it seemed so obvious that Hester should never have dreamed she could compete with such excitement—and it was her own fault for imagining otherwise.

'He can never have felt that way towards me. Perhaps there was some mild attraction, but he has shown me beyond all doubt the value of his promises and what his priorities truly are. If I ever thought myself one of them, I'm ashamed to own it.'

Her mouth felt parched, but no drink of water would make a difference. Humiliation and regret welled up to claw at her throat as she thought how easily Nathaniel had fooled her yet again, perhaps his every smile a lie.

When she recalled the times she'd delighted in his touch, in the strong circle of his arms as they came around her, her gut fluttered with anguish like a trapped bird and she had to clench her jaw to keep the torment inside.

'But, Hester… Are you certain there can be no mistake?'

Diana's forlorn hope might have broken Hester's heart all over again if it hadn't already been crushed by expensive boots. Lady Lavendon had never known the searing sting of rejection and Hester found she was grateful for that at least, hoping her little sister would never feel as desolate as she herself did now.

'Impossible. He has *chosen* to go. He doesn't have to—he explained to me himself there's no cause for him to sail. It's the same situation as before, but worse now. Five years ago he left without so much as saying goodbye, but this time he has broken his word on top of everything else.' Her voice quavered slightly and she reined it in at once, hardening herself against rising emotion. 'I should have known he couldn't change. When he first arrived I had suspicions, but I allowed myself to be persuaded. What is this if not proof of the real man inside? The one behind the charm and the handsome face I thought was finally mine?'

A priceless collection of rings glittered on Diana's slim fingers and she twisted them as she thought, her sharp mind searching for a solution even as Hester knew there was none.

'But he might only be away for a short time. There's nothing to say it will be years.'

'It isn't the duration. It's the principle. He doesn't care enough to honour his promise to me. The pursuit of wealth is his first concern and all else a poor second, despite his assurances. Actions speak far louder than words and there can be no confusion.'

'Could you not ask him to stay?'

Hester settled her own wedding ring, its gleam suddenly almost mocking. 'No. He's made his choice. If I was foolish enough to think there was something between us that meant he had changed, then I won't embarrass myself further by begging him not to leave.' At her sister's attempt to interrupt she held up a weary hand. 'It isn't pride—I know that's what you're thinking. It's self-preservation. I won't keep throwing myself down the same well when I know the only outcome is drowning.'

She turned back to the window, unable to bear the sorrow in Diana's eyes. Clouds were gathering on the horizon, their swollen grey bellies threatening rain and casting shadows over Farleigh's pristine grounds. They were the perfect mirror for Hester's state of mind, bleak and dark and blocking out the sunlight Nathaniel had once brought to her life.

'So what will you do?'

'What is there to be done other than wait for him to return? I managed well enough alone before. There's no reason I shouldn't again.'

'This time things are different, though. Given all that has happened these past months and how I know you feel...' Diana didn't finish her sentence but she didn't have to. Hester knew exactly what she meant.

Memories of her time with Nathaniel would haunt her relentlessly, this separation nothing like the last. A small spark of the pride she'd denied flared at the insinuation that she couldn't do as well on her own, but it fizzled at the undeniable fact that Diana was right: Nathaniel's essence hung in every room, his laugh a silent echo and the image of his face lurking just out of sight. He would be everywhere and nowhere at the same time, and being at Shardlow without him, now she had known what she had thought was his love, would be a torture she didn't know if she could endure.

Inner strength was one thing. Living with inescapable regret every day was quite another, and fresh despair swept over her just as the first drops of rain spattered against the glass.

But she hadn't reckoned on her sister's determination to make a plan.

'Why don't you come away with me for a while? Lavendon's house in Canterbury is so lovely and you've never been. We'd already thought to leave tomorrow morning, just for a couple of weeks, and a change of scene might do you good.'

Hester tried to find a smile, failed, and grimaced instead. 'You're kind to offer, and I truly appreciate it, but the very last thing I want to do is bring gloom into another of your houses. You and Lavendon go—I would far rather you enjoy yourself.'

But sometimes speaking with Diana was like talking to a wall. If there was something she didn't want to hear she would simply ignore it, just as she did now, carrying on as if Hester hadn't even opened her mouth.

'If you went back to Shardlow now to pack

your things we could leave promptly after breakfast tomorrow. The journey to Canterbury is so pretty, even if this rain keeps up, and only a very few hours long.'

More heavy droplets dashed against the window and Hester watched them skate downwards towards the ledge. For once she didn't have the energy to argue. Like a doll with the stuffing removed she felt empty, a husk with a splintered heart, and she had no desire to do anything but sleep and not wake up. Trying to stand against Diana was difficult at the best of times, and nigh on impossible when her sister's will so outweighed her own.

Hester attempted to find some last vestige of resistance. 'Shouldn't you at least speak with Lavendon before you issue an invitation? I can't imagine he'll want his sister-in-law tagging along on a romantic time away.'

Diana's nose wrinkled, as if she'd never heard anything more ridiculous in her life. 'He'll be delighted. You know how much he enjoys your company.'

It was hardly a surprise that the morning room door opened at that moment, Lord Lavendon's handsome head appearing round the jamb in search of his wife. He and Diana might have shared some kind of psychic connection, with the very man in question appearing at just the right time.

'Hester!' Lavendon's eyebrows rose as he caught sight of her hunched on the window seat. 'This is a fine and early visit. How are you and N—?'

Out of the corner of her eye Hester caught the minute shake of Diana's head, her white lace cap quivering ominously. Lavendon checked at once, glancing from one sister to the other before moving—with obedience if not understanding—to withdraw.

'Ah… Please excuse me. I recall I have something to do…elsewhere…'

'Wait. Before you go…' Diana rose quickly and rustled across the room to intercept his escape. 'You've no objection to Hess joining us at Newchurch Manor, have you? She's never seen the house, and I hope she will come with us tomorrow.'

With her back to the room Diana's face was hidden, but Hester knew exactly what unspoken message her sister must be conveying with her eyes. Lavendon looked to be reading her lips, obviously appreciating the gravity of the situation when a touch of concern so genuine it made Hester's throat constrict entered his expression.

'None whatsoever. The more the merrier.'

Hester took a second to smooth down the lap of her gown, partly to cover having nothing to say and partly to avoid having to see the look of tenderness passing between man and wife. Nathaniel would never look at her so fondly ever again—she knew that with hopeless certainty. Not now he had turned away and the home she'd thought they had been making was revealed to be clearly built on sand.

'You see? No problem at all.' Diana allowed Lavendon a gracious smile as he disappeared, closing the door behind him as gently as if a baby slept inside. 'He wants you to come and so do I. There's really nothing more to say on the matter other than *yes*.'

Clearly Diana considered the case settled. Hester, now tracing the sprigged pattern of her skirts, could feel a bright blue gaze waiting for her nod, but her head refused to do anything other than hang down like a wilted flower.

If she left in the morning Nathaniel wouldn't yet have returned from London. She wouldn't see him before he went, and would have no chance to wish him a safe passage and a swift return home. Ironically enough they'd be like ships in the night, sailing past each other without meeting or exchanging any words at all.

But her fingers tightened among the folds of her dress as another cold truth trickled down her spine, chilling her as it went.

Surely he wouldn't care whether she was there or not? If he had been bothered about being in her presence he wouldn't have chosen to leave her all alone, disappearing once again for a length of time neither of them could know for certain. At least if she was away herself she'd be spared having to say goodbye, risking traitorous tears and a voice that would shake far too much to conceal her feelings. It was small comfort to think her pride might remain intact, but it was the only one she had—the only life raft to cling to when all else was sunk.

Diana still watched her expectantly, worry etched on her face despite an encouraging smile. Her love for Hester was pure and uncomplicated, unwavering and fiercely real—everything Nathaniel's was not, and, although it shredded her soul to admit it, Hester knew there was only one choice.

'If you're truly sure, then, yes. Thank you. I'd be happy to go with you.'

But she didn't mean it. Even as Diana came to take her hand, holding it with the unbreakable affection only a sister could show and then gathering Hester into her arms, it felt as though something inside her had died.

In truth, Hester didn't believe she'd ever feel happy again.

Nathaniel barely noticed anything during the ride back from London, his mind so full of Hester he hardly knew which road he was taking. For the most part he let his horse do the navigating, the grey gelding heading instinctively in the direction of Shardlow and the woman Nathaniel half longed and half dreaded to see.

What kind of reception to expect once he reached her seemed obvious, although a minuscule ember of hope stubbornly remained to make him wonder if, by some miracle, Hester might have realised how little he wanted to leave.

If she could just see he had no choice perhaps she would think better of him, and her fledgling affection would remain steady, proving his father wrong. She had such a warm and generous spirit when her outer shell was cracked that for a moment Nathaniel almost believed his own desperate wish—until he recalled how her face had fallen at his news, clouding over and the gleam of promise in her beautiful eyes dimming at once.

The weight that had sat in his gut for the past two days grew heavier and he clenched his fists on the reins, gripping so tight his knuckles cracked. With every hoofbeat he drew nearer to Hester, and yet they would never be close again. Either his absence or her eventual revulsion would drive them apart and they were doomed either way.

Ever since the disastrous meeting with his father Nathaniel had racked his brains to think up some escape from such a miserable fate, but as the grey sky opened up above him he knew there was none.

Either I go and risk Hester resenting me, or

I stay and be disinherited. She'll learn the truth about Algiers from my wretch of a father, and then I'll have neither wife nor business to turn to.

Rain pattered down onto his hat and shoulders, soaking into his coat and spreading its chill, but Nathaniel hardly felt it. Any discomfort was what he deserved for allowing himself to be backed into such a corner and he should take it without complaining, the hurt he'd caused Hester unbearable in comparison to anything else. Doubtless she thought he was just as selfish and inconstant as ever, and there was nothing he could do to convince her otherwise without revealing the truth that would damn him all the same.

He gritted his teeth on a growl, bending his head to keep the rain from stinging his eye. Thame Magna was only a few miles away, and woodland was already turning to the well-kept farms that surrounded the town. Soon enough he'd have to face Hester and see her disappointment all over again—both in him and in herself, for allowing him that precious second chance.

How much would she regret her lapse in judgement, with any feelings for him growing sour until they were gone without trace? There was only one way of knowing and it made him want to keep on riding until he ran out of road—anything but arrive at Shardlow and see the answer for himself.

The wind had picked up, throwing great handfuls of water into his face and plastering the hair below the brim of his hat to his brow. On either side the trees bent and shook their naked boughs, the prospect of fresh new leaves still some weeks away, even as last year's turned to mush among the mud. With his head down and the wind whistling in his ears Nathaniel could hardly see nor hear the road ahead—until the sudden whinny of his horse made him look up and squint through the rain, pulling up sharply as a carriage appeared through the gloom.

Evidently riding a grey horse on a grey day hadn't been a good idea. The coachman reined in hard, and the carriage juddered to a halt so abrupt Nathaniel heard the occupants inside cry out even above the roar of the driving rain. They must be startled and he felt rattled himself, his breath coming faster as he gathered himself and spurred his horse forward.

'A near miss! Are your horses well?'

'Aye, sir.' The coachman peered through the rain to check the pair of handsome black mares who stamped and fretted at this unexpected stop. 'No damage here. Yourself?'

'None. I hope the same can be said of your passengers?'

The words were no sooner out of his mouth than the carriage window slid up and a face appeared at the glass. Belatedly Nathaniel realised who it was, although it was the passenger beside her that made his heart suddenly leap into his throat.

'Nathaniel? Is that you?'

Diana called out to him, but it was Hester's face that drew his eye like an arrow to a target. She stared back, colour rushing into her cheeks alongside a look of surprise that, with a harsh blow to his innards, he saw was not of the pleasant kind.

She glanced swiftly away again, jaw tight and set so determinedly that he knew, without a shadow of a doubt, that all hope was lost.

'I felt for sure we'd had an accident. Are you unharmed?'

From somewhere he found a mute nod, unable to tear his attention from Hester's face even to speak. She was gazing steadily past him, the pale oval of her face luminous in the carriage's shadowy interior and her lips pressed into a grim line. There was no warmth, no smile, no outward sign at all that his presence was in any way wanted; and Nathaniel felt his heart split in two, cracked from top to bottom and the pieces cast out like a pan of ash.

'And your horse? Is he hurt?'

He shook his head, this time managing a hoarse reply. 'No. Your driver stopped just in time. Another few feet and I think we'd all have been in trouble.'

Diana inclined her head, for once seeming ill

at ease. She slid a loaded glance towards Hester, who returned it with one as dark as pitch; but she allowed her sister to slip away to the other bench, removing the shield between Nathaniel and herself, although when she leaned closer to the window it was with a reluctance he felt in his bones.

'Are you going somewhere?'

Her nod was as curt as if they were passing acquaintances and nothing more.

'Diana has invited me to her house in Canterbury. I shall be away from Shardlow for a few weeks—not that it will make much difference to you, of course. You'll have gone by the time I return.'

Seated high up in the saddle, Nathaniel felt dizziness sweep over him and he clenched his fist around the pommel to anchor himself in place. He had no grounds whatsoever to object to Hester going away, but for her to do so without a word told him all he needed to know.

'I didn't realise you'd made plans. I wouldn't have seen you before I left.'

She swallowed, the tell-tale movement of her throat drawing Nathaniel's eye at once. 'In truth I didn't think you'd care. It wouldn't be the first time we'd parted without saying goodbye.'

Heavy droplets of rain still fell all about him, but nothing was as cold as Hester's tone. It took him right back to the moment he'd arrived in her parlour all those weeks ago, when she'd been unbending as granite and then swept out as though she couldn't bring herself to look upon him any longer than she had to. The same sensation gripped him now—the feeling that she wanted to be far away from him—and it sent a knife into the very centre of the defenceless place meant only for her.

'Hester...please.'

He knew there was desperation in his voice, but he couldn't make himself care. The coachman watched impassively and secreted inside the coach Lord and Lady Lavendon could hear every word, but Nathaniel's whole world was held in Hester's hand and it was only to her that he directed his heartfelt plea.

'You need to understand...'

'I understand everything.' The first hint of a spark appeared, glinting among the frozen depths of her otherwise icy façade. 'More, even, than you apparently think me capable of.'

Another man might have recoiled but Nathaniel refused to back away. For all he knew this might be his final chance to try for a stay of execution, and he hurled everything he had into his argument for clemency.

'It isn't like last time. *I'm* not like I was last time. Surely you can see things have changed? You can't believe all is the same?'

Her lips parted, and for half of one wonderful second he thought she might agree. How could that mouth remain so coolly aloof when he knew the heat of its kiss? How soft the skin was that he'd mapped with his own? After everything that had passed between them Hester must know he was telling the truth—or at least part of it, his feelings for her never a lie.

He looked down at her face in the window and his very being ached for one smile, one tiny curve of her lips as a reason to live. She was everything and there would never be another—not even if he was forced to grow old without ever again feeling the precious touch of her hand.

Ask me to stay.

Despair welled up in an unstoppable tide just as relentless and real as the rain that drenched Nathaniel to the skin, every moment that ticked by increasing his fear of what Hester might say next. She had all the power, and suddenly even his father's threats seemed as nothing compared to what his wife might decide, like a Roman emperor choosing the fate of a fallen gladiator.

Ask me to stay. If you ask it of me I'll do it, and hang whatever comes next.

But she didn't.

Hester's jaw remained set and her eyes were cold, holding his gaze with that same unwavering courage he'd come to admire more than she'd ever guess. Perhaps her life wasn't at stake this time as he was leaving, but her heart was, and it seemed she wasn't willing to take the risk.

'I believe you are exactly as you always were, and indeed as you will always be. Some things change, and some people too, but others...others will never be anything different.'

The finality with which she delivered the blow was as clean and brutal as a guillotine's blade, although the words sounded curiously far away to Nathaniel as he sat high on his horse and tried not to fall. Something inside him broke like a glass shattered against a cold stone floor as he watched Hester's lips move, beautiful but deadly, and knew that he was lost.

She was still speaking, and he tried to hear, although the buzzing in his ears made it quite impossible. Through the window Nathaniel could just make out her hand—her gentle, slim-fingered little hand—clenched so tightly the bones stood out beneath the skin, unable to drag his eye away from it as she reached up to knock on the carriage's ceiling.

'I wish you safe travels, Nathaniel.'

For the briefest moment their gazes met, uneven green looking into blue, both colours vivid with a pain neither knew how to quench. He longed to leap down and scoop her into his arms, to carry her off and never let go; but then the carriage began to move, and he could do nothing but watch as Hester was borne away and disappeared amid the rain.

* * *

By the time Jacob tracked him to a chair in a dimly lit corner of Shardlow's library, Nathaniel was on his fourth glass of Scotch.

'Are you drinking the whole decanter?'

'Perhaps. I can spare a glass or two, though, if you've a mind to seek your own ruin.'

He stared into the unlit grate, a half-full tumbler cradled in one hand. The other traced a scatter of stubble across his chin, the idea of something so banal as shaving almost laughable when his life lay in tatters of his own making.

'Only one, then, just to be sociable. Never did get a taste for Scotch, ironically enough.'

Nathaniel waved absently to a table beside the empty fireplace. 'Help yourself.'

Taking another mouthful, he felt its warmth flow down his throat and into the gaping chasm of his chest, although it couldn't melt the ice around his heart. Every beat was an effort, and he wondered whether it was true one could die of misery, with the pulse ceasing to skip when all felt so bleak.

There was a gentle splash and the clink of cut glass and then Jacob dropped into the armchair opposite, his concern unspoken, but tangible nonetheless. He held his head to one side, studying his friend before he delivered his verdict with the same no-nonsense candour Nathaniel had come to expect.

'You could have told her. Taken the power off your father and seen what happened when you told your wife the truth.'

'No, I couldn't.' Nathaniel pressed his fingertips against his forehead. The skin there was tender from a frown so painfully etched it might never smooth out. 'She'd have been revolted. Hester might hate me, but I think even that is preferable to disgust.'

'I don't think you give her enough credit. When has she ever given you cause to believe she'd react like that? She strikes me as far too sensible a woman to think ill of someone for things they couldn't help.'

'You don't understand.'

Nathaniel sat back, fixing Jacob with one bloodshot eye. He was the best friend Nathaniel had ever had, yet it was difficult to put into words how their experience had left him feeling so polluted, with a lingering sense of shame he never wanted Hester to see.

'We were treated like animals. How many times did we go weeks without being able to wash, being fed scraps and forced to work until we almost fainted from the sun? We were barely human by the time we were rescued. How could she still want me after knowing all that? A woman like Hester deserves the best of men—not someone reduced to life in the gutter.'

Jacob took a tentative sip of his drink and

made a face like a child being forced to swallow medicine. The scar at his lip stretched as he drank, pulling his mouth into a terrible smile that only reminded Nathaniel all the more of what they had endured.

'I suppose you know your wife better than I do, but if I were in your place I'd still take the chance. Nothing and no one would come between me and Mrs Morrow.'

'But you're not in my place. And, furthermore, there *is* no Mrs Morrow.'

'Not at present… Hannah is looking a better prospect each day, though. I might not be a bachelor for ever.'

'Who?'

'Hannah—Arless to you.' Jacob's mouth twisted a little more, although this time the smile was intentional. 'And I tell you now: I wouldn't keep a secret from her. When I marry it'll be with a clean slate.'

With a flick of his wrist Nathaniel downed the rest of his drink in one quick gulp and reached out again for the decanter. What did Jacob know? Their situations couldn't be more different, and neither could the women about which they each spoke.

'Arless—*Hannah* is a servant. Her expectations won't be as high as Hester's. She's used to finer things—and finer people.'

For the first time the ready sympathy in Morrow's face dimmed a little, replaced by a shadow of impatience. 'You think class makes a damn bit of difference to a woman's heart? There's good and bad in all walks of life, Nathaniel. I thought you'd learned that by now?'

Jacob was an employee in name only. His reprimand was from one man to another and Nathaniel felt its sting. Leaning forward, he pushed the Scotch away, its influence clearly making him slide into foolish self-pity he wouldn't indulge.

'You're right. I'm sorry. That was a stupid thing to say.'

Irritation disappearing as quickly as it had come, Jacob shrugged. 'No offence taken. But think of what I said.'

'There's little point. What can I do now? Hester's gone away, and I doubt she'd agree to see me even if I did decide to come clean.'

'You'd give up that easily?'

Nathaniel gave a humourless laugh. If he needed more proof that Jacob didn't know the extent of his problems, that question was enough to show it for certain.

'Once Hester has made a decision it might as well be written in stone. She doesn't trust me. Anything I tell her now will fall on deaf ears, or she'll write it off as another untruth. My word holds no weight with her, and for that I can only blame myself.'

'Your word is nothing?'

'After the number of times I've said one thing, only to do another, hurting her in the process? Exactly so.'

It was only a repetition of what he already knew, but to say it out loud was like another kick in the stomach. He felt bruised, winded, and although he refused to act on it his fingers itched to reach again for the decanter that might grant him solace in drunken sleep.

'There's nothing I can say that she'll listen to now. I don't have a hope in hell of persuading her that I've changed from the selfish boy I was into a man who wants nothing more than to cherish her... Not that I deserve that, of course.'

'But you *have* changed. Who would know that better than me?' Jacob finished up the dregs from his tumbler and set it aside. 'You're nothing like the pathetic creature I pulled out of the sea and I'm glad of it. I wouldn't have enjoyed throwing you back in.'

Despite the anguish that sapped his strength Nathaniel mustered a wry smile. 'Thank you. Your compassion is so warming to the soul. But it's Hester I'd need to convince, and she will never accept anything I say again.'

'I understand.'

Jacob looked away, his brown eyes fixed on the cold hearth just as Nathaniel's had for un-counted hours. He might have been thinking anything or nothing at all, his face inscrutable as ever, weathered and scarred but still hiding one of the kindest hearts Nathaniel had ever known.

'I understand completely.'

Chapter Fourteen

Rain fell in a relentless deluge for the entirety of Hester's first week at Newchurch Manor, all of Canterbury sodden and grey. Diana sighed and bemoaned the impossibility of venturing out, but the howling wind and bullish clouds suited Hester just fine.

There was nowhere she wanted to go, nothing she wanted to do. Food had lost all its flavour and wine was sour. Even sleep was elusive, and refusing to give her any release from the thoughts of Nathaniel that tormented her. She felt like a ghost walking the halls of the great house and knew she must look like one too, pale and silent as she drifted from one room to the next, seeing her sister and brother-in-law exchanging worried glances whenever she appeared.

They meant well, and Hester appreciated their concern, although the sight of them sitting on the same sofa, heads close together in intimate conversation, drove a shard of agony directly into her chest and she much preferred to be alone.

Escaping soon after breakfast on the seventh day, Hester wandered the impressive gallery, tracing her own steps back and forth until she lost count. An uninterested glance outside showed the rain had finally stopped, the storm's fury spent, and the Manor's grounds were at last emerging from their gloomy shroud. They would be beautiful, no doubt, once the sun came out, but Hester's thoughts turned instead to Nathaniel, the constant ache beneath the bodice of her gown increasing as she conjured up his face.

How terrible it must be, tossing and turning on rough waves. I pray the better weather here makes its way to the sea and keeps him safe.

She pressed her lips together so tightly it hurt, another surge of bitter regret rising in her gullet. Her last words had been so cold—what if they really *were* the final ones she'd ever speak to him, laced with hurt and anger she hadn't been able to control? Perhaps he hadn't deserved an affectionate farewell, but his expression as he'd watched the carriage take her away was burned into her mind, and every time she recalled it another pinprick of pain drove into her skin.

But there's nothing to be done. He set sail days ago and must be miles away at this very moment.

Forcing her spine straighter, she pulled her shoulders back, not realising how much they had slumped into a miserable curve. Nathaniel had gone to sea, just as he'd said he wouldn't, and Hester could only wait for his return. It might take weeks, months, or even—if last time was any guide—years for him to walk back through her door, and the prospect of tolerating her heartbreak for all that time made her grit her teeth on a cry of despair.

They had come so close to finding a home in each other—or so she'd thought—and to have it ripped away from her was an agony like none she had known before.

'How could he leave me?' Hester murmured to her reflection in the gallery window, another set of grave blue eyes returning her stare. 'How could we have had so many wonderful moments that in the end meant nothing at all?'

That morning spent out on the ice, Nathaniel's cheeks pink with cold and his grin from ear to ear as he took his first wobbly strides...

Diana's ball, when he'd appeared as if from nowhere to surprise her after she'd thought he wouldn't come...

His candlelit face in his bedroom, burning with desire but still holding back until she gave him permission to proceed—and then what had come after, sensations so vivid she could still feel their essence even now...

Screwing her eyes shut, Hester wrapped her arms tight around her body as if she could ward

off the memories that came from all sides, each
one a jagged knife seeking somewhere soft to
stab. They hurled themselves against her defences, wearing them down in a merciless battle of attrition that left her gasping and desperate
for somewhere to hide.

'Ma'am? Are you unwell?'

As though from a great distance away Arless'
voice cut through the clamour and Hester's eyes
snapped open at once. She didn't know when her
maid had entered the room, but she'd never been
more relieved to see her—a welcome distraction
from death by a thousand cuts.

'No, no. I'm perfectly well. Were you searching for me?'

Arless didn't look entirely convinced by the
denial, but she was far too well trained to probe
further. Instead she held out a letter, the sight of it
sending a sudden flurry through Hester's nerves.

'This came for you, ma'am.'

Hester's pulse quickened as she took the en-
velope and turned it over, willing her fingers not
to shake—although in the next moment disappointment settled heavily on her chest. It wasn't
Nathaniel's bold, sweeping writing, and for one
long, horrible beat Hester thought tears were
going to spring up in her eyes at how sharply
her hopes had leapt upwards.

But for what reason would he write to her?

And how would he manage to send a letter from the middle of the sea?

Unhappiness chasing out all but the vaguest curiosity, Hester nodded to the waiting maid. 'You must be itching to get out now the rain has stopped. I don't feel much like venturing outside but take the rest of the morning yourself if you'd like.'

Arless' brow twitched into a frown of concern at Hester's bleak face. 'Thank you, ma'am. Is there anything I can do for you before I go? It hardly seems fitting to leave when you seem— forgive me—so unsettled.'

The same rigor mortis smile Hester had forced for the past week became necessary once again. 'I'm not unsettled in the least. Please do go and enjoy yourself.'

The maid hesitated, on the very brink of a refusal, but then her usual tact won out. 'If you're sure, ma'am. Thank you.'

Hester kept the smile stitched in place until Arless was safely out of the gallery and then allowed it to fade, the corners of her mouth turning down until not a trace remained. She'd almost forgotten the letter in her hand, but slowly she sank onto the window seat, breaking the seal and beginning to read with barely any interest at all.

That was…until she reached the second paragraph.

* * *

Hands clasped behind his head, Nathaniel lay back on his bunk, staring blindly up at the wooden ceiling. He knew every knot by now, every imperfection in the rough boards that he'd studied for nearly a week already and would for months to come. The *Luna* hadn't even left harbour yet, with foul weather keeping the ship stubbornly docked, so there was nothing for him to do but wait—wait and endlessly torture himself with memories of Hester in those times when her smile had lit up both the room and his life.

He closed his eye, a sigh coming all the way up from his boots. What would she be doing at that very moment? She'd still be in Canterbury, most likely. Only twenty miles away, but it might have been on another planet for all he could reach her. Hester was beyond his grasp now and would be even if she'd stood right next to him, his fatal mistake driving a wedge between them there was no hope of overcoming—as she had made agonisingly plain.

That final glimpse of her through the carriage window would have to last him, and still with his eye firmly shut Nathaniel tried to picture her face.

Even when rigid with repressed emotion the lines of her countenance had been beautiful to him, Hester's profile carved from marble or snow or something else cold but no less a work of art for its chill. She'd held his gaze until the very last moment, two chips of blue ice boring into his soul and leaving him in no doubt that what they saw there was wanting.

The desire to race after her and declare his love had gripped him like an iron fist, but he'd found he couldn't move, and then she was gone—disappeared through the rain, leaving him alone but for the resounding jeers of his own regrets.

Ship bunks weren't known for their comfort, this one being no exception, and Nathaniel shifted in a vain attempt to ease his aching back. Every muscle was strained and his neck was tight as a bowstring, getting worse every time he wondered how Hester fared. The only consolation he could find was that Jacob had finally agreed to stay behind at Shardlow. His willingness to weather another hideous sea voyage had been a true testament to his friendship, but it was something that Nathaniel hadn't, in good conscience, been able to allow.

There was no call to separate him from his Hannah, if marriage is indeed where that's headed. At least with Jacob at home there will be somebody to look out for Hester when she returns...not that I imagine she would appreciate such a thought.

If he couldn't be with his wife himself, Nathaniel mused grimly, Jacob was the next best thing. Hester wouldn't be completely alone, a trustworthy pair of hands waiting to scoop her up even if she didn't know it. There was nobody on earth more fit for the task than Morrow, but it was still small comfort for Nathaniel as he waited, with rising impatience, for the wind to change.

If he *had* to go he'd rather it was now. The sooner he left, the sooner he could return and try to mend whatever remnants of their relationship Hester might have been merciful enough not to throw on the refuse heap.

A tap on the door of his tiny cabin roused him from his unhappy thoughts.

'Yes?'

'Captain said to tell you the wind's changed, Mr Honeywell' came a gruff voice from outside. 'The storm's passed on and we'll be fit to sail today.'

The scuffling of footsteps moving away again told Nathaniel no reply was required, which was probably just as well. Relief rose at finally being able to break this accursed waiting, although the knowledge that he would soon be miles from Hester made his chest ache all the more.

With an effort he forced himself up from his bunk, stooping immediately as the low ceiling of his cabin attempted to greet the top of his head. He was barely able to turn around in the cramped space. A bed, two shelves and a minuscule desk were the only things squeezed in, apart from himself, with no room to spare. It was more a cupboard than a cabin, and a pitiful home for the weeks and months to come.

Making for the deck, Nathaniel had to hunch his broad shoulders to fit through the narrow gangways and stairs until he clambered out into the cold air, darkness replaced at last by pale sunlight filtering through cloud.

A salty tang danced on the breeze, all about him a flurry of activity as the crew readied the *Luna* to weigh anchor. By the look of it he was the only one whose spirits hadn't lifted at the turn of the wind: rough laughter and shouts rang across the port, some men swarming up to check the rigging and others rolling laden barrels across the glistening deck, but all working with a cheerfulness the driving rain had made impossible. At this rate they would be ready to sail within a few hours, and Nathaniel's hand curled into an involuntary fist as he scanned the bustling harbour, hoping without hope to catch a glimpse of dark blonde ringlets.

If Hester appeared he'd jump right off the ship to meet her, and hang what his father might think—but there were only sailors in place of beautiful *vexing* women and, choking back another sigh, Nathaniel went in search of the Captain.

He found Captain Bright standing near the wheel, watching proceedings with the unflappable calm only many voyages could bestow upon a man. He glanced over his shoulder as Nathaniel approached, acknowledging his presence with a nod.

'Mr Honeywell. Ready to sail?'

'More or less. It's about time—I don't see how there can be any rain left.'

'Never say that.' The older man took an unhurried puff on the unlit pipe clenched between his teeth, his attention still fixed on the bustle unfolding around them. 'The weather gods like to play their tricks when you least expect it. I'd have thought you the last person to tempt fate after what happened last time. The *Celeste* sank without trace, didn't it?'

'I'd be surprised if lightning struck the same place twice. Or perhaps once was enough and the men already call me a Jonah.'

Captain Bright removed the pipe and levelled a shrewd look at Nathaniel's tight face. He wasn't the least bit cowed, too weathered and world-weary to fear any man's bad temper. 'No, sir. Not in my hearing at least.'

Nathaniel rubbed his brow, slightly ashamed of his terse response. It wouldn't be surprising if the crew thought him bad luck, considering the fate that had met the *Celeste*. Seafaring men were a superstitious lot, and having one among them who had gone down with a ship was never going to make him popular—even if he could hardly be blamed for it running into the jagged rocks that had led to him and only a handful of survivors being captured.

'I suppose that's something to be grateful for. I can't say I'd appreciate the men plotting to throw me overboard.'

'Of course not.' The Captain leaned forward and spat a stray shred of tobacco neatly over the side. 'Even so... I hope you found time to say your goodbyes? None of us ever knows which voyage might be our last.'

Under cover of straightening his hat, Nathaniel allowed himself a swift grimace. Perhaps *he* was the superstitious one. Captain Bright seemed to have sensed the unease nestling in his chest, uncannily reading something in him that Nathaniel wanted to hide. His farewells to his mother and Jacob had been painful enough, but Hester's...

If that was the very last time they would speak he'd die an unhappy man indeed, doomed to be haunted by the echo of her frozen face for eternity, or whatever awaited him beyond the mortal veil.

Her image would be the thing that accompanied him at that moment—the last memory flashing through his mind as life slipped from his grasp and everything grew dark. He might not always have loved her, but now that he did nothing would ever wrench her from his heart: not his father's scheming, nor a thousand miles of ocean, not even Hester's own disgust. She owned him now, his soul tethered to hers, and no matter what happened it would be her name he whispered with his final breath.

'Only a few hours more and all this will be behind us.' Captain Bright took a deep breath of sea air, contentedly stretching out his arms as if he was more at home on the ship than on land. 'In truth I yearn to be off again. There's nothing here to keep me, and I have nobody wanting me to stay.'

'No.' Nathaniel allowed his eye to stray to the horizon, and then to the waves rising and falling in a steady rhythm he would have to learn to endure. 'Neither do I.'

'Read it again, Hess. Slowly this time.'

Diana sat so close to the edge of her seat that Hester might have worried she'd fall if her thoughts hadn't been so completely absorbed by the letter in her trembling hand. Both sisters' eyes were wide, unable—or perhaps not daring—to believe something so astounding could possibly be true.

'I'll try, but I'm shaking so much I don't know if I can.'

Hester laid a hand over the place where her heart leapt in a frenzy, each beat so powerful she felt it all the way down to her slippered feet. Taking a shuddering breath, she tried to steady herself against the parlour chair she had collapsed into, both Diana and Lavendon starting in alarm when she'd burst through the door.

Rereading the letter might help her to understand it herself, too bewildered to comprehend it while her head spun with more questions than answers.

The first paragraph was unremarkable. Only once her unexpected correspondent's pleasantries were out of the way did he move on to make her jaw drop and the earth stop turning on its axis.

I beg you will excuse my writing, but concern for my closest friend, your husband, makes it impossible for me to remain silent any longer. A sea voyage is a dangerous undertaking, and in the event he doesn't return it would be wrong for you to be left without an accurate understanding of both his recent actions and his true feelings.

Under any other circumstances I wouldn't presume to interfere. The depth of Nathaniel's misery at the prospect of parting from you, however, was more than I could bear. Our bond is now a brotherhood, and if there is even the smallest possibility my interference can bring about a happier situation I must act.

In the hope that this letter might show the real man, rather than the man others

*have forced him to appear to be, please
allow me to share the story of our time in
Algiers—and how Nathaniel Honeywell
saved my life.*

Hester swallowed, stumbling over the unfamiliar handwriting and her mouth dry. She knew what was coming, but still hardly believed the evidence of her own eyes as they travelled the folded page, skittering across words and spattered ink.

On one side she sensed Diana listening with bated breath, Lavendon on the other just as intent as his wife.

I believe you know the Celeste *was sunk
off the coast of Algiers. What I think you
weren't told was that I was the one who
pulled your husband from the sea and
dragged him ashore.*

*Although I meant to help him, I'm afraid
he was destined for the same fate I'd lived
for the past year: to be captured by slavers
and sold into servitude with little chance
of escape.*

To her left Hester heard Diana's soft gasp, although her own breaths came too shallow for there to be any to spare. *Her* Nathaniel—her witty, handsome, aggravating Nathaniel—sold

like cattle to labour beneath the burning sun...
The very thought of it pierced her like a savage blade, cutting through the despair of the past weeks to slice down to the bone. Emotion too intense to name flared like a bonfire, the protective side of her spirit blazing hotter than the sun that someone had *dared* treat him with such disdain.

Her palms prickled with sweat, the parlour fire cold in comparison as she gathered the courage to continue.

I'll spare you the details of our day-to-day lives. Suffice to say it was a cruel existence that left scars on both body and mind which will never fully heal. Some of our fellow slaves died from exhaustion and disease, and those who survived often wished they hadn't.

The only thing that kept us going was the glimmer of hope that we might one day be rescued and a sense of camaraderie that gave each other strength. It took Nathaniel a while to realise the value of both leaning on and caring for others, but once he had seen the light he changed from a selfish youth into a dependable man that I was, and still am, proud to call my friend. Where once he thought only of himself, he began to consider those around him, although I

*had no idea just how deep this consider-
ation would run.*

*I apologise in advance for any distress
caused by what comes next, but if you are
to learn the full truth of your husband's determination to better himself I can't leave
it unsaid.*

Hester looked up, needing a moment to ground
herself before she could carry on. Even having
read the letter twice over she had to steel herself,
flames still lapping around her that crackled with
rage and pity and the sudden crystal-clear yearning to fold Nathaniel in her arms.

Diana was like a statue, waiting for her to
speak, the parlour so silent Hester could hear
every rustle of the breeze outside.

*One day I was tasked with carrying a
load of stone from one place to another.
The foreman was displeased with me for
some perceived slight, and as punishment
nobody was permitted to help me. By the
time I had made five or six journeys I was
dehydrated and weak. The sun that afternoon was unendurably strong, and Nathaniel could take it no more.*

*Disregarding the foreman's orders, Na-
thaniel took over my task so I could rest,
ignoring my pleas not to risk punishment*

and carrying the rest of the stone himself. When the foreman learned what was happening he came in a fury, swinging his whip and swearing to beat me bloody.

The end of the whip caught Nathaniel's eye, resulting in the wound covered by his patch, but despite his own agony Nathaniel stood over me and wouldn't move away. I have no doubt that in my weakened state a beating would have killed me and that your husband saved my life, even though he knew the penalty for such disobedience was the severance of a finger.

The foreman was so distracted that he forgot about me, allowing me to live until the British Navy came with their almighty bombardment and we were finally freed.

Out of the corner of her eye Hester saw Diana reach for Lavendon's hand, gripping it so firmly her fingers turned white, and nausea turned in Hester's stomach as unwanted images ran like wildfire through her mind.

One after the other they streaked past, sickening in their lurid brutality: Nathaniel's face running red with blood from his ruined eye, a half-dead figure at his feet and another raising its arm with a blade flashing in one hand. Her heart pounded against her ribs and her hands still shook, her revulsion second only to the an-

guish of imagining how much Nathaniel must
have suffered.

*You know better than anyone that your
husband is a proud man. He believed that
if you knew how far he had fallen your feelings for him would change, so ashamed
was he of how low he had been brought
that he believed he was tainted and unworthy—something his father has held him to
ransom with, alongside the threat of disinheritance. For my part, I feel his actions
in Algiers were heroic, not shameful, and I
confess I can't imagine what more convincing proof there could be that he is capable
of far greater things now than he was when
the Celeste set sail.*

*Before leaving Shardlow House he ex-
pressed sorrow that his word will mean
nothing to you now he has felt forced to
break it. I pray that mine might have some
weight instead, and that you will believe
your husband's devotion to you is as real
as his change for the better. Perhaps your
maid, Miss Hannah Arless, could vouch
for whether I am considered trustworthy,
should you wish to satisfy yourself on that
count?*

*Once again, I beg forgiveness for pre-
suming on subjects you doubtless feel are*

*not my concern. My only excuse is the de-
sire to save my friend unhappiness born
out of misunderstanding, and to assure you,
in the strongest terms, that this latest absence is neither his highest priority nor of
his choosing.*

*There is only one place Nathaniel would
ever choose to be: next to you. Whether
there's any hope of his love being returned
or not.*

*I remain, madam, your most obedient ser-
vant,*

Jacob Morrow

Hester sat back in her chair, the letter hanging
from numb fingertips. Nobody said a word. None
of the three people sitting in the parlour could
think of any way to respond—three minds blank
with horror and amazement that robbed them of
all possibility of speech.

They must have remained like that for some
minutes, although it felt like hours before Hester could break from under the spell that held
her in place.

'Nathaniel a slave. All this time and I never
knew.'

Slowly Lavendon rubbed the back of his neck,
looking every bit as stunned as Hester felt. 'None
of us did. He never gave so much as a clue. To
have endured all that without mentioning it

once... If everything written there is true, there can be no doubt he's changed beyond all recognition.'

A curious warmth filtered through Hester's blood, even as shock and dismay still ran riot. Could Mr Morrow indeed be telling the truth? Surely nobody could tell such macabre lies, a tale that horrendous too awful to be anything but fact. If Jacob could be trusted it would turn every assumption she'd made on its head, bringing the faint gleam of a hopeful dawn where once she'd seen only endless night.

One word had jumped out at her from the untidy scrawl: *love.*

Jacob writes that Nathaniel wants me to return his love.

In uncharacteristic silence Diana rose to her feet and moved unsteadily to the bell rope hanging at one wall. Without even needing to ask, Hester knew exactly what she was going to do, almost able to read her sister's mind as her own began to pick up speed and range over what might not be impossible after all.

A white-capped head appeared round the door and Diana spoke as normally as she was able. 'Would you fetch Miss Arless, please? It's extremely important she's brought here at once.'

'Yes, Your Ladyship. She mentioned going into town but she hasn't left yet. I'll bring her now.'

The maid withdrew, her swift footsteps echoing away down the corridor, and then Arless' quiet voice brought with it a welcome sense of calm.

'Yes, ma'am? Do you need me to stay after all?'

Hester attempted a smile, although her muscles seemed to have frozen stiff. 'No, no. I'm sorry to call you back for a moment. I just want to ask you something before you leave.'

Arless came fully into the room and stood beside the fireplace, waiting obligingly for Hester to continue. She seemed mildly curious, but not uneasy, and her steady presence gave Hester a gentle nudge to proceed.

'I believe you're well acquainted with Mr Morrow?'

The maid blinked in surprise, a giveaway trace of colour creeping into her cheeks. 'Yes, ma'am, but only in the proper way. Mr Morrow is a gentleman, and would never attempt anything untoward.'

'Of course. In truth I'm glad you know him so well. Could you tell me more about his character?'

'His character?'

'You know…' Hester pressed further, trying not to let her rising eagerness show in her tone. 'Is he honest? Trustworthy?'

'Oh, yes.'

Arless' face glowed pinker still, suddenly so

unlike her usual reserved self that Hester's smile softened into something infinitely more real.

'Mr Morrow is the very best of men. I'd have no hesitation to take him at his word, and he's so kind. Funny, too, ma'am, and good to his mother... He speaks fondly of his sisters, all three of them, and I've never once heard him exchange a cross word with anyone.'

It seemed her lady's maid could wax poetic about Jacob Morrow all day, but Hester had heard enough. 'I understand. Thank you, Arless. Please go and enjoy yourself—I think you might take the afternoon as well as the morning.'

Clearly at a loss as to why the interrogation had taken place, Arless dipped a curtesy and left the parlour—perhaps before she could be asked any more compromising questions. Hester watched her go, her hands clutching the letter so hard the paper was in danger of being torn clean in half.

'Well. It would certainly appear this Mr Morrow is a man of his word.'

Lavendon stretched out an arm and gathered Diana to him, anchoring her at his side with instinctive concern. Hester wondered if her own face was as pale as her sister's, as the two regarded each other with matching bewildered blue eyes.

'I agree. Arless has been with Hess for years.

She wouldn't lie, even if she didn't have such an obvious fancy for him.'

Hester took a deep, shuddering breath in an attempt to order her thoughts. Every sense seemed to have abandoned her, only dizzying wonderment left to fill the gap left by everything else. That one word—*love*—came to her over and over again, the sweetest whisper in her ear that Hester had ever heard, and the longing to believe it was so strong it burned beneath her gown.

'So what are you going to do? How will you act now you know Nathaniel didn't choose to leave, but rather was blackmailed into it by his wretched father?'

A touch of the old spark had resurfaced in Diana, nothing able to keep her down for long. She leaned forward to look into Hester's face, keen as a hound following a promising trail, but Hester could only helplessly shake her head.

'I don't know. I don't know what to think. Even if Jacob is right—and that's a colossal *if*—Nathaniel sailed days ago. He must be miles away by now.'

'Not necessarily.'

Lavendon leaned forward just like his wife, the pair of them alight with an excitement that sent shivers through Hester's insides. It was infectious, setting her caution alight and tempting her to send it up in smoke.

'The weather has been appalling right up until

this afternoon. There's a chance Nathaniel may still be stuck at Dover, waiting for a favourable wind.'

Hester's breath caught halfway out of her body. 'That can happen?'

Lord Lavendon nodded. 'It can. Given how stormy this past week has been, I wouldn't be at all surprised if Nathaniel is still there.'

Hester sat motionless, like a statue perfectly still apart from the rise and fall of its chest as she reminded herself to breathe. It would be easy to forget such an inconsequential thing while so many other thoughts clamoured for her attention, horror and compassion mingling with that tentative glint of hope she hardly dared allow.

Why hadn't Nathaniel told her what had happened, instead of allowing his father to hold such sway? It made her stomach roil to think of him bearing such unimaginable pain—pure, white-hot rage simmered that somebody had inflicted it upon him, although admiration tempered the very worst of her wrath. The old Nathaniel would never have sacrificed himself for the sake of another, throwing doubt on the conclusion she'd thought so settled and making her wonder if, perhaps, she had made the most terrible mistake.

She had to know for certain.

There was only one question to ask and it slipped out before she realised her lips had even moved, her mind already racing on to what might lie ahead if she was brave enough to reach out and seize it. There was no other way, and although it would take all her courage Hester knew what she must do, instinct guiding her onwards like the gentle hand of fate.

'Diana, Lavendon...please may I borrow a horse?'

Chapter Fifteen

Cold wind whistled past Hester's ears, but she spurred the mare on regardless, paying no mind even when her bonnet was snatched from her head and sent bowling back the way she'd come. She was so close now and stray millinery wouldn't deter her, not so much as a moment to lose as she bent lower and felt the horse lengthen its stride.

'Good girl. We're almost there.'

She'd practically flown the past eighteen miles, only stopping at Barham to change mounts and then ploughing on as though fleeing the fires of hell. A carriage would have been more comfortable but far too slow, tangled hair and wind-burned cheeks a small price to pay for the chance—however unlikely—that she might reach Nathaniel in time.

Now, as she sped along the road to Dover, Hester tightened her grip on the reins, her heartbeat so fast it matched the thundering of her horse's hooves.

Don't have left. Please don't have left—not before we have a chance to speak.

With eyes screwed against the air buffeting her face, Hester watched a town begin to rise in the distance—an indistinct jumble of buildings set against the bleak sky. Stretched out beyond lay the impossible expanse of the Atlantic Ocean, although she tried not to look at it as each hoof-beat brought her closer. Nathaniel might already be crossing that vast blue span and the thought she might be too late was more than she could bear, trying to force that fear behind her and urging the horse onwards for the final mile.

Galloping flat out, horse and rider entered Dover far more quickly than they should have. A couple taking a leisurely walk leapt out of the way as Hester tore past but her apology was lost on the breeze, not able to pause for a second to beg pardon or even truly notice the shops and houses on either side. All she could think of was Nathaniel, his face overtaking all else and his voice a whisper calling her name.

She *had* to get to the harbour to see if he had already sailed, carrying her heart away with him to the other side of the sea and perhaps leaving it there if she couldn't undo her mistake.

The smell of salt water assailed Hester's senses and she felt her pulse leap higher. The harbour was near. Even above the sound of horseshoes on cobbles she could hear the chime of ships' bells, seagulls crying out as they wheeled overhead and the coarse shouts of sailors in languages Hester couldn't understand.

Turning one last corner, she saw water spread out in a sparkling cloak, boats bobbing up and down on their moorings and tall masts reaching towards the sky, the huge vessels bigger than anything she'd seen before.

She pulled up short, hesitating as she cast her eyes this way and that. Which ship was Nathaniel's? Perhaps none of them were—the notion struck her like a physical blow and she laid a hand on her chest as if it might calm the ragged pace of her shallow breaths.

A brawny, weather-beaten man in sailor's garb passed close to her and Hester called out, hoping her dry mouth would allow her to speak. 'Excuse me, sir. I wonder if you could help me?'

The man stopped and squinted at her, sitting high up on her horse, before removing his cap, exposing straggly hair tied up with string. 'I will if I can, miss. What's the trouble?'

'I'm looking for a ship. I don't know its name, or that of its captain, but it's bound for Spain on behalf of the Honeywell Trading Company. Would you happen to know of such a ship, or if it's already left?'

The sailor's brow creased, and immediately Hester's spirits dropped like a stone.

'That would be the *Luna*. Captain Bright was caught in the harbour for the best part of a week, but now the weather's turned they've gone on their way. You've just missed them, I'm afraid, if that was the ship you wanted.'

Hester's lungs emptied of air as the sailor's words hit home. 'Just missed them...?' she repeated faintly, barely a murmur coming from disbelieving lips.

The harbour around her grew dim, all the colour and noise retreating as she felt her hopes dashed to the ground. She'd ridden so fast, tried so hard, and it hadn't been enough. Nathaniel had already left, and her cold dismissal was the final memory he would have of her until he returned—assuming he ever did. Her chance to make amends had slipped through her fingers, and Hester closed her eyes as despair seeped into her very bones to make them feel like ice.

'Aye...'

She heard the man speak but couldn't make herself look at him.

'That's the *Luna* over there. The big one—just leaving now.'

Hester's head snapped up. At the far end of the harbour a ship was gliding steadily away, moving slowly until there was room for it to pick up speed. It was sailing parallel with the seafront,

and it might even be possible to ride alongside—
as Hester saw with a great swell of amazement,
sudden urgency and resolve a heady cocktail that
made her act before she could think.

'Thank you, sir. Thank you very much!'

Without pausing to hear his reply Hester
turned her horse and tapped it into a canter, not
a thought in her head other than to reach the ship
now sliding smoothly towards the sea. Heart racing and jaw set, she sent the horse flying forward, hooves clattering and Hester's hair rippling
out behind her, scattering pins as she went but
caring for nothing. Curls crowded into her face
and she brushed them aside with impatient haste,
straining for a glimpse of a familiar figure as she
closed the gap between her and the *Luna* and
drew alongside.

Her eyes raked the vast vessel, noting how
many men stood on its deck. All of them seemed
busily going about their tasks without any tall,
broad-shouldered person among them, Hester's
desperation growing by the second, until—with
a sense of instantaneous calm only *he* could possibly inspire—she saw him.

Nathaniel.

He stood at the prow, staring out over the
water like a figurehead and apparently oblivious to the hive of activity around him. With arms
folded he was motionless, his golden hair stirring
in the briny breeze but apparently miles away

as his gaze fixed on something Hester couldn't make out, and she could only pray he would be able to hear her when she shouted his name.

'Nathaniel!'

He didn't move. His profile remained stiff as ever, and he continued to stare dead ahead, as if deaf to anything but whatever was running through his mind. If he didn't see her soon Hester would run out of harbour, and even desperation wouldn't give her the power to ride on water.

Taking a deep lungful of sea air, she gathered all her might for one more try. There was no time for another attempt if this one failed and summoning all her strength Hester bawled his name once again.

'Na—than—iel!'

The blond head turned. For the briefest of moments Hester saw him look through her as though she was a ghost: but then his eye widened and his hands gripped the rail in front of him, and relief flowed through her like a crystal stream.

He'd seen her—seen that she'd come for him in the end, and although she would have to watch him sail away he would know that all was not lost. Even if she had to stand there until the *Luna* disappeared over the horizon, a tiny black dot among the interminable blue, Hester knew she would do it if it meant Nathaniel would realise he was loved.

Slowing to a stop, Hester slipped down from

the horse, never taking her eyes from Nathaniel. The distance between them grew steadily, but they might have been locked in an embrace for the intensity of that stare, crackling unbroken across the water in a connection neither had to speak to understand.

Words weren't always necessary, Hester learned in that moment. Sometimes one long look was all that was needed, every emotion captured and shared as with a raw throat and bursting chest she slowly raised a hand to wave goodbye.

Longing clawed at her insides and tears gathered on her lashes, but she swore he wouldn't see her cry, determined not to send him on his way with a heavy heart. If he had to leave then it would be with a smile, not with regrets and guilt he would have to endure for however many countless weeks until she was with him once more.

However, it seemed that Nathaniel had made a decision of his own.

Before Hester could fully take in what he was doing he had stepped up onto the side of the ship, torn off his hat—and dived, head first, into the sea.

She froze, unable to believe what she'd just seen until his head appeared above the surface, hair darkened and slicked to his brow but coming towards her with a steady, unstoppable stroke. On the *Luna*'s deck the sailors gathered, their shouts of alarm turning instead to rapid interest as, together with Hester, they watched Nathaniel reach the harbour wall and haul himself up, hand over hand as easily as a monkey climbing a tree until amazingly, *wonderfully*, he was before her, dripping wet and breathing heavily, only a few paces away and handsome as ever despite it all.

Astounded, Hester spread her hands wildly. 'Why did you do that? You could have been killed!'

Nathaniel pushed sopping hair from his forehead and raked it back, not looking completely sure himself. His sodden shirt clung to every contour, making it difficult for Hester to concentrate on anything else, and a pool of seawater gathered slowly about his ruined boots.

'I had to know why you'd come. As soon as I saw you I knew you must have good reason.'

Hester's lips parted to reply—until she realised with a start that she had no idea what to say. Reaching Nathaniel had been her only goal, and now he was in front of her she didn't know where to begin, hope and confusion and a thousand other emotions fighting to make themselves heard.

'Can you truly not imagine what that reason might be?'

She saw his throat contract in a hard swallow, his neck moving and crying out to be kissed.

Hester ached to do just that…to feel his skin on hers…but first she had to be *sure*.

Nathaniel took a slow step forward, closing the gap between them, but not enough to touch. Warily he met her searching gaze, his eye narrowed as if trying to read some hidden message in her face.

'I know what I'd like it to be. Perhaps you could tell me and put me out of my misery.'

Behind Hester the borrowed horse huffed and blew impatiently, although it barely registered in her crowded mind. Trying to think how to start was all she could focus on—something made harder still when Nathaniel took another step forward and she saw his hand twitch, as though curbing the urge to reach out.

She had to say *something*, anything to break the unbearable suspense holding them both so tightly wound—and so, casting caution to the wind, Hester took a leap of faith.

'Won't your father be very angry? I thought this voyage essential—yet it seems you have decided it isn't so very important after all.'

Nathaniel looked down at her, his expression unreadable, and Hester felt a tense stillness fall over her. He seemed so serious, a hundred miles away from the provoking clown she knew he could be when he chose, and the unblinking fire contained in that one emerald eye raised every hair on her nape with a nameless animal thrill.

'No,' he murmured eventually, his voice low and soft like velvet at midnight. 'I think, on balance, perhaps it is not.'

When he took that final step, at last closing the distance between them and reaching out to take her in his arms, Hester's bones all but melted away, nothing but his capable strength holding her upright as raucous cheers rang out from the retreating *Luna*. She might have been embarrassed if she'd heard them, but all she was aware of was the rhythm of Nathaniel's heart as she leaned into his chest, her dress immediately damp from his wet clothes but not caring one bit. Nathaniel was all there was, all there would ever be, and as they stood entwined she felt the last poisonous dregs of doubt drain away.

Now she had him she would not be letting go, any uncertainty vanishing without trace at the honest adoration written on his face, and as he bent to kiss her she reached up on tiptoe to meet him halfway—just as she always would, for however many years they had left together, now she could be sure his love was true.

Nathaniel's lips came down on hers as gently as a butterfly landing on a petal and made them tremble. He tasted of salt from the sea and his skin was cold, although Hester would have accepted anything to be near him as she reached up to push shaking fingers through damp hair and pull him closer still. Once she'd feared she would never again feel the warmth of his mouth, and relief—pure, simple relief—flooded her until she could barely breathe. She hadn't lost him: he was there with her, the man she'd wanted since she was a shy girl of eighteen, but a better version now and one who would never hurt her again.

Breaking the kiss, she held his face in her hands, palms cupping rough cheeks covered with a week's worth of stubble. She'd have to make sure he sorted *that* out as soon as possible, but there was something far more important to discuss, and with her lips close to his ear she whispered three little words.

'I know everything.'

Nathaniel drew back, still holding Hester a willing prisoner in his arms, but immediately wary. 'What do you mean *everything*?'

'Everything.' Hester nodded gravely. 'Your Mr Morrow wrote to me. About the slavery, your injuries, how your father tried to blackmail you into sailing… I know it all. I think he deserves an increase in pay, given the service he has done you. He's a good friend indeed.'

She watched Nathaniel's jaw clench, apprehension and dismay fleeing in rapid succession across his countenance, and compassion shot through her like a burning arrow. Whatever memories he had been left with, whatever scars, they clearly ran deep indeed—but, ironically, the secret he'd tried to keep from her was the very thing that would save them in the end, the most unlikely silver lining to what must have been unendurable suffering.

'I wanted to tell you.' Nathaniel sought her gaze earnestly, apparently keen that she understood. 'I wanted to tell you the truth...'

'And so you should have. How could you have imagined it would turn me away? I had no idea I'd wed such a simpleton. Surely you must know there's nothing you could tell me that would make me respect you less? It would be difficult, in fact, for me to respect you more, given what I know now. Your ordeal does nothing to devalue you and everything to prove how good a man you have become.'

He blinked quickly, apparently taken aback; but then he smiled, a curve of his lips that in his joy stripped away the years and made him look almost a boy again. It was the face Hester had fallen in love with, but a good man wore it now, kind and dependable where once it had been a mere handsome façade.

'If that's the case I praise it for a miracle. I should have trusted you, and I'll always be sorry that I did not. There will never be any secrets between us ever again.'

Hester raised an eyebrow, attempting to look stern even as her own mouth began to lift. 'Is that a promise?'

'Madam, that is a vow.'

He tightened his grip on her waist and Hester yielded without argument, allowing him to gather her in and sink his nose into her tousled curls. She must look a state, she thought vaguely, with her hair in disarray and her gown half drenched, although the notion mysteriously died as Nathaniel carefully tilted her chin up to kiss her again. With her heart fluttering like a soaring bird and her mind empty of everything but bliss it occurred to her dimly that she still hadn't told Nathaniel she loved him…

But she would, eventually. When she found the time.

Three months later—six years to the day since Nathaniel had so fatefully boarded the *Celeste*—he followed the sound of laughter down the sunlit paths of Shardlow's gardens. His morning had been spent double-checking accounts and he'd earned a rest, enjoying the warmth on his back as he walked beneath trees laden with glossy leaves and the scent of flowers hanging heavy in the air.

He already knew where he'd find Hester, even without her laugh pointing the way, and as he drew nearer he couldn't help a flutter in his chest at the beauty of her smile.

'Nathaniel! Have you come to join us?'

She sat on the grass beneath an ancient oak, with his mother reclining nearby on a blanket spread over the ground. Both upturned faces shone with life and happiness, and his own unconsciously copied them as he folded down beside his wife.

'I have. I think I've done enough paperwork for one morning.'

'More than enough, I'd say.' Hester relaxed against him, as naturally and comfortably as though she'd never known anything else. 'And so would my papa. He didn't invite you to form Townsend & Honeywell to spend such a lovely day indoors.'

Nathaniel bent lower, laying one cheek on the top of Hester's head. Her curls glowed like dark gold, and he had to stop himself from burying his face in them, rosewater and soap so tempting it tested even *his* self-control.

'I know. I just don't want to let him down. I'm already a disappointment to one father.'

The smallest twinge tried to catch at him, but he brushed it aside, gathering Hester closer instead. Leaving the Honeywell Trading Company had been a wrench, and he couldn't deny it, but he would never regret his choice. *People over profit*—that was his new mantra, even if his father couldn't understand it, and a treasure far greater than any money was his reward for turning his back on selfishness and greed. Going into business with Hester's papa had solved many problems, but Mr Honeywell remained a silent spectre, reminding Nathaniel that there was so much more to life than trade.

He felt Hester shake her head, but it was his mother who spoke first.

'You will never be a disappointment. Perhaps your father might have desired a different outcome, but for my part I've never been prouder to call you my son.'

'Nor I to call you my husband.'

Hester laid a gentle hand on his knee, sending a ripple of sensation through him all the way to his chest.

'Although after everything we've learned of you lately, I can't see how we had much choice.'

His mother smiled, looking from one to the other with a satisfaction he knew she felt in her bones. As tactful as ever, she rose to her feet, holding up a stern finger when Nathaniel moved to help.

'I'm not so in my dotage that I can't fetch my own parasol. I'll return to the house for a moment to find it, and ask for some tea to be brought down while I'm there.'

She walked away, picking carefully along the gravel path until she rounded a corner and disappeared in the direction of Shardlow's impressive walls.

The moment she was out of sight Nathaniel scooped Hester onto his lap, winding an arm round her waist and revelling in the gasp that escaped when he found her ear and nibbled at the lobe. He murmured into it, feeling her stir at the softness of his breath tickling sensitive skin and his own nerves tingling at holding her close.

'You ought to be careful about saying such nice things about me. Too much praise might go to my head.'

She twisted to give him an admonishing frown, although the quirk of her lips spoiled the effect entirely. 'I'm not too worried. Jacob will be back from his honeymoon soon, and I feel sure he'll put you back in your place should you need it.'

Nathaniel snorted, his hands still locked around the narrow span of Hester's waist, waiting for the chance to drift further. 'Just as Hannah reminds him of his, I imagine. I dread to think what working with him at Townsend & Honeywell would be like without her influence to keep him in line.'

'True. She'll make him an excellent wife— though I can't pretend I won't miss her being at Shardlow. I'd like to be her friend if she'd have me.'

Hester's face brightened with sudden mischief, and Nathaniel narrowed his eye.

'After all, there was a time when hers was the only friendly face in the whole house. But I don't suppose you remember.'

He groaned, well used by now to her teasing. With each day that passed he learned more about his complicated wife, building a fuller picture of who she was that only made him love her more. She was in equal parts clever, exasperating and kind—and *his*, now: something he gave thanks for every morning, when he woke to see her sleeping face on the pillow beside his own.

'There's no need to remind me. I'm determined to make up for my transgressions every day for the rest of our lives.'

Still smiling, Hester cupped his cheek with one hand, her palm warm and smooth against the scars he no longer even considered.

'You already have. I can't imagine a better husband or even a better man.'

Lifting her chin Hester kissed him sweetly on the mouth—a familiar feeling by now, but never any less thrilling—and settled herself in the strong circle of his arms. Nathaniel held her tight, listening to the steady sound of her breathing, until with the sun on their faces both he and Hester fell asleep—to dream of each other, most likely, neither wishing for anything more.

* * * * *

COMING SOON!

MILLS & BOON

Coming next month

THE EARL'S INCONVENIENT HOUSEGUEST
Virginia Heath

Rafe tugged his shirt from his waistband. He tried to undo the knot in his cravat with one hand, and when it wouldn't budge, tried to assist with his bad arm and his torn shoulder screamed in pain. Frustrated he tugged on the stupid thing while cursing Archie's too-tight knot, only to tighten it worse as he wrestled with it.

In desperation, he stalked to the washstand to grab his razor, and was about to cut the dratted thing off when he remembered that his good hand wasn't his good hand at all. It was his left hand, and Rafe was right-handed. If he were incapable of untying a paltry knot with his left hand, he'd likely cut his own throat if he attempted to slice it off in a temper.

Annoyed, at both his predicament and his lingering arousal despite the long lecture with himself, he marched out of his bedchamber intent on waking Archie to help him, but as the door slammed behind him, it was Sophie who emerged onto the landing.

'Is everything alright, Rafe?'

As his necktie now resembled a noose and he was clutching a cutthroat, it clearly wasn't so there was no point in lying. Worse, if indeed things could get worse, the vixen had unpinned her hair and it fell in soft waves to her waist to taunt him some more. 'I can't undo Archie's blasted tie!'

She laughed at his anger. A soft, feminine, come-hither sort of sound which played havoc with the unruly, awakened beast in his breeches.

'Let me help.' She invaded his space to study the source of the problem, sending an alluring waft of soap and Sophie up his nostrils as she tackled the knot.

When her fingertips brushed the exposed skin above his collar, he almost groaned aloud, so channelled the sage words of his favourite colonel instead to help him withstand the torture.

Stay calm…

Remain in control at all costs.

It didn't help, so he gritted his teeth as hard as he could until the blasted knot finally came free.

'There… all done now.' Like a wife, she smoothed his lapels, and he made the fatal mistake of gazing into her gorgeous big brown eyes. That was when something odd happened in his chest. Something odd and unsettling and wholly unexpected.

Because he wished, just for a split second, she actually was his wife—and that scared the living daylights out of him.

Continue reading
THE EARL'S INCONVENIENT HOUSEGUEST
Virginia Heath

Available next month
www.millsandboon.co.uk

MILLS & BOON

THE HEART OF ROMANCE

A ROMANCE FOR EVERY READER

MODERN

Prepare to be swept off your feet by sophisticated, sexy and seductive heroes, in some of the world's most glamourous and romantic locations, where power and passion collide.

HISTORICAL

Escape with historical heroes from time gone by. Whether your passion is for wicked Regency Rakes, muscled Vikings or rugged Highlanders, awaken the romance of the past.

MEDICAL

Set your pulse racing with dedicated, delectable doctors in the high-pressure world of medicine, where emotions run high and passion, comfort and love are the best medicine.

True Love

Celebrate true love with tender stories of heartfelt romance, from the rush of falling in love to the joy a new baby can bring, and a focus on the emotional heart of a relationship.

Desire

Indulge in secrets and scandal, intense drama and plenty of sizzling hot action with powerful and passionate heroes who have it all: wealth, status, good looks…everything but the right woman.

HEROES

Experience all the excitement of a gripping thriller, with an intense romance at its heart. Resourceful, true-to-life women and strong, fearless men face danger and desire - a killer combination!

To see which titles are coming soon, please visit

millsandboon.co.uk/nextmonth

JOIN US ON SOCIAL MEDIA!

Stay up to date with our latest releases, author news and gossip, special offers and discounts, and all the behind-the-scenes action from Mills & Boon...

 millsandboon

 millsandboonuk

 millsandboon

It might just be true love...